TANGLE with FIRE

BOOK ONE *of the Flame Series*

THERESA GAGE

ACKNOWLEDGEMENT PAGE

I wish to thank my writing coach, Keven T. Johns for all his help in getting this story together. I'd like to also thank my beta readers, especially Rachel, and my critique group. I couldn't have gotten this far without you.

Chapter One

Planet Xan, year 2150

I RUBBED THE KNOT ON THE BACK OF MY HEAD AS I stood on the bridge that overlooked the

Hope River and stared at the water while waiting for my friend. Clouds blocked the light of the red sun-like star, and pink and lavender colors tinted them. The breeze tousled my hair as I inhaled the fresh air and listened to the Harmony Waterfalls that plunged two hundred and seventy feet through a gorge near the south end of the bridge. Dad generated electricity from the falls for the realm. I wished that power belonged to me. Then I'd show that bully what I was made of.

How many times must I ask Mother to allow me to learn fighting skills? Her answer was always no. For some stupid reason she wanted me scholarly and my brother brawny. If I knew how to fight like the warriors, maybe I would get respect from the men and not called a wuss behind my back. I had to survive. Didn't she understand? I wanted to be accepted.

Did Mother know how Santurin treated me? If she did, she probably didn't care. I couldn't do anything right in her eyes and my brother could do no wrong. Someday Santurin will be king. Where did that leave me? My future looked bleak. Where is my place in this world?

Voices startled me, and I thought Santurin and his friends were after me again. Didn't I sustain enough bruises for one day?

I turned around and saw my friend, Varick stroll outside. But his Aunt Darshana and my mother walked out with him! That wasn't the plan.

I didn't want to hear Mother's prattle about my studies. Today I wanted to relax. I grabbed Varick's arm and dragged him to the stairs away from the women. Mother called my name, but I blocked her out, and ran down the stairs.

Two rowboats waited in the river with a guard standing by. "Good day, My Prince. What mischief are you up to?" Sir Jayel asked. His cheeks rosy from the crisp air, he was a roly-poly man that rotated stations, according to what Dad needed for the day.

"We'd like to take one of the boats out and do a little fishing," I said.

"Good show. Take the red one. It's equipped with fishing gear already. King Arin reeled in a fat trout this morning, Perhaps, you'll do one better, hey?" Sir Jayel said.

"Is that a bet?" Varick asked.

Varick loved to gamble and play games. It's probably the reason we got along. *Maybe I should have bet Santurin we would bring in a bigger fish than him? And if we didn't, he would never let it down.* I shook my head. *After hours of studying, I developed a headache, and Santurin punching me didn't help any. If I told Dad, I'd be known as a squealer. I got called enough names without that.*

"Come on, Varick. Forget your bets," I said. "I get limited free time without Mother caging me like a pet bird."

Varick climbed inside the rowboat after me and Sir Jayel pushed us out. I grabbed an oar and paddled us further out. Waterfowl flew over with their incessant squawks and cries. We found an area away from the other fishermen and pulled in our oars. My father had stocked the river with various fish. My grandfather had brought some species from Earth.

We skewered a worm on each of our fishing hooks, then cast out our lines, and waited for a fish to bite. It didn't take long before Varick got a nibble. I grabbed the net while Varick reeled in his line. He looked hysterical with his tongue protruding through his teeth and his eyes nearly crossed as he struggled with the weight of the fish.

"Help me, Aidan. It's bending the rod," Varick said.

I set the net down and placed my hands over his on the fishing rod. We tugged and pulled, yet that fish didn't give up. We kept at it, even though our arms ached. The fish took the line out more and Varick reeled it back in. It was like a game. Give a little, pull back, out more, pull back. Finally, we yanked the biggest freshwater bass into the boat, and it flopped around. While Varick held it down, I removed the hook from the fish's mouth. Varick dropped the bass inside the wicker basket.

"Nice one." I felt a bit jealous. I hoped to reel in my own that surpassed Varick's prize.

The boat rocked with the waves of the river. It almost lulled me to sleep. My thoughts wandered. *What position could a second son of a king have? Mother wanted me to become a scholar. That didn't interest me. Reynard, the high priest said they always needed more high priests, but I didn't see myself that way either. I wouldn't mind becoming a soldier. That wouldn't sit well with Mother, and I didn't know a thing about warrior skills or how to fight.*

I don't know how long we sat waiting for a bite, but it seemed an hour passed. I stood and stretched. Varick pointed behind me. My fishing pole skidded across the floor. I raced over and grabbed it. Something weighed my pole down. I pulled and reeled my line in several times but couldn't get that damn fish. I leaned closer to the water.

"Let it go, Aidan before it breaks the fishing rod!" Varick yelled.

"Why? So, you can brag how you best me? No way." I kept struggling with the fish.

Then the unspeakable thing happened. The fish jerked me in the river, and my pole slipped from my hands. The cold, frigid water took my breath away. Water splashed my face as I wrestled to breathe. I bobbed up and down as the current dragged me further away from home.

I reached for a boulder and missed. "Wretched rock!"

"Aidan!" Varick called. "I'll get help." Instead of rowing to me, Varick paddled back to the dock.

"Don't leave me!" I shouted.

He probably didn't hear me. I should have listened to Varick and wouldn't find myself in this predicament. I had to save myself or die trying. Who knew how long help might arrive? Certainly not my brother to the rescue. He'd probably love to get rid of me.

I could hear it now; Aidan couldn't even stay in a boat and catch a simple fish. Probably thought he could outsmart it. Probably faked his death too.

The river rose higher than normal with the rainy season upon us. The shoreline flooded in some areas. I was a speck in the belly of the river and rode high on the crest of a wave. I attempted to swim out of it, but floundered, and the river laughed as it pulled me downstream.

Nothing but water met my eyes for miles. My heart hammered. Was this my doom?

The river chilled me to the bone. My teeth chattered and I shivered. My eyes darted around. I grasped at anything floating to stall my progress. Twigs, grass, leaves slipped through my fingers. Nothing solid to hold onto. I kept my head up, treading water.

A log plowed into me and knocked me under. I kicked out and surfaced, gasping for air. I coughed and spat out a mouthful of water.

Bushes and bramble, ripped from the shoreline, drifted towards me. I climbed on top of a bush, but its needles dug into my hands, and I lost my grip. The bush weaved around me and continued down the current. Rain lashed down and made it hard to see anything.

Tears sprung to my eyes. I'm too young to die. My regret was not ever to see my father or my friends again nor to experience love. How could Varick just leave me? I sniffed and wiped the water from my eyes. One good thing if I died, Santurin can't mock or bully me anymore. Who would he pick on then?

After some time passed, the rain ceased, and I blinked several times to view my whereabouts. Trees blurred by. Nothing looked familiar, until the jagged teeth of the gate overlooking the city of Fallow appeared ahead. My back slammed into a boulder and knocked the wind from me.

To my surprise, my fishing line tangled around that huge rock and the hook still pierced a big trout. The pole bounced with each wave. I held onto the boulder with one hand and leaned back, removing my knife from the side pocket of my boot. I cut the line and grasped the trout before it fell.

I glanced around. The river lowered the closer it neared Fallow and I waded to shore. Water dripped from my clothes. My boots sloshed and crunched across gravel. I sat down on a tree stump, with the fish in my lap, and dumped the water from my boots. My toes curled from the chilly air and goosebumps formed on my arms. I wrung out my clothes and my hair.

Smoke puffed in the sky, and with it a putrid odor. I don't know what the scientists were up to, but it couldn't be good. Dad banished them here after they refused to abide his laws, and they continued in their strange experiments and with chemicals.

When our people first arrived on Planet Xan, my great-great- great grandfather used the people of Fallow to mine the minerals and ore to build our fortress and our airships. Together the slaves and the scientists bore a hatred for the Azurins. I had to get out of here fast. My boots squished as I strode down the path. I had miles to cover to get home. The mud from the road clung to me. If nothing else, it kept the insects away.

Tall, deciduous trees, sparse at first, turned to yards of green. I loved the rich, earthy smell and the peacefulness of the woods. Birds broke out in song. I knew wild animals lived here, some grotesque from the experiments, yet I hoped they stayed their distance.

I'd been on the road for an hour when the clouds burst with rain again. Great. I'll die of pneumonia before I make it home. The wind blew through my soaked clothes, and I shivered and sneezed. I ducked under the skirt of a funnel tree. The warmth of a fire sounded good, but I had nothing to start one with. I had survived Santurin's beatings and drowning only to die from the elements? No. I don't know where my life leads, but I won't give up that easily.

Sir Jayel showed me once how to use flint to start a fire. He was nice to me, not like the other men. I searched the grounds until a piece of flint glittered on the ground. I gathered some sticks and brush from under the trees, and piled them together. Pulling my knife from my boot, I struck the flint until sparks lit the brush. I blew on it until a small fire started. Holding my hands over it, the warmth felt good.

By the time the rain relented, nightfall hit. The twin moons shone through the darkness like eyes and the night filled with twinkling stars. A twig snapped behind me and danger rippled down my back. Someone watched me. I peered through the trees. Whoever it was, hid well.

Hating to lose the warmth, I scooped dirt over the fire, and hurried down the path. Someone followed me at a distance and their steps were heavy and clunky. I had no idea what they wanted, but no way was I sticking around to find out.

A light burst the darkness up ahead.

Chapter Two

The next day

ONLY THE CANDLES, ABOVE THE MANTLE, AND THE light from the artificial gas fireplace lit the room of the main lounge. I ducked behind the couch and peered around the edge. With a girl on each arm, Santurin strolled down the two steps that led into the lower half of the main lounge.

How does he do it? Two girls at once? Do they think they are worthy of princess material? Ha! Little do they know the queen choses his bride. In fact, Mother is in Zavion doing that now. If I had Santurin's muscular physique, the girls would flock to me too.

Santurin and the girls sat down on the couch, and I clamped my hand over my mouth.

Crack.

"Bloody bells!" Santurin jumped up. "What's that wet mess on the back of my breeches?"

"Looks like eggs, My Prince," one of the girls said.

"Aidan!" my brother's voice roared.

I laughed and slipped into the hall. I ran down the hallway and rounded the corner, smashing into Councilor Wings' big belly.

"Umph. Young Prince, why the hurry?" he said. The councilor towered over me, and I counted the hairs in his sharp nose. Not a pretty sight.

"Some strange beast chased me," I said.

Councilor Wings raised his thick, bushy brows. "Another one of your fabrications?"

"There he is!" I cried and pointed behind me.

Santurin's blonde braid whacked his back as he charged in my direction. I rushed ahead and hung a right at the end of the corridor. I snuck inside the open elevator and punched the second floor. The doors slammed shut. I sighed and leaned against the wall as the elevator zoomed up.

I knew better, but my brother was a sucker for pranks, and sometimes I couldn't help myself. If he didn't mock me in front of the men and his friends, maybe I'd stop. Better to escape now before he pounded me again.

The elevator dinged and the doors opened. I ran to the stairwell, on the opposite side from the elevator, and raced down the stairs. When I hit the bottom step, I was pulled into a headlock. I struggled, but it didn't do any good. Packed with muscles, from practicing warrior skills every day, Santurin held me tight, and rubbed his knuckles into my head until it burned.

I gritted out, "Let-me-go."

Returning from her trip, Mother walked in on the scene. "What is going on?"

"I told Aidan he needed to trim his hair." Santurin smiled and ruffled my hair.

Now who is lying? I thought.

"Who is the lovely lady with you, Mother?" Santurin asked.

The two girls, Santurin brought into the lounge, stood in the hallway, scowling at the new girl. She was a beauty with small green eyes, high cheek bones, a good figure, and an erect posture that commanded attention.

Too lovely for my brother. A pang of jealousy ripped through me.

"May I present your bride-to-be, Mori of Zavion," Mother said to Santurin.

My brother looked dazed as if he couldn't believe his bachelor days were numbered. He coughed to cover his shock.

Didn't Santurin realize that was why Mother took a trip to her home village? Maybe he didn't take it seriously.

"Show her around, Santurin," Mother said. "Get to know one another."

The other two girls followed behind Santurin and Mori, calling out, "What about us, My Prince?"

I felt sorry for them. My brother ignored them and walked on.

"Am I to get a bride too, Mother?" I asked.

"You're not old enough nor do I feel you are ready. Your time will come, though. Run along to the conference room. Your father wants a word."

I cringed. *Was I in trouble for lying to Santurin last night?* He didn't believe someone followed me, so I exaggerated, and told him some man kidnapped me, but I escaped. Once I got started weaving my lie, it stretched into this drawn-out fish tale. I should have stopped, but it was fun. *Maybe I should become a traveling storyteller?*

I ran up the stairs to the second floor as Mother left my side. The conference room stood on the left of the queen's chambers. The door slid open as I walked towards it. Darkness met me. *What happened to the lights?*

I heard whispering and someone shushed them. *Was this a trick of Santurin's to get back at me?* "Hello? Anyone here? Dad?" Goosebumps rose on my arms as someone breathed on the back of my neck. I whirled around and bumped into someone. "Who is there?"

The lights popped on and people jumped up from their hiding spots. "Surprise! Happy birthday, Prince Aidan."

"Got you, son." Dad grinned, and his ice-blue eyes twinkled. A thin crown of gold pulled his long, white-blonde hair back. He wore a cobalt blue tunic over his thin, six-foot frame with matching breeches over his knee-high leather boots.

I stood to his shoulder and gazed up at him. "I forgot it was my birthday. I thought I was in trouble."

Dad arched a brow. "Why?"

"Because I lied to Santurin that someone kidnapped me."

"You know everyone worried when Varick told us you fell in the river. Why lie to your brother if it wasn't true?" Dad asked.

"How can anyone believe a word he says?" Councilor Wings said.

The people murmured in agreement.

Varick sidled to my side. "Let's get this party started!" He pulled me away from them and over to the table with the cake.

"I'm grateful you interrupted them," I said.

"No problem. Besides I'm eager for you to open my gift," Varick said.

The people gathered around the table and sang happy birthday. I blew out the candles. The servants sliced pieces of cake and passed them around.

Dad patted my back. "Hard to believe you're fifteen already. Time flies. I know you've wanted to learn warrior skills like your brother. I'll teach you, but only if you learn how to hunt with me first. My gift to you."

I hugged him a bear hug. "You're the best. What about Mother?"

"She can come along if she likes."

"That's not what I meant."

Dad grinned. "We both know she hates hunting. We won't tell her what we discussed. Hush now. Here she comes."

With her ruffled collar up to her ears, her dark hair slicked back, and her black gown swaddled around her like a blanket, Mother reminded me of some hideous bird of prey. Her brown eyes narrowed into slits as she approached us. "What are you up to now?"

"Nothing. Dad plans on teaching me how to hunt." I smiled.

"Really? And when were you going to inform me this bit of news, Arin? I cannot stop a grown man from chasing wild animals, but our son is a different matter." Mother poked Dad in the chest. "If anything happens to our son, I promise you that will be your last hunting trip."

"Mother, it's my birthday gift. Dad won't let anything happen to me."

Dad glared at her and stormed off. *He was king. Why not tell Mother off?*

Mother plastered a fake smile on her face, then joined her friend, Lady Darshana, and some other women.

She didn't even say happy birthday to me. Why did she care if Dad took me hunting?

Juliana, Varick's cousin and Lady Darshana's daughter, strolled over to me with a piece of cake. She looked nothing like Varick, except her green eyes. "Here. Better get some before it's all gone. Happy birthday by the way."

"Thanks." I inhaled the cake's spicy aroma, then scooped a forkful in my mouth. "Yum, pumpkin spice."

"Here, I made you something." Juliana handed me a parcel.

I unwrapped the tissue paper and removed a cobalt blue vest with pockets. I pulled it on.

"See. I embroidered your name in the upper corner." Juliana pointed out.

"A thoughtful gift." I kissed her cheek.

"I don't know what I'd do with the vest if you had drowned." Juliana smirked. "Your mother wants you to open her gift and I'm curious to see it. Come on." Juliana pulled me by the hand.

"There you are son." Mother handed me a wrapped package.

I yanked the paper off and examined my gift. *A book? She doesn't get me at all.*

"It's a book of poems written by your grandmother," she said.

I glanced at a few pages. *Seriously? A book of poems? At least give me a book with pictures depicting how to fight.* I handed the book to Juliana, and she flipped through it. "Thanks, Mother."

"Here. Open mine," Varick pushed an odd-shaped box in my hands.

I ripped off the paper and opened the box. "Wow."

A drum lay inside made of goatskin and tightened to a wooden rim. I pulled it out of the box and struck a beat. *Ta-da. Ta-da. Ta-da-dum-dum.*

I hit it again and got into the rhythm. The people swayed and danced as I played.

Mother held up her hands. "Enough! You can play more in your room."

Silence engulfed the room, and the people stared at Mother.

"An amazing gift, Varick." *None of the other gifts compared to my drum.*

Santurin strode over and handed me a wrapped package. "Happy birthday, brat."

I couldn't believe he got me something and tore off the wrapping. I wrinkled my brows and held up the breeches stained with eggs.

"A prank for the prankster." Santurin laughed and walked away.

I shook my head. It's always something with him, but I deserved it. I tossed the stained breeches on the table. Someone tapped my shoulder, and I turned around.

Chapter Three

WILEY, MY FRECKLE-FACED, NERDY FRIEND, WITH A NEST of unruly red hair and rumbled clothes like he just climbed out of bed, felt uncomfortable around the royals and chieftains, so we walked out of the conference room and down the stairs. We strode outside and stood on the bridge over the Hope River. Wiley shoved a polished board in my hands.

"What is it?" I turned the board around.

"Put these on." Wiley gave me a headset.

I pulled them over my hair.

"Not like that. It's an EEG headset and it works on your brainwaves, man." Wiley adjusted the headset to the temples of my forehead. "Step on the cloud-board and tell it what to do."

"Stand on a piece of wood? You're joshing me," I said.

"Enlighten me, My Prince."

"I stepped onto the board and pointed up. "To the roof of the security building."

Blue lights circled around the rim of the cloud-board and metal clasps locked my ankles in place. Before I uttered another word, the cloud-board zipped over the bridge. I put my arms out wide for balance and landed on the roof of the two- story building. "Whoa."

I stood on the edge of the roof and stared down at the turbulent waters below. Only yesterday, I fell in the river and almost drowned. Ice filled my veins and I shivered.

"Hey, man. Did the river hypnotize you or what?" Wiley yelled.

"What happens if I fall?" My voice squeaked.

"You won't. Remember you control the cloud-board. The electro encephalogram measures your brain activity and sends it to the micro-controller through the dongle. It controls the movement and speed of the cloud-board."

"Hmm, sounds like a mouthful of nonsense, but you're the tech expert, not me." I swallowed hard, closed my eyes, and then dropped. The air blew in my face, and I snapped my eyes open. I swooped down towards the waterfalls. Water sprayed my face and my arms, and then I pulled up. I wove in and out of the posts underneath the bridge. I circled back, landing at Wiley's feet. "Great gift. I love it."

"I'm thrilled it works. Enjoy. Gotta run." Wiley waved and hurried through the fortress doors.

I gazed up at the vast, sprawling fortress with its high towers that gave the impression of a foreboding presence. A glass dome centered between the towers. I flew to it and grasped a spire from its roof, spinning around, and soared back to the river. Santurin strode onto the bridge, and I whipped in front of him, startling him, before zipping across the sky again. I backflipped in the air. "Wahoo! Did you see me, Santurin?"

My brother's eyes widened. "Bloody bells! You want to join our ancestors in the afterlife? Where did you get such a contraption? I should outlaw it."

"It was a gift. I control the movements of my brain. It's safe," I said.

"If that thing relies on your small pit of a brain, then you're in trouble," Santurin said. "Mother wants you to thank our guests for attending your party."

I landed on the bridge and removed my headset. The clasps released my ankles, and I carried the cloud-board under my arm. I looked up at my brother. "Has anyone followed you?"

"Several girls, infatuated with me, follow me around. Why?" he asked.

"That's not what I meant. Someone followed me home from the river. Yes, I lied about the kidnapping part, but not the other. What if someone plans to sabotage us, one by one?" I asked. "The scientists and the people of Fallow hate us, you know."

"You're imaging things, Aidan. Run along before Mother blames me for your delay." Santurin left my side as we strolled inside the fortress.

I better watch my back since no one else will. What if the kingdom was at stake and not just my life? Some people hated the Azurins because they feared our technology and others resented our wealth. I saw it on some of the guests' faces and the younger councilors from poorer families as I opened my gifts.

I shoved my cloud-board and the headset inside the hall storage unit, and then ran up the stairs to the conference room. The doors stood open, and I walked in. "Thank you, everyone for your gifts and for attending my party."

"You're quite welcome, Young Prince. Your father arranged a hunting trip on my lands," Chieftain Yewande of Volney said. "I shall see you on the morrow." Her paper-thin ebony skin made her look fragile but beware the man that thought her weak. Her bracelets jangled as she hobbled with her walking stick.

Others said their farewells and I thanked them all again. I turned to Varick and Juliana. "Wait until you see what Wiley made me."

"Sorry, I can't stay. Mom has a meeting," Varick said. "I'll talk to you later."

"Show me your gift," Juliana said.

"Hold on. Maybe Wiley has an extra one you can borrow. Come on," I said.

"You haven't told me what it is yet," Juliana said.

"You'll see."

We raced down the hallway to the elevator. We rode it to the third floor and walked to the furthest end north until we stood in front of an arched wooden door. Dad kept this area for the computers and the techs. I knocked on the door. A few minutes later, a metal piece slid over the peephole and a blue eye appeared.

"State your business," a voice said.

"It's Prince Aidan. I'd like to talk with Wiley a moment."

The slider closed, and the door opened.

"What's up, man?" Wiley asked.

"Do you have a spare cloud-board Juliana could borrow?" I asked.

"Come in. I was putting on the last touches of my own." Wiley led us to the back of the room. Gadgets hung from the ceiling and on wires.

Lights blinked from various computers and a continuous buzz emitted. Wiley stopped at a table with a cloud-board decked out in bright green colors and yellow zigzags. The smell of paint lingered in the air.

"Wow. I love the colors. What else does it need?" I asked.

"The finishing touches on the lights." Wiley stuffed sections of wires inside small holes around the board, then screwed tiny bolts in. He applied an EEG headset and stood on the cloud-board. "Go forward. Easy now." Red lights circled around the board before the clasps held his ankles. The cloud-board ventured forward at a slow speed. Satisfied with its progress, Wiley removed the headset and the clasps released. He handed the cloud-board and headset to Juliana. "Keep it, pretty lady. I'll make myself another."

Juliana gushed, "Thanks."

We raced down the stairwell and out the side doors. We tramped across the metal ramp to the security building and climbed the stairs to the roof. I stood on my cloud-board and Juliana on hers.

"Your brainwaves control the cloud-board. Put the EEG headset on and tell it what you want to do. Let me demonstrate first." I pulled on my headset and flew across the sky. Turning around, I zipped back to Juliana. "Your turn."

She tilted on the edge of the roof. Juliana applied her headset, and then spread her arms out. The Harmony Waterfalls pounded like a drum roll as I held my breath in anticipation. My heart leapt as she dropped. I looked down and the clouds swirled in vivid pinks, then twisted into a deep purple. Juliana opened her eyes and glided across the sky.

"You did it!" I waved my arm in the air.

A squeak behind me was the only warning as Santurin punched my shoulder. "Did you dare her, Aidan? Her father is my best pilot. If anything happens to her—"

Where did he come from? Quiet as the first flake of snow. I swan-dived off the roof and sailed around Juliana.

"Show-off," she said.

Santurin called, "Good thing I'm the eldest. At this rate, Aidan you won't live long enough to be king."

"What kind of king will you make? You're afraid to take risks!" I shouted.

"Juliana is right. You're all show." Santurin pivoted around and climbed down the stairs.

I gazed at the spire atop the glass dome roof, sharp like Santurin's remarks. My brother needed some fun in his life, and I don't mean beating on me. If he took risks, he might relax. I flew in and out of the waterfalls, then flung my wet hair from my face. Water dripped down my hooked nose.

Juliana flew closer to me. "I want to try that too." She ducked under the falls and came out the other side. She wiped the water from her eyes, and I gawked at her. "What? Did I do something wrong?" Juliana nibbled her lip.

I brushed a damp red lock from her face and counted six tiny freckles across the bridge of her pert nose. I didn't mind looking at her near nakedness through her wet tunic, but it wasn't right. Juliana was a family friend.

"We should get back."

"Why the rush?" Juliana asked. "Why not cloud-board further east or west?"

"Uh, I can see through your top," I said.

Her cheeks flamed red, and she covered her chest with her hands. "Don't look." Juliana sped over to the bridge and tossed her headset down. She left the cloud-board on the bridge and tore down the path. The fortress doors opened at her approach and Juliana disappeared inside.

I never meant to embarrass her. How could I make it up to her? I flew over to the bridge and picked up her headset, shoving it in my pocket. Removing my own, the clasps released, and I carried both cloud-boards inside. I placed them in the hall storage unit.

Dad carried his bow and a quiver of arrows over his shoulder and strode down the hall towards me. "Packed anything for our hunting trip, Aidan?"

"Not yet."

"Why so glum? Something happen?" Dad asked.

"I didn't mean to, but I embarrassed Juliana," I said.

"Flowers always cheer the ladies. Why not pick some?"

"Great idea, Dad." I pulled my cloud-board out of the storage unit and applied my headset. I ran outside and jumped on my cloud-board. "To the meadow beyond the falls."

A field of wild daisies, mint, and buttercups grew in the meadow. I glided closer and stooped down, gathering a bouquet. My neck prickled. I whirled around, but no one stood there. I glimpsed a shadow departing from a thorn tree.

Whoever it was didn't follow me as I hastened back to the fortress. I landed on the bridge and tore off my headset. Shoving the cloud-board under my arm, I raced inside the fortress with the bouquet in my hand.

I found Juliana, by the fireplace in the lower main lounge, playing her guitar and singing to her younger sister, Olivia. They both had auburn hair, but Juliana's had red highlights in hers that dazzled in the firelight like copper. Olivia's hair curled where Juliana's waved down her back. Juliana resembled her mother while Olivia had her father's violet eyes and freckles. I sat on the couch and listened to them harmonize. When they finished their song, I tossed flowers at them from the bouquet.

"Look, Juliana. It's raining flowers," Olivia said. She picked up some mint and inhaled it.

"They are lovely, but such a waste on the floor," Juliana said.

"I didn't mean to embarrass you," I said. "Forgive me?"

"What did he do, Juliana? Are you going to spank him?" Olivia asked.

"Let me talk with Aidan. Go to the dining room and ask the cook for a sweet. I'll join you in a minute."

"You're in trouble." Olivia ran up the two steps into the upper section of the lounge.

"Aidan, I had a wonderful time cloud-boarding until you spoiled it. When you pointed out that you could see through my clothes, I felt dirty, and wanted to hide. Flowers won't erase my embarrassing moment, but thanks. Enjoy your time with your father hunting tomorrow. The break from each other will ease things. If you'll excuse me." Juliana stood.

"Wait," I said to her back as she rushed up the stairs.

Chapter Four

The next day

FLAT, LAVENDER CLOUDS STRETCHED ACROSS THE HORI-
zon of the Volney savanna. Heat suffocated the morning air. Sweat rolled
down my sides as I held the *dragmulen's* hard leather reins. *Dragmulens*
were a four-legged hoofed creature with a wide girth for carrying things
on their back and they had a long snout that narrowed at the end. *How
was this teaching me how to hunt by holding the reins of the pack animal?
Shouldn't I hold a weapon too instead of standing here?*

Dad loaded an arrow on his bow and raised it. He aimed and pulled
the string taut. Dad crept closer to the black and white Tuxedo wildcat
that napped in a crooked tree. He loved the adventure of stalking prey
with basic tools. At home in Azure, Dad owned advanced weapons like
lasers and guns, but the Volney people preferred a simple life and lived off
the land. They feared technology and Dad respected that.

The dragmulen snorted, and the wildcat's ears perked. The hairs on my
arms rose as the cat's tail swished back and forth. The wildcat opened its'
golden eyes and I felt trapped in place. My heart thundered in my chest.
*What if Dad missed and the wildcat charged at the dragmulen and me? I
didn't have anything to protect myself.*

A dark-hooded man appeared behind my father. *Where did he come from? The man wavered like a lens out of focus. He aimed his knife at Dad's back.*

A chill cast over me at the man's intent. "Dad, look out!"

The Tuxedo wildcat leapt as Dad released his arrow while that stranger stabbed my father. I raced over without thinking of the consequences. The hooded man vanished. Dad and the wildcat collapsed in a heap on the ground.

I pushed and shoved the wildcat's body to get to Dad, but its' dead weight made it impossible to move. The pole-thin guide, Jamar rolled the wildcat on its side, showing an underbelly of spots, and he checked a pulse in Dad's neck.

Jamar looked up at his friend, Mongo, and shook his head. "Da king is gone."

"No!" I pounded the ground, sending up dry dirt. My mouth filled with its gritty taste. *Why kill Dad? Everyone loved him. Who would stand up for me now? Dad was my hero. I couldn't imagine a day without him.* Tears flooded my face.

"What are we going to do?" Mongo, a chubbier version of Jamar, except he had a diamond-shaped scar on his forehead, glanced around. "We'll be blamed for his death."

"Da boy witnessed it. Get a grip," Jamar said. "Other dings more worrisome."

The Volney men picked Dad's body up and laid him across the drag-mulen's back. They removed the arrow from the wildcat and tossed its' body next to Dad. I stood up and pulled on the reins, and the dragmulen followed me. Jamar led us back to camp and Mongo brought up the rear.

I looked back at Dad's body. I found it hard to believe he was gone. Tears rained down my cheeks as I plodded along.

Crows cawed above from overhanging trees. I hated the noisy, pesky things, even though as an Azurin, we didn't harm or eat birds. We were cloud-dwellers because our fortress loomed among the clouds, and we relished watching the birds.

My grandfather had brought a pair of crows with him through the portal from Earth to this planet eons ago and the crows multiplied. One of the pesky birds landed on Dad, and I shooed it away.

"Go bother some other dead critter!" I yelled. *They weren't going to feast on Dad nor the wildcat after all my father's efforts to hunt it, if I had anything to say on the matter. I would rather they feasted on that hooded stranger that killed Dad, whoever he was.*

A herd of Kirin ate the lower leaves of thin trees as we walked by. Tufts of fur wrapped around each of their legs. Their bodies, covered from head to hoof in carp-like scales, glistened in the light. Long, flowing manes and a single antler topped their heads. Handsome creatures. Better than a damn crow.

The day wore on. The air was stuffy, and my shirt clung to my back. The longer we trudged on, my boots weighed down my feet. *It wasn't fair. Dad had promised to teach me warrior skills and now he's gone. Who will teach me now? Somehow, I'll find Dad's killer and make him pay for his dirty deed.*

I gazed at the guides. Their eyes scanned the territory and they seemed nervous. It dawned on me we had fresh meat. Predators stalked us. Jamar rushed us on, but not quick enough. Mongo cried out. I whipped around. A young female Brobdingnagian raced out of the brush and bit the back of Mongo's neck.

Jamar grabbed Dad's rifle, from the saddle of the dragmulen, and fired at the hairy beast. He missed and the Brobdingnagian roared, showing her massive fangs. Her paws were bigger than my head. She dropped her prize and stalked towards us.

Fear pulsated through me, and I trembled. Nowhere to go and nowhere to hide. Out of a bush, bounded a Sward. They were humpbacked, muscular creatures with green fur that were smaller than a Brobdingnagian, yet this one aimed its head and charged at the bigger beast. Growls and snarls amidst spit and pieces of fur flew as they fought over Mongo. The Sward didn't have a chance. One swipe of the Brobdingnagian's paw and the Sward sailed across the dry grass and didn't move again. The Brobdingnagian dragged Mongo's body through the brush. I didn't know the man, but Mongo didn't deserve to die like that. *Am I next?*

Another Sward snatched Dad's body from the pack animal's back. Something broke inside me, and flames shot from my fingers at the creature. The Sward shrieked and ran off with his stubby tail beneath him. I gazed at my hands. *Nothing like it ever happened before. No burns.* What did it mean?

Jamar stared at me and crossed himself.

Great. He thinks I'm a demon or something. The only demons I was aware of was the belief they lived in the fissures of Fallow. I struggled with Dad's body, trying to get it back on the dragmulen, when Jamar ran over and helped.

We headed down the path, and Jamar peeked at me now and then. He didn't speak to me and that was fine with me. Grief weighed heavy on my shoulders and confusion at what transpired with my hands. No one I knew had any powers. I couldn't ask Dad either. I bit my fist as the tears plagued me again.

Dad saved me from boredom and took me on travels with him to the other villages. He taught me how to fly an airship too. *How can I live without him?* All this seemed like a terrible nightmare.

We trudged on. I was tired of walking in this heat. Not a puff of a breeze. *How can anyone live here?* The few trees barely gave any shade, and I inhaled dirt like air. Grabbing the canteen from the saddle, I drained the remainder of my water. It didn't quench my thirst either.

"Jamar, how do your people survive in these conditions?" I asked.

"Da Baobab dree holds water for long periods of dime. Have you seen a pinkish gray dree dat looks like someone planted it upside down?"

"Can't say I noticed," I said.

"No? Da Baobab is our dree of life. Every part is useful. Da bark cures cough and brings down fever. Many stories abound from its history," Jamar said.

"Like what?" I asked.

"When da world young, da Baobab lorded over da lesser growths with haughtiness. Da gods became angry and uprooted dem. Dey shoved dem back in da ground with dare roots up. Evil spirits haunt da Baobab's flowers and anyone dat picked dem died from its bad smell," Jamar said.

"And you believe that?" I smirked.

"Da dead cannot speak and no one alive chances it." Jamar stared at me.

I wanted to hear about the other legends, but the flag of the king's pavilion waved ahead. At least Jamar's story kept my grief away for a short spell. The dark- skinned Volney people, in their colorful fabrics and beads, mumbled amongst themselves as we grew closer.

Damira, my old nursemaid, covered her mouth and paled at the sight of my father's body. She stood next to stocky-built Twain, her husband and Dad's advisor. Damira ran to my side and hugged me to her. "My poor boy. What happened?"

Before I uttered a word, Jamar said, "Da wildcat killed King Arin."

"Not true. A man killed Dad." I glanced at Damira, and my chin quivered.

She rubbed my back. "What man?"

"Da boy is in shock. Dere was no man," Jamar said.

"You're wrong!" I glared at the guide. "A man plunged a knife in Dad's back, before the wildcat fell on him. He vanished afterwards."

The crowd murmured.

I wound my hand in Damira's midnight hair. "You believe me, don't you?" I searched her warm, brown eyes.

"I believe you saw something." Damira patted my hand.

I witnessed everyone's stares and heard the whispers behind their hands. *I'm not crazy.*

Damira stirred something in a drink and handed it to me. "Something to calm you."

If anyone else gave the drink to me, I'd toss it. I drank it down without question. After a while, it was hard to keep my eyes open and I crawled inside Dad's cot. I inhaled his musky scent off his blanket and cradled it close.

The Volney people sang of my father joining the great kings in the sky. I drifted to sleep.

Later, Damira woke me. Jamar handed me the soft fur of the wildcat. I climbed in the passenger seat of our airship and held the fur to my chest. Wrapped in huge leaves, Dad's body lay in the back seat. Twain piloted the airship, and I peered out the window. Damira waved. A tall girl, around my age, with white-blonde hair and ice-blue eyes, watched me. She dressed like the Volney people, yet she resembled a cloud-dweller. *Who was she?* I leaned back in my seat.

If I had known I had special powers, I could have saved Dad. *Why did they develop after the fact?* I traced the letters, *Dad* in the fog on the glass. Sadness overwhelmed me and tears dropped off my cheeks into my lap. I rubbed the fog off with the back of my hand.

Lost in my thoughts, and dozing off and on, soon the Azure Fortress peeked through the clouds ahead. Twain glided the airship onto the track leading inside the hangar. He parked next to the other airships with the Azurin insignia, then lifted the safety hatch. I clutched the fur and climbed out. Twain walked over to the security crew, and they assisted him with Dad's body. I tromped across the metal ramp and the doors to the fortress opened. I ran past Mother and her friend, Lady Darshana.

"Aidan, slow down!" Mother called.

I hastened to my chambers, at the end of the long hallway, and raced inside. The doors shut behind me, and I flung the fur on my bed. Pulling my drum close to me, I pounded away until exhaustion wore me down.

An hour later, someone knocked on my door.

Chapter Five

SANTURIN PEERED AROUND MY BEDROOM DOOR AS HE opened it.

"Go away! I want to be alone." I glared at my brother.

"He was my father too." Santurin sank down on the end of my bed. "What happened?"

"You'll think I'm nuts too." I folded my arms over my chest.

"Try me."

"Why? So, you can mock me?" I frowned.

Santurin brushed stray golden-blond hair away from his brown eyes. "I promise not to laugh."

"It's my fault." I looked at the floor.

"What do you mean?" Santurin arched a brow.

"After Dad released his arrow into the wildcat, a man stabbed him in the back, and then he vanished. I could have saved Dad," I said. "No one told me I had special powers."

"What are you jabbering about? People don't disappear. And what makes you think you own powers?" Santurin wrinkled his nose and picked up a dirty sock off the bed. "If you did, you should clean your room. It stinks like sweat." He tossed the sock in the wicker hamper in the corner.

"Not funny. Besides, we have servants for that." I looked away for a moment. *Did it smell in here? Maybe I'm used to it.*

"Anyway, I knew you wouldn't believe me. I'll show you." I thrust out my hands and flames shot from my fingers, igniting Santurin's braid.

"Bloody bells!" Santurin clapped his hands over his braid. The smell of burned hair filled the room.

"Phew!" I waved the air. "Computer, open the window."

The curtains lifted into a compartment in the ceiling, then the window slid open. The smoke dissipated out the window.

"Say, I believe you. Describe this man," Santurin said.

"About six-foot tall, thin build, and he wore a dark-hooded cloak. I only saw him a moment," I said. "He was out of focus or something, and then he was gone."

"Almost anyone with that description. Anything else happens, come see me. I'm the man of the fortress now."

Was Santurin preening? Geez, Dad's gone only hours, and my brother acts like he's king. I massaged my forehead. "How is Mother taking the news?"

"A lot like you. Hiding in her chambers." Santurin looked at me. "Not another word about the strange man. Father died because of a wild-cat. Understood?"

"You want me to lie?" I stared at him.

"Not exactly. Omit parts of your story. It saves face."

"You sound like Mother. Always worried how others view us." I frowned.

"With power comes responsibility. The people trust us." Santurin rubbed my knee. "Isn't it better than telling them a killer is on the loose?"

"I suppose. What about my magic?" I asked.

"Talk to Mother about it. I'd wait though. She's grieving."

"And I'm not?"

"I didn't say that." Santurin picked up the fur off the bed. "The famous beast that killed Father."

I snatched it from his hands. "The same cat, but a different monster killed him."

"Aidan, we talked about this."

"No, you told me to omit the truth. People already call me a liar." I held the fur to my cheek and glanced at my brother. *He seemed devoid of grief.*

"Come out of your room and eat something. You'll feel better." Santurin coaxed.

"How can you say such a thing?" I sniffed. "Don't you care that he's gone?"

"Of course, I care, but I'm worried about you and Mother. I shoved my emotions aside to stay strong for everyone else." Santurin paused. "Do me a favor and join me for supper."

"I'm not hungry." I pouted.

"Sit by me anyway. I hate to endure the stares of everyone and eat alone," Santurin said.

"What about your bride-to-be?" I asked.

"She is giving me space to deal with everything."

Was she really or was Mori upset with him for the other girls tagging along? I found it hard to believe he requested me by his side after all the punches and mockery I endured.

We strode down the hallway and into the main lounge. Drapes covered all the windows and shrouded the room in gloom.

Black candles sat in a tray atop the glass table in front of the red couch. A black wreath hung over the neck of the elk head displayed over the mantle of the artificial gas fireplace. Dad had been a boon of light in every room he visited. He wouldn't want this gloom. He told stories of his great adventures and hunting trips. People flocked to his side and drew in his energy. Now everywhere I looked, death followed me. My throat clogged and I fled down the hall.

"Aidan, where are you going?" Santurin called.

I raced outside and stood on the south end of the bridge, watching the Harmony Waterfalls. The roar of them cushioned the sound of footsteps behind me minutes later. I flinched when a hand touched my shoulder. *Was it the killer?* I turned around slowly.

Mother stared into my face. "You saw a man stab the king?"

She probably wondered if I told the truth or not. "Yes, but no one believes me."

"Security was briefed, although we don't know much about him. Keep this news to yourself," Mother said.

"What about my new powers?" I asked.

"Your brother didn't mention it. Explain yourself."

"Flames shot from my fingers. Santurin saw it," I said.

Mother leaned against the railing of the bridge. "I hoped your grandfather misread your future."

"What do you mean?" I asked.

Mother held my hands. "Magic skips generations in our family. Usually during puberty, it manifests. When nothing happened during your thirteenth or your fourteenth year, I assumed you didn't possess any magic. Sometimes trauma triggers it."

"Do you possess any magic?" I asked.

"No, son. And before you ask, you cannot bring the dead back to life. Your father is gone, and we must accept it," Mother said.

"What good is magic?" I furrowed my brows.

"Everyone in my family, with the ability, would tell you it's a gift and a curse. Magic is unreliable at times, especially if you are exhausted," Mother said. "Do not depend on it to get you out of trouble either. And you cannot use it for personal gain."

"How do I control it?" I asked.

"Trial and error and lots of practice. I'll see if the druid will instruct you. For now, resume your studies."

"Yes, Mother." I had other questions, but she dismissed me.

Usually, I dragged my feet to class, but today I wanted to tell my friends about my new powers and rushed inside the fortress. I rode the elevator to the second floor, then strode to the north end and entered the classroom. I took the last empty seat in the row of desks behind Varick.

Master Lindy cleared his throat, and everyone looked straight ahead. He flapped his black cloak sleeves as he paced back and forth in front of the class.

A blackboard hung on the wall behind him. "Who can tell me how we arrived on this planet?"

I stretched my arm and waved it around. Master Linton called on me. "My great-great-great-grandfather brought our people through a portal he had discovered on Earth."

"Anything else?" the instructor asked.

"Yes, his many great grandfathers called the kingdom, Azure and granted himself the title king. Although, he didn't have a speck of royal blood in him," Juliana said. "A bit conceited if you ask me."

"No one asked your opinion, cousin," Varick said. "The grandfather also brought vegetation, animals, birds, and other specimens through the portal."

"Good. You've paid attention to our history lessons. Why do some of the people live away from Azure?" Master Linton asked.

I raised my hand. "That's easy. They were scared about the technology."

"Right. Some preferred the savanna territory, while others liked the forest or the rivers. Can anyone name any of the chieftains?" Master Lindy asked.

"I know!" Varick raised his hand.

"I believe Master Linton asked me," I said.

"Tell him then, know-it-all." Varick crossed his arms.

"Never mind." I hated it when people called me that. *Forget telling Varick about my new powers. Maybe I'll show him instead.*

"Yewande of Volney and Sylvia of Zavion," Juliana piped up.

Varick glared at her.

"What? You were too busy quarreling to answer," Juliana said.

I leaned out of my seat like I dropped something and pointed my fingers under Varick's chair. Flames burst from my fingers and warmed Varick's seat. Beads of sweat rolled down his neck.

Varick jumped up. "Wart's breath. What did you do, Aidan?"

"Me? Whatever are you rattling on about?"

Varick punched me in the nose.

"Boys!" Master Linton yelled. "Cease your fighting at once."

"But Aidan set my seat on fire," Varick whined.

"I only warmed it a little." I held my hanky over my bloody nose. "Can I go to the doctor's office?" Sadness filled me. *I couldn't tell Dad about my new powers or the prank I played on Varick.*

Master Linton scrunched his nose. "My Prince, this doesn't excuse you from your studies. I expect an essay on my desk on why I should be kind to my fellow students."

Varick snickered, and I stormed out of the classroom.

I breathed in and out like my meditation teacher taught me to ease my anger and stood in front of the picture window that overlooked the courtyard. Santurin wielded a sword against huge, muscular brutes in fur-lined vests over bare chests. Envy rippled through me. *Mother's logic sucked. Santurin learned warrior skills at my age. Why can't I?*

Santurin swung, but one of the big bruisers blocked his sword, and another cut him. My brother clutched his side and blood oozed between his fingers. He slumped to a stone bench and his sword clattered to the ground.

I forgot my bloody nose and ran down the back stairs and out the doors to the courtyard.

Santurin looked up at me. "It's only a flesh wound."

"That looks worse than that." Worry twisted my gut. *If Santurin died, I'm next in line for the throne. I don't want that responsibility. Was this an accident or was someone plucking off my family one by one?*

Doctor Panphilia arrived and peeled my brother's fingers away from his wound. Santurin hissed. The doctor cleansed the wound with saline, and he winced.

"You can hold my hand, if you want, while the doc stitches you," I said.

My brother gripped my hand, and I bit my lip. The doc sutured his side, and then applied a fat dressing. When she finished, I shook out the numbness from my fingers. Santurin didn't know his own strength.

"Can I tell you a secret?" Santurin whispered.

I nodded.

I was scared," Santurin said.

"You? Why?" I asked.

"Imagine if you will, these big brutes coming at you, then one slip, and you're down."

"I'm glad you didn't die."

"Remember this, if you ever fight—bloody bells, what happened to your nose?" Santurin asked.

"Varick punched me. It's nothing," I said.

"As I was saying, act brave, whether you are scared or not. It might save your ass." His face contorted as Santurin stood.

I grabbed his arm, yet Santurin pushed me away when Sir Edrei strode over.

"I'll take him from here, Young Prince."

Why treat me different with the men around? I stomped off.

Inside the fortress, I found Varick and Juliana playing chess at one of the game tables in the upper section of the main lounge. I peered over each of their shoulders and gauged their next moves. Juliana touched her rook, and I shook my head. She saw an open area and captured Varick's king. He swore and dumped the board.

"You're a sore loser." Juliana said.

"It doesn't matter. I'm moving to Waverly," Varick snarled.

"Why didn't you inform me?" I asked.

"I planned on it, until you gave me a hot seat. Mom wants to build her shipping business by the ocean. Promise you'll come visit," Varick said.

"Promise," I said.

We shook hands, then Varick strode away. Sadness filled me. *First Dad died, and now my best friend moves away. Life wasn't fair. Who would I pal around with now? Wiley built me that great cloud-board, but he was always busy with some project.*

I squatted down and helped Juliana pick up the wooden chess pieces from the floor. "I never showed you my new powers. Watch this." I pointed a finger at a rook and set it on fire.

Juliana's eyes widened. "How did you do that?"

"Mother said magic runs in her family but skips generations. She was surprised as me when I told her flames shot from my fingers when some wild beast snatched Dad's body off the pack animal." I picked up a glass of water off the table and doused the chess piece.

"I thought magic was some nonsense adults told to scare us," Juliana said.

"I heard stories about magic from my grandfather, but never believed them. Who knew they were real? I want to ask Mother more questions about it," I said.

"I'll go with you." Juliana stood and followed me out into the hall and up the stairs.

Chapter Six

THE QUEEN'S CHAMBER DOORS STOOD AJAR. MOTHER sat in a quilted high-back chair surrounded by girls. She promised their families good status and prominent prospects for the future husbands of their daughters, and they signed contracts with Mother. She picked several for handmaiden positions.

"Why does she need that many?" I whispered to Juliana.

"The queen feels insecure since her husband died. My mother is in there."

"She's a little old for a handmaiden." I snickered.

"Silly. Mom probably signed Olivia or me up. Father wants a good match for us."

"You want to be a servant, Juliana?" I arched a brow.

"No, but the position teaches one humility. You don't think I can do it?" Juliana frowned.

"I never said that. It takes away your freedom enslaved to another," I said.

"Why not get a better husband through the queen's connections?" Juliana said.

"No one takes away my freedom." I pushed my shoulders back.

"You're a prince. With power comes responsibility. You're not free."

"You sound like Santurin." I scowled. "Mother is too busy to answer my questions about magic."

A voice slithered from behind me. "I could teach you a few things about magic."

Juliana stared up at the man in white councilor robes and shuddered. She hurried inside the queen's chambers. I didn't understand her fear. *Did she sense something?*

The man had olive skin, an aquiline nose, and wiry hair, but it was his piercing brown eyes that held my attention.

"Who are you and what do you know about magic?" I asked.

"Grimshaw is my name. I learned a few tricks in my youth that I could show you if you like." He pulled a coin from behind my ear.

"Parlor tricks? That's not true magic." I frowned and turned away from the man. I slid in a patch of ice on the floor and landed on my bum. *Where did that come from?* I looked back at Councilor Grimshaw.

"Watch who you scoff at, boy. You may fall on your ass." Grimshaw smirked.

I stood and felt the dampness on my breeches. "That was uncalled for, sir. I am a prince of the realm and demand respect."

"Respect must be earned and goes both ways, you little snot." The man stormed off.

"Are you okay?" a lean, athletic girl, with toasty skin and sun-bleached hair, rushed to my side. She was a little taller than me, and quite beautiful. I knew her from somewhere, yet I couldn't place her. She smiled and

I saw a gap between her front teeth. Some might call it a flaw, but it gave her character. The scent of cinnamon wavered off her.

Perhaps we'll hit if off? "Some of these councilors think they're above everyone else and don't respect the royal family. Never mind that jerk. I am Prince Aidan, and you are?"

"Astra of Volney, at least I was, until the chieftain kicked me out. Have you seen Lady Darshana? I seemed to have misplaced her."

"Come with me." I held out my arm and she entwined hers in mine. We walked inside the queen's chambers, and I brought Astra to Juliana's mother.

"There you are," Lady Darshana said. She walked Astra over to my mother. "Your Grace, may I introduce you to Astra? Chieftain Yewande sent the girl here because she believes Astra is a cloud-dweller and should stay with her own kind. One of our airships crashed on Volney and the pilot died." Lady Darshana flipped her dark hair over her shoulder. "The child, Astra wandered away from the ship and a clanswoman took her in many years ago. The clanswoman died yesterday."

"Why wasn't the child brought here before now?" my mother asked.

"Veda begged Yewande to raise the child as her own. Veda was barren," Lady Darshana said.

"Ah, Yewande washes her hands off her then. Come here, girl. Let me look at you." Mother peered down her beak of a nose at Astra. "How old are you, my dear?"

"Fifteen."

Juliana walked over. "Hi, I'm Juliana. You look familiar." I joined their side and Juliana looked from me to Astra. "Wow, your eyes are the same ice blue as Prince Aidan's."

Lady Darshana and my mother whispered amongst themselves and strolled to the back of the room.

Really? Would I ever get a word with Mother? Always busy. I glared at her backside.

I'll try later. What else can I do? Swallowing my annoyance, I asked Astra, "What do you like to do for fun?"

"I love to run. I beat most of the boys in races on Volney." Astra smiled.

"With your long legs, I'm not surprised," I said.

"I bet we could beat you at cloud-boarding," Juliana said.

"What are you talking about?" Astra scanned our faces.

Juliana and I locked gazes.

"You'll see. Follow us," I said.

We ran down the stairs to the first floor. I removed the cloud-boards and the EEG headsets from the storage unit. We raced outside to the bridge.

I placed an EEG headset on Astra's forehead and Juliana handed her a cloud-board.

Astra rolled the cloud-board over and over. "Is there a button or something to push?"

"The headset works on your brain waves. Stand on the cloud-board and tell it what you want to do. Watch me first." I applied my headset and stood on my cloud-board. The blue lights circled around the board, before my ankles locked in place with the clasps. "To the sky." I sailed over the railing and soared across the sky. I circled back. "See? You try."

Opening the gate to the railing, I assisted Astra through, and she closed her eyes looking at the river below. Astra held her arms up and commanded the board, "To the building across the way." The cloud-board lifted her up and Astra wobbled at first, getting her bearings, and then flew to the security building's roof. She landed on it and opened her eyes. "I made it!"

"Way to go!" Juliana shouted. "Come back."

Astra looked straight ahead and flew towards Juliana. "How do you stop this thing?" She rammed into Juliana, and they fell in a heap on the bridge.

"Are you all, right?" I cloud-boarded over to them.

"A bit tangled," Juliana said.

Astra removed her leg from Juliana's shoulder and rolled over. I leaned over and pulled Juliana to her feet.

"Astra, remember you control the cloud-board. Tell it to slow down before you plow into people." Juliana brushed off her hands. "Are you hurt?"

"Abrasions on my knees. Nothing I can't handle." Astra grimaced as she stood.

Determination on her face, Astra zipped across the sky, without looking down. She circled around me, and I gave her the thumbs up. Astra chased some shiny green birds with big bills and nabbed their tail feathers. It squawked and pulled out of her clutches. Astra laughed.

I flew over to her. "As a cloud-dweller, we honor the birds, not abuse them."

"No harm done." Astra frowned. "How about a race? To that spire up there."

"Juliana, count to three for us." I squatted down.

"On the count of three. One…two—"

"Three!" Astra raced across the sky and touched the spire. "You didn't have a chance, My Prince."

"You cheated," Juliana said. "I didn't finish counting."

"Whatever!" Astra ripped across the sky again, then backflipped.

My mouth dropped open. I looked at Juliana. "Do you believe that?"

"Aidan, are you sure she never did this before?" Juliana asked.

"Must be a natural."

"Astra, I want a turn," Juliana called.

"Hold on. I'm not done yet." Astra crossed her arms over her shoulders and spun in a circle.

"Show me how you do those tricks," I said.

"Imagine you're a top twirling around." Astra demonstrated.

My spin seemed clunky. I needed more practice. Juliana groaned, and I glanced her way. Her lips tightened in a firm line and guilt poked me. I valued my friendship with Juliana, yet Astra's natural skill amazed me. I felt pulled between the two girls. Juliana marched down the bridge.

I glided over to her. "Please don't go."

Juliana stopped and said to me, "I wanted some time to cloud-board too, but Astra is selfish."

"I heard that," Astra said. She zoomed closer. "Go away, crybaby."

"You'd like that. You want to hog the board and the prince all to your-self." Juliana shoved Astra.

"Don't touch me." Astra seethed.

"Girls, I know a way we can all have fun," I said.

"How?" Juliana searched my face.

"It calls for a leap of faith. Climb on my back." I faced my backside toward her.

"You're jesting. I'll fall." Juliana stepped back, shaking her head.

Astra squawked and flapped her arms around.

"Never mind her. Juliana, I'll help you." I held out my hand and Juliana grasped it.

"Climb on my shoulders and I'll hold your feet." I steadied myself with the extra weight and bent my knees. "Here we go. Steady." I flew over the waterfalls and circled back.

Astra flew near us. I glided slowly, so I didn't frighten Juliana when I felt her rock backwards. She plummeted down and clawed at the air. Astra had a smug look on her face, and I wondered if she pushed Juliana. To make matters worse, one of the royal airships sped towards Juliana.

"No!" I cried. *How do I prevent Juliana from smacking into the rocks below? I had to do something and quick or lose Juliana forever.*

I cringed as the airship flew closer to Juliana. Time was ticking. I swooped down, yet I knew I wouldn't be quick enough. An Ascension bird, with a huge wingspan, flapped its wings near me. I caught its attention and stared into its obsidian eyes. "Save Juliana." I sent a telepathic picture in the bird's mind of her.

When Juliana and I took meditation classes together, we found out we could communicate with each other and some creatures telepathically. I hoped this worked.

The Ascension bird dove down and snatched Juliana with the fabric of her tunic. The bird flew back to me and dropped Juliana in my arms. Juliana cried into my shoulder and hugged me tight.

I rubbed her back and whispered, "I've got you. You're safe now." I glided us over to the bridge and Juliana climbed through the opening in the gate.

Seeing Astra nearing me, I glared at her. "Juliana almost died because of you."

"Me? What did I do?"

"Don't play games. I know you pushed Juliana off my shoulders. Such behavior is not tolerated." I frowned. "You should respect us for teaching you to ride a cloud-board."

"I only gave her a little nudge to scare her. I didn't expect her to fall. What is Juliana to you anyway?" Astra asked.

"She's a close family friend like a sister." I snatched the headset off Astra's head and the clasps released her ankles. I handed the cloud-board and headset to Juliana.

Astra grasped the railing with one hand and dangled in the air. "A little help?"

Chapter Seven

A WEEK LATER, THE MORNING BROUGHT FOG AND A slight chill. Held on the grounds, near the mausoleum, the funeral progressed on the back of the Azure property. Dad, dressed in his favorite purple jacket over matching breeches, was lying on boughs of balsam fir inside the wooden casket. He wore a thin crown of gold on his head and his long, white-blond hair was braided.

Multitudes of people from various villages arrived last night and everyone dressed in their best finery in honor of Dad. I wore the Tuxedo wildcat fur around my shoulders, over my black velvet jacket, and matching breeches. Mother, dressed in a black gown, stood at the head of the casket with Santurin and Mori, his bride-to-be. I stood on the right of Santurin. The chieftains sat near the councilors and Mother's handmaidens. The guards and the soldiers scattered around in a protective circle. The rest of the people gathered on the lawn. Mother nodded to the high priest.

The high priest, Reynard lit some incense, inside a brass container, and the smell of Frankincense filled the air. He waved the smoke over Dad. "By the fire, Arin is on his way. Remember him." The priest put the brass container on the ground and held up a chalice of water. "By the rain, Arin is on his way. Remember him." He splashed some water on Dad's forehead. He set the chalice down and picked up some loose dirt. "By the earth, Arin is on his way. Remember him."

He tossed the dirt on Dad's body. The priest blew over Dad's face. "By the air, Arin is on his way. Remember him." The priest nodded to the casket bearers.

The king's men lifted the casket. They turned four times from east to west and then south to north. They chanted, "Protect the king, O goddess, and guide him to the afterlife and fulfill your duty." The men put the casket back on the ground.

The high priest looked at Sir Edrei, Mother's champion, and Juliana's father. "Light the fire."

Sir Edrei nodded to the archers. They lit their oil-slicked arrows and shot them into the casket. Mother and some other forest-dwellers sang a song about how we will meet again. Tears flooded my face as Dad's body burned.

Santurin hugged me to him. Shocked at the display of emotion from him, I welcomed this change. I didn't want to remember Dad shriveling into a waxy glob, and I squeezed my brother's waist. I believe the act brought comfort to him as well. For once, he didn't push me away.

I wiped my face with my hanky, before I followed Mother, Santurin, and Mori back to the fortress. I nodded to everyone who gave their condolences. It was too hard to converse without breaking down again. Juliana walked in silence next to me and I managed to give a weak smile for her. The people followed behind us.

I hoped to see Varick at the funeral service, but he didn't show. Probably still unpacking and getting situated at his new home. I glimpsed Astra with the handmaidens, but I wasn't in the mood for her theatrics.

After the incident of her pushing Juliana to her doom, I eventually helped Astra up on the bridge that day, but I scratched her off my list as girl-friend material.

Juliana and I walked inside the main lounge and climbed up the two steps to the upper half where the cook had prepared food for the guests.

Chieftain Yewande wandered over to me. "Sorry for your loss. I shall miss King Arin's vivid stories. He loved a good hunt, but you may come and hunt on Volney whenever you wish, My Prince."

"Thanks, Chieftain for the offer, but I can't imagine doing that at the moment," I said.

"I understand," Yewande said.

"Excuse me." I left the chieftain's side and found Juliana and Astra sitting on the couch in the lower main lounge.

Astra gazed at her reflection on the glass coffee table. "You're jealous, Juliana because all the men fall for me. Don't you think Prince Santurin dreamy? We'd make the perfect couple, and our children would be beau-tiful like us."

"Whoever wants you, can have you and all your faults, but the prince already has a fiancé." Juliana shot up from the couch.

"What did I do now?" Astra wrinkled her brow.

"After you tried to kill me, I don't want to hear your prattle." Juliana twirled around and plowed into me.

Not expecting the blow, I fell over the footstool.

"Sorry, Aidan. I didn't see you." Juliana's lip curled as she peered back at Astra. "It seems the prince has fallen for me, instead of you." Juliana stepped over me.

I grabbed her foot. "Wait. Where are you going?"

"Away from her." Juliana slapped my hand away from her foot and rushed away.

I ran after her. "Please don't go. This place is depressing. Care for a ride on one of the airships?"

Astra tiptoed behind Juliana and twisted her arm. "We'd love to go. Right, Juliana?"

"Where to?" Juliana gritted through her teeth.

"It's your choice," I said. *I hadn't intended for Astra to go, but maybe she was trying to be nice.*

"Really? Even if I say the wastelands?" Juliana said.

Astra snorted. "Why go there?"

"Because I'm curious and never been there."

"You like a little danger. I like this side of you." Astra let go of Juliana's arm.

I frowned. "You don't have any other choices?"

"No," the girls chorused.

I groaned. "You won't enjoy the scenery, believe me. Dad worried the scientists might contaminate the rest of the kingdom and had Fallow separated."

It was good the girls got along again, but I hated the idea of traveling to the wastelands.

We tramped across the metal ramp leading to the airship hangar. We walked to the end of the line and approached a red airship.

"Don't tell me we're going in that old can. Does it even fly?" Astra spat.

"This was Dad's ship. It's an older model, but it works." I pushed a button on the key bob and the airship's doors swung outward.

The girls clamored inside, and I jumped in the pilot seat. I pushed another button and the safety hatch clicked in place over us. I engaged the engine and the airship shot across the track and into the sky.

Juliana peered over my shoulder. "What are all those fancy gadgets? Can you teach me to fly?"

"Your father would peel my skin across the tracks if he caught wind of you piloting."

"You exaggerate, Aidan. Father isn't that harsh." Juliana giggled.

"I'm not teaching anyone. We're on an adventure, remember?" I steered us north.

Fallow was almost two hours by foot. It was much quicker by airship. Tall iron gates, resembling jagged teeth, blocked the entrance by foot. I flew over it and cast a look at the bleak, scorched wastelands. Weather-worn rocks and sparse, stunted plants dotted the tough environment. I headed northeast and the heat generated from the fissures in the ground. The survivors from the last war hung out here and heated their food. They tossed rocks at my airship, and I flew higher. They blamed the kingdom for their circumstances.

We headed further inland. Shells of buildings spread across the land-scape. Gigantic holes gaped in the ground. Uprooted trees twisted into odd shapes. Thousands of bones littered the dry dirt. Nothing green grew on the land.

"What happened here?" Astra questioned.

"Politics and war. The scientists experimented with various chemicals and explosives. Dad tried to end it when he saw the effects on the land, but they refused to stop. They wanted their own independence and started a war. Dad took it hard when many people died. He feared the scientists would destroy us all and built a wall around Fallow.

"I've seen enough. Take us home," Juliana said.

From a nearby cliff, the light glimmered off some metal and it blared into my eyes.

"What's that?" Astra pointed.

I shielded my eyes with one hand. A skull-like figure aimed a weapon at us. I shifted gears and swung the airship around. Something struck the side of the ship and rocked it.

"Get us out of here!" Juliana yelled.

I dipped the airship between some rock formations and escaped from Fallow. Soaring across the sky, I headed south.

"That was a stupid idea, Juliana. Next time, I pick our destination." Astra glowered.

"There isn't going to be a next time when Santurin sees the damage. I hadn't asked permission to take the airship out. No one would know our whereabouts if that figure attacked us. Who knows what kind of mis-shaped monsters live out there?" I said.

"What are you saying, Aidan?" Juliana shuddered.

"Don't tell me you're scared." Astra cackled.

"Shut up." Juliana hugged herself.

We left Fallow and flew home in silence. We glided into the airship hangar of Azure, and I parked the airship next to the others. I lifted the safety hatch and the girls climbed out. We didn't speak of the incident. The girls headed to their units. I walked inside the fortress and hastened to my room. Guilt gnawed at me. I expected Santurin to call me and explain the damage of the airship any time. I entered my chambers and took my frustrations out on my drum.

An hour later, I received a summons.

The ticking of the clock, on top of the mantle, inside the main lounge, grated on my nerves. I drummed my fingers on an end table. As usual, Santurin was late. Always in some meeting or other thing, yet he summoned me. The couch felt like a thousand thorns poked through it. I don't know why Mother kept it. I jumped to my feet and paced the floor.

Above the mantle, the wildcat trophy head, replaced the elk, and its golden eyes bore into mine as if it knew my anguish. I sniffed back a tear. How long must I wait for my brother? I raised my hands to the artificial gas fireplace, but not much warmth came from it.

Half an hour later, Santurin strode down the two steps into the lower half of the main lounge. "Ah, Aidan, do you know how Father's airship got damaged?" Santurin pierced me with eyes the same boring brown as Mother's.

"Straight to the point, I see. Can't say hello or how are you doing?" I scowled. "I want respect too. You've kept me waiting for some time."

Santurin seemed taken aback by my remarks. "I have a wedding to plan, and I've taken over Father's duties. Someone must take responsibility around here. Not play around like you." He blew out his breath. "Security reported seeing you enter Father's airship and now it's dented. What happened? And don't feed me a lie."

Juliana and Olivia barged into the room.

"We're here, Prince Santurin," Olivia said.

"Good day, ladies," I said. "Where are you off to?"

"Your brother promised us a venture. He's to show us the animals on Volney." Olivia jumped up and down.

"Why go there so soon after Dad's death?" I asked.

"I'm taking Chieftain Yewande back and asked the girls if they wanted a ride. Olivia is eager to view any animal." Santurin chuckled.

"Yes, I see that."

Santurin turned to Juliana. "I need a word with Aidan first. You may wait with the chieftain at the hangar.

"Is this about the airship? Someone shot at us," Juliana said.

"The assailant wore a mask and was armed," I added.

"And you're just telling me this news? Where were you at the time?" Santurin frowned.

My shoulders slumped. "In Fallow."

"You took Juliana to the wastelands? You know it's forbidden. What were you thinking? Your impulsiveness could have gotten you and she killed." Santurin pounded his fist on a nearby table.

"It's not his fault. I talked him into it," Juliana stared at the floor.

"Don't lie. It's beneath you." Santurin lifted her chin.

Astra strolled into the room. "She's not. I was there too." She shoved Juliana out of her way. "I don't believe we've met. I'm Astra." She extended her hand.

Santurin ignored her outstretched hand. "And what do you know of this?"

Astra clung to his side anyway. "I like a little danger, but this was an irresponsible, stupid idea of Juliana's. I have never seen such destruction." She paused. "Where are you going?"

"Santurin is taking Chieftain Yewande back home and the girls are joining him," I said.

"May I tag along?" Astra batted her eyes at my brother.

"Not this time." Santurin turned to Juliana. "Come on, before I change my mind. Your father will need to hear about this too."

"Great." Juliana grabbed her sister's hand and followed him out the fortress doors.

"Safe travels!" I called.

Astra glared at Juliana's back. She turned away and wound her arm in mine. "What is beyond the Harmony Waterfalls? Last night while I stood on the balcony, I saw some lights flickering beyond them. When I asked Sir Edrei about them, he told me they were reflections of the stars on the water. I doubt that."

"Let's check it out," I said.

Chapter Eight

WE CROUCHED LOW ON OUR CLOUD-BOARDS AS WE neared some crushed metal that sufficed for an airship. We floated over the ground in search of survivors. A person, in metal armor, lay on his side. I hopped off my cloud-board and walked over to the figure, rolling him over.

Astra gasped. "It's the same skeletal creep that shot at us from Fallow."

I unlatched the side of his mask. "He's a boy."

"He's a replica of you, except the scar on his cheek and his shaved head. No wonder he wore a mask. Why did he attack us? We meant him no harm." Astra held her hand under his nose. "The boy is breathing, but he has a bad wound on his head. Can we carry him back to the fortress?"

"What if we dropped him?" I said. "Wait. I have an idea." I ran over to the smashed airship and dragged a large piece of metal over.

We removed the boy's armor, then rolled him onto the slab of metal. Blood soaked through the side of the boy's thin shirt and bruises encircled his arms. I removed my shirt and wadded it into a ball, pressing it against the wound, and the boy moaned.

"Astra, search the airship for a rope," I said.

She raced over to the airship and tossed things out, until she found a rope and a shirt. Astra hastened back and kneeled next to me. She tore the shirt in strips. "Lift him up."

I pulled him up and Astra weaved the strips around the boy's waist and chest. She tucked in the end piece. Astra grabbed the rope and threaded it around the boy. "Lift the metal part up and I'll tie the rest of the rope around it."

"Hurry. It's getting heavy," I said. She finished tying the rope to the metal and I laid the boy back down.

"Cut some branches of cedar, Aidan. We'll cover him to keep him warm," Astra said.

I hiked over to a cedar tree and cut some lower branches. Hurrying back, I spread the cedar over the boy. "I'll drag him through the woods to Azure."

"No, My Prince. He might die by the time you got there. Fly on your cloud-board and get help."

"Astra, I won't leave you here by yourself. I'd never forgive myself if something happened to you. What if an animal mauled you or some bandits attacked you? I'll stay with the boy, and you get help," Aidan said. "Ask Tano, the pilot to bring an airship here. He's usually cleaning them or working in the security building."

"Will he listen to a girl?" Astra questioned.

I pulled off my tanzanite ring. "Show him this and he'll come."

Astra grasped the ring, and then jumped on her cloud-board. "Take me to Azure."

After she left, I glanced at the boy. His shaved head glistened in the meager light between the thickness of the trees. Something on the boy's arm caught my attention. I raised it up and looked closer. *What did it mean?* The boy had the birthmark of a bird on his inner arm like mine.

I plopped down on the ground and crossed my legs. Something rustled behind me, and I twirled around. A heavy branch smacked the side of my head and I plunged into darkness.

Sometime later, the smell of ammonia gagged me. Juliana held a bottle of Spirit of Hartshorn as I sat up.

Her father, Sir Edrei squatted down. "What happened, Young Prince?"

"Where is Astra?" I asked.

"We pulled into the hangar and Astra flagged us down. She told us about the boy and his condition. She stayed at the fortress to give us more room," Juliana said. She handed me my ring.

"After Astra left, someone struck me with a heavy branch." I massaged the side of my head. "Where is the boy?"

"Gone and his airship too," Juliana said.

"Describe your attacker," Sir Edrei said.

"It happened too fast. It's a blur, but he was tall and bulky built. Did Astra tell you; the boy looked like me?" I stood up and everything spun around.

Sir Edrei caught my arm. "Easy." He guided me to his airship.

I climbed inside the airship and Sir Edrei handed my cloud-board to me. Juliana placed the broken pieces of my EEG headset in my hand.

I hoped Wiley could replace the parts. Whoever hit me, didn't want me to escape. Probably imagined me dying from the elements. Why take the boy though?

Sir Edrei flew around the area. Light flashed in the distance, and I pointed it out. Sir Edrei flew lower over the rivers. A strange vehicle rumbled across a dirt road.

Sir Edrei flipped a switch and spoke in his microphone. "Pull your vehicle over by order of the king!"

A short, thick man raised his fist in the air. "I know my rights. Find your own junk."

He steered a long, motorized cart with the wrecked airship on board. Steam escaped from a side port of the cabin of the vehicle, before the man halted.

Sir Edrei landed his airship in a meadow. "You two stay put." He climbed out and swaggered over to the man.

I listened for any information about the boy.

"Did you pick up a boy with this airship?" Sir Edrei asked the man.

"Someone paid five pieces of silver to haul this airship away. No child about. What do you want with him?" The man stroked his chin as if calculating a deal.

Their voices lowered and I couldn't hear a blasted word. Sir Edrei inspected the airship. He flipped a coin to the man. Sir Edrei swaggered back to us after the man climbed back in his vehicle and continued down the road.

"You're allowing him to keep the airship? Why?" I asked.

"I told him to keep the piece of junk, but I expected him to notify the kingdom if he sees a boy that resembles you. It benefits the kingdom to hold the people's ears and eyes open." Sir Edrei climbed inside the airship.

I kneaded my forehead as a headache came on and looked out the window.

"Father, can't we search the woods for the boy?" Juliana asked.

"I won't risk your life, besides the prince needs medical attention," Sir Edrei said.

We flew home and soon the fortress rose through the clouds. Sir Edrei guided the airship onto the track of the backside of the hangar. He parked it next to the other airships and lifted the safety hatch. I climbed out first and assisted Juliana down. As dizziness overcame me, I leaned into Juliana, and she helped me walk to the fortress doors. Once inside, she put my cloud-board inside the hall storage unit, and I staggered down the hall to Dr. Panphilia's office. I held onto the wall as dizziness claimed me again. I knocked on her door.

The smell of antiseptic assaulted my nose in the white, sterile room. Jars of cotton balls, tongue blades, gauze, and lollipops lined the counter.

I cleared my throat. "Someone smacked me with a heavy branch. My head and face ache. I'm dizzy too."

The doctor flashed a light in my eyes. "Your pupils aren't uneven or dilated." She pressed around my eyes and cheekbones.

I flinched.

"Open your mouth, please." The doctor probed a tongue blade around the inside of my mouth. "No teeth broken. Any problems moving your jaw?" Her hands felt around the back of my ears and along my jawline.

"It's sore, yet I can open and close my mouth," I said.

"You had a mild concussion. Rest and ice your face. I'll give you something for the pain." The doctor unlocked her cupboard, pulled out a prefilled syringe, and injected my shoulder. "If your symptoms worsen, come back and see me."

I walked back to my room and squinted at the light flooding in from the window. "Computer, shut the shades." A compartment opened in the ceiling. The shades dropped down and darkened the room. I pressed a button on the far wall. "Send some ice."

Minutes later, the pneumatic tube system whooshed through the chambers of the fortress and dropped a pack at my station. A red light flashed. I opened the glass door and removed the sealed pack of ice. Flopping on my bed, I applied the ice to my face and closed my eyes.

I must have dozed off. Fifteen minutes had passed by, and my cheek felt numb. Too many questions plagued me about the missing boy, and I left my chambers.

I plopped down in a rocker in the lower section of the main lounge. Feeling weary, I closed my eyes, while I waited for Astra. Someone shook my shoulder, and I opened my eyes. Mother and Councilor Wings stood over me.

"Aidan, your face is one large bruise," Mother said.

"Someone surprised me and struck my head with a branch. Didn't Sir Edrei inform you?"

"No, Councilor Wings and I walked in the meadow and just returned. Did you see your attacker?" Mother asked.

"He was a big brute, but it's all a blur," I said.

"Keep a low profile. I don't want our guests to panic," Mother said.

"Do you care only how others view us? What if I died? Would you shed a tear?" I asked.

Mother gasped.

"Do not speak to the queen in that insolent manner," Councilor Wings snapped.

"Mind your own business. You're not my father." I glared.

"Someone should have paddled your behind a long time ago." Councilor Wings frowned.

"That is enough!" Mother shouted. "Leave my side, Councilor."

"As you wish, Your Grace." Councilor Wings bowed, before he strode down the hall.

"Is he courting you, Mother?" I asked.

"Yes, and Councilor Grimshaw too. It's quite flattering. You think I'm too old?"

"You could do better than those two," I said.

"I've known Wings a long time. Grim was a friend of your father's. Never mind." Mother flung her hand in the air. "I don't understand why someone wants to harm you, Aidan. Unless… it's because you witnessed your father's murder. Are you sure you don't know who it was?"

"No, Mother. The figure wore a hooded cloak, but he was leaner than the person that knocked me out with the branch. Maybe they're working together?" I said.

"Inform Santurin," Mother suggested.

"He won't believe me," I said.

"Tell him I sent you then."

"All right." I left her side and hurried up the two steps to the upper lounge. I walked down the hall to Santurin's office and knocked on the door.

"Enter," he called.

Santurin had removed all of Dad's animal heads from the walls, but a shadow of an outline remained. His collection of spears and other things no longer existed in the corner of the room either. Sadness filled me at the loss.

My brother sat in Dad's old leather chair behind a mahogany desk. He looked up as I strolled in. "Bloody bells! What happened to your face?"

"Astra and I found a wrecked airship near the Lithadora Woods. She left to get help for the injured pilot, and I stayed with the boy." I glanced around the room and noticed Santurin had removed the animal skins Dad had decorated the floor. "Anyway, some big brute swung a branch at me and knocked me out. When I woke, the boy and the airship were gone."

"Describe the pilot," my brother said.

"He looked like me, except for his shaved head and puckered scar on his cheek," I said.

"Then the rumors are true," Santurin mumbled.

"What rumors?" I stared at him.

"Father had affairs."

"Take that back. Dad was an honorable man."

"You are too naïve, Aidan. Our parents hadn't been happy in a long time. A man has needs. You'll understand when you're older. Excuse me, but I have a meeting. I'll investigate your situation." Santurin glanced at his clock.

"I knew it was pointless to see you. Nothing I say or do means anything." I scooted my chair back.

"I never said that. We can talk later," Santurin said.

"Don't bother. I'll find the boy on my own." I charged out of the office.

Chapter Nine

The next day

I GLUED MY FACE TO THE GLASS OF THE AIRSHIP FOR ANY sign of the boy. Something glistened in the light, and I pointed it out to the pilot, Tano. "Follow that glider boat. I have a feeling the boy is in there."

Tano veered to the right and followed it. As we closed in, I looked at the contraption. A rowboat shape glided across the sky with sails. A person, covered from head to toe in a thick cloak, steered it. On the floor, a blanket was wrapped around a figure.

"It's heading towards Meadowlark," I said. "Why not return to Fallow?"

"You saw that place, Prince Aidan. I believe the boy was held against his will. When he saw an opportunity, he escaped," Astra said.

"You're probably right. But why not go to Azure?" I said.

"Maybe he felt unwelcomed in Azure?" Tano said. "After the war, any straggling survivors stayed on Fallow."

"What if the boy planned an attack on Azure?" Astra voiced.

"Maybe he's the one spying on me?" I pulled up my sleeve. "That boy had the same birthmark as me."

"I have that same one on my arm," Astra said.

"Santurin told me Dad had affairs, but I didn't believe him. And what does the boy have to do with you? Did you have a brother, Astra?" I asked.

Astra pulled a necklace from beneath her top. "I was found with this locket." She showed me the pictures inside. "I don't know the boy in my locket. Veda said they only found me."

"Santurin never mentioned he had any birthmarks, but he keeps mum on a lot of things." I shielded my eyes from the glare of the sunlight. "Look." I pointed. "The glider boat landed in that field. Take us down, Tano."

He landed in the field, then raised the safety hatch. We hopped out and strode to the glider boat. The hooded figure lifted the boy out and turned around. The hood slipped off.

"Damira?" I asked.

"Prince Aidan, what are you doing here?" she asked.

"I could ask you the same thing. Are you part of a conspiracy against the kingdom?"

Damira carried the boy to the grass and knelt. "Cosmo is my son."

"He looks like me. Did you have an affair with Dad?" I asked.

"No. Your mother had twin boys. Something went wrong during the birth of your brother and the side of his face was damaged. Your mother couldn't look at him and told me to get rid of him. I raised him as my own in secrecy on Fallow and named him too."

"He's not my twin then?" Astra questioned.

"No, dear. Skyla bore only you. Forgive my deceit. I placed that picture in your locket when you were little to protect Cosmo from harm,"

Damira said. "I could never kill a baby. I don't know who shot your mother's ship down, Astra. Although, I have my suspicions."

"Maybe Mother feels guilty every time she looks at me?" I said.

"It's possible, dear." Damira glanced around. "I must protect Cosmo. He escaped Fallow and now his life is in jeopardy."

"Thanks for sparing my brother's life. Who wants Cosmo dead, besides Mother?" I asked.

"Grimshaw and Twain are the only ones that know Cosmo's history. At first, Grimshaw took a liking to Cosmo as a boy, but recently, something happened between them," Damira said. "Cosmo won't talk about it, but I saw the bruises on his arms. Don't share your knowledge about him with your mother, Prince Aidan. I beg you. Grimshaw is too close with the queen. I'll keep Cosmo here on Meadowlark for now."

"Mother and I were never close. I can't believe she was heartless though. To send away your own baby?" I said.

"How is Tiana getting along with the queen?" Damira asked.

"She's Mother's personal handmaiden," I said.

"I made a pact with the queen. For getting rid of her son, she promised my daughter a good position. Prince Santurin doesn't know Twain is my husband nor Tiana's father. We thought it best to keep him in the dark since he's close to your mother." Damira turned from me and faced Astra.

She held Astra's hands. "I know it's hard to hear. King Arin was attracted to your mother and Queen Willow turned him away from her bed. At the time, the queen delivered the twins and Skyla delivered you not long afterwards. I overhead the queen and Twain talking. She wanted to get rid of Skyla. I don't know if he was involved in the shooting of your mother's airship."

Damira glanced around. "I told Skyla to get out of Azure for her own safety. I arranged with Chieftain Yewande to hide Skyla and you on Volney. My heart cracked when I heard the news of the crash," Damira said.

"How can I trust anyone?" Astra bristled.

"You can trust me, honeypot," Tano said.

"I don't know how I feel about anyone right now. I want to scream." Astra stomped her foot.

"If it makes you feel better, go ahead and scream," I said. "I'll scream with you."

"Me too," Tano piped up.

Astra burst out laughing.

We traipsed through the tall blue-green grass of Meadowlark. Tano carried Cosmo over his shoulder. About a mile from the field, a village of oblong cement structures raised on wooden poles appeared. Six small, square windows looked out from each one. On the side of the structures, a pulley mechanism assisted people in and out of their homes. The back of the structures faced the river edge. The river-dwellers learned from their past experiences and adapted. The river brought them food, but it also brought floodwaters during the rainy season.

Astra leaned close to Tano and picked up Cosmo's hand. "You can trust us. You, Prince Aidan, and I share the same father. We'll talk more after the healers fix your wounds."

A warmness filled me. I had a sister and another brother. Too many secrets kept from me.

I could understand Cosmo, but why not tell me about Astra?

Damira led us to some white tents down the path. "Tano, put Cosmo on one of the empty cots."

A healer, in a winged cap and a white robe, ran over to Damira and she told her, "The boy crashed into a cliff."

"Besides his head wound, the boy has a wound on his flank," I added.

The healer nodded and set to work on Cosmo.

"Tano, wait here with Astra," Damira said. She interlocked arms with me. "Walk with me, My Prince."

We strolled to the center of the town outlined in steppingstones. A wooden stage stood off to the left far corner with rows of benches in front of it. To the right, a building marked, *General Store* stood on blocks of stone with a bakery, a bait shop, a clothing store, and an herbal shop next to it. Damira led me to the backyard of the herbal shop and stopped at a round-shaped structure. She pressed a remote and the shield lifted. She waved me in, and we sat at a table with chairs. Damira hit a button and the shield enclosed us.

"You're free to talk in here. It's made of soundproof glass." Damira continued, "Your father feared the scientists might clone you and your siblings. You have the gift of sight. Your father wanted you to remember, in case something happened to him, and placed a special design behind your ear."

"Why didn't you tell me this before? No one believed me when I said a man killed Dad."

I furrowed my brows. "I've been called a liar, yet everyone around me has deep secrets. How can I trust anyone? If I had this gift, why didn't it warn me about Dad's demise?"

"We can't change the future, My Prince. I don't know how your gift works, but your father insisted I tell you about it," Damira said. "Press the design. Perhaps it will answer your questions."

Did I really want to know? I held my breath and pushed the design behind my left earlobe. The round enclosure and Damira disappeared. Gray clouds enfolded me, before it cleared. A vision of me holding the reins of the *dragmulen* appeared. Dad aimed his arrow at the Tuxedo wildcat. A figure materialized behind Dad. I recognized him now. Grimshaw held a dagger and stabbed Dad as my father released his arrow. The scene clouded over once more, and my view returned to the present.

"Grimshaw killed my father. Why? He was friends with Dad. Mother told me Dad gave Grimshaw the position of councilor too." I stood and paced inside the enclosure. "Is he a sorcerer? How else could he materialize, and then vanish? I knew it was a man, but I couldn't explain why he was out of focus and shimmering. No one else saw him, but me." I rubbed my forehead. "And he's courting Mother!"

"The guide claimed he didn't see anyone. I'm sorry I didn't believe you," Damira said.

"I should get back to the fortress. I'm surprised security isn't searching for me," I said.

Damira pressed the remote and the shield lifted. I hugged her, then strode down the path. The stark whiteness of the healers' tents drew my attention up ahead. My fingers itched to smear grass on it to add some color. I dug my nails in my palm to stop my impulsiveness. I was angry at Grimshaw, not these people.

I inhaled and blew out my breath, before walking inside the tent. Cosmo's eyes were closed, and I turned to walk away, when his hand shot out, and halted me.

"A question burns within you. Speak. I'll answer if I can," Cosmo said.

"Did you ever meet our father?" I asked.

"I met him once, by accident. He came to Fallow with my stepfather, Twain. I slipped out of my hiding spot, and he spied me. He looked surprised. At first, he thought I was a clone of you." Cosmo cleared his throat. "My adopted mother, Damira took him aside and explained the circumstances. He never knew I existed. I never saw him again." Cosmo looked away a moment. "I thought he was ashamed of me until I learned later; he died in a hunting accident."

"Grimshaw murdered him. It wasn't an accident," I said.

"But I heard—"

"All lies. I was there. Nobody believed me either. Sorry, it's a sore spot."

"Grimshaw wanted me dead too," Cosmo said.

"What? Why?" I asked.

"I overheard Grimshaw talking with a man. He said I stood in his way of becoming king. I had to save myself and piece together that airship from scraps of metal. By sheer luck, I flew that far. Something struck the side of my ship and I plowed into the cliff."

"I assumed Grimshaw lived in the councilor chambers on Azure," I said.

"I know he travels back and forth between Fallow and Azure. My stepfather and Grimshaw converse a lot with the scientists on Fallow," Cosmo said. "I've seen you before, in the meadow picking flowers. I was curious. You resembled me. I was afraid to come any closer. Twain told me the people of Azure hate us. You don't look any different than the people of Fallow."

"How do they survive those harsh conditions?" I asked.

"Maybe I've said too much." Cosmo turned away.

"Rest, brother. We'll talk later." I left his side and trekked down the path.

Tano and Astra stood by the airship.

"Ready to go?" I asked.

They nodded. We climbed inside the airship. Tano put it in gear and the airship rocked across the field, and then lifted into the air. The scenery blurred as the airship flew away. Information from Damira and Cosmo swirled around my mind. It brought more questions than answers.

Tano glided the airship inside the Azure hangar forty minutes later and parked it. The safety hatch rose, and we climbed out. Our boots echoed in the quiet. We strode through the security building and onto the metal ramp that led to the fortress. The doors opened.

Santurin stood in the middle of the hallway and tapped his foot. Astra and Tano ran off.

What did I do now to earn that look from Santurin? I thought.

"Where have you been?" My brother glared.

"Can we talk in your office?" I asked.

"Fine." Santurin waved me in front of him. He smacked the back of my head.

"Hey! What was that for?"

"For worrying Mother."

I deserved that, but I refused to walk in front of him after he hit me. Santurin strode inside his office and sat behind his desk.

I pulled up a chair. "Remember when I told you a man killed Dad?"

"Yes. What of it?"

"It was Grimshaw," I said.

"How long did it take you to make up that story?" Santurin stared at me.

"It's the truth. Damira told me Dad placed a design on me because I have the gift of sight. When I pressed it, a vision of that day appeared. I'm telling you, Grimshaw murdered our father."

"Aidan, you expect me to arrest him on a vision?" Santurin slapped his desk. "I need solid proof."

I leaned across his desk. "Did you know Grimshaw and Twain plan something against the kingdom with some scientists?"

"Now you add Twain to your conspiracy theory?" Santurin asked.

"I tried to warn you. You should worry as he's courting Mother." I left his office and stormed down the hallway. Not looking where I was going, I slammed into the back of Astra.

Chapter Ten

ON THE THIRD FLOOR, I STRUCK A PANEL ON THE WALL, and the lights flashed on. A series of holograms appeared. I stood in front of the hologram of Dad. He wore the tawny fur of a Luca cat he had hunted for two days in the Fang Mountains.

"I will see justice for your murder, Dad. No one believes me, not even Santurin. Somehow, I'll prove it." I wiped a tear from my cheek.

"There you are, Aidan." Santurin walked down the hall towards me. "Father was proud that day, wasn't he?"

"Yes, did you need something?" I asked.

"I'm sorry if I've been rough on you, but I've had a lot on my plate, since Father is gone and my upcoming wedding, then you throw me a curve about Father's friend killing him. Can we put our differences aside for a day? I'd like you to be my best man. What do you say?"

"Are you serious? Why not ask one of your men?" I asked.

"Because I'm asking you and its tradition. The others will be there too as escorts for the girls that Mori selected as part of the wedding party. We've already sent out the announcements and hung the banners. Mother wants the kingdom stabilized," Santurin said.

"Tell me more about your bride-to-be," I said.

"You've seen her. Small, green eyes with flecks of gold in them, fiery red hair with blonde highlights, and skin soft as down feathers. Mori is the eldest in her family too." Santurin's eyes sparkled as he talked about Mori. "She loves nature and paints for pleasure. Her mother educated her in herbal therapy and groomed her in the ways of running an estate. We stood on the balcony and watched the birds this morning. I think we'll get along."

"What about all your other girlfriends?" I asked.

"They only wanted a title. I can see myself settled down with Mori," Santurin said.

"You sound happy. Okay, I'll be your best man. When is the wedding?" I asked.

"In two days. Mother already arranged our outfits. In the meantime, try to stay out of trouble." Santurin walked away.

He had to dig in that last remark? I shook my head, then strode to the elevator when Astra walked out.

"Hey, I heard there was a hologram of our father here. Can you tell me about him?" Astra entwined her arm into mine.

I led her down the hall where the holograms lined the wall. Stopping at the first one, I said, "This was my great-great-great grandfather, Celestas Azure. He was a geologist, an explorer, and a grand wizard. Mother thinks I favor him."

"You have his hawk nose and brown hair, but your eye color is different," Astra said.

"His wife, Storm shot lightning from her eyes according to the rumors," I said.

"Creepy," Astra said.

"Grandfather Celestas wrote the history of our people in the book below his hologram." I read it aloud: "The people of Earth learned of their impending doom and sought refuge. While researching claims of alien history, Celestas found a portal that led to this exoplanet."

"Where is this portal?" Astra asked.

"No one knows," I said.

"Maybe your grandfather hid the portal out of fear someone might use it," Astra said.

"Why return to a planet that was dying?"

"It doesn't say it was dying, Aidan. It talks of impending doom. What if they were wrong?" Astra pushed her hair behind her ears.

"We'll never know," I said.

We walked further down and stopped at my father's hologram.

"This was King Arin. He had a passion for life, and it showed in everything he did. I really miss him," I said. A tear slid down my cheek and I brushed it away.

Astra looked closer. "You have his eyes and his smile." She turned around, and I realized the rumors were true. Next to Dad's hologram, Astra had the same long, white-blonde hair, crystal blue eyes, and the same height. No one could deny she was his daughter.

Did Mother find out and had Astra's mother, Skyla killed? "You are my sister. The resemblance is uncanny to Dad," I said.

"Is that why the queen hates me?" Astra asked.

"She pretends nothing happened between your mother and my father. It was long ago, and Dad paid attention to Mother since then. If he had other affairs, I don't know about them. I'm sorry if she hurt your feelings," I said.

"I was treated differently on Volney too. It doesn't stop the hurt." Astra glanced at her fingernails. "Every time I get upset; I bite my nails off. Councilor Grimshaw offered to make me a queen. What do you think of him?"

"I really don't know the man, but the councilors think they run the fortress. You know he still courts Mother, right?" I looked at Astra.

"The scoundrel. He's too old for me anyway. I was dazzled by the idea of becoming queen." Astra sighed.

"I think Grimshaw killed our father, but I don't have any proof. How was he going to make you a queen anyhow?" I asked. *Was he planning on killing Mother? Would he get rid of Santurin and me too, so he could become king and Astra his queen?*

"I don't know. Wings and Grimshaw skulk in the shadows and Twain remains friendly with those two. Any one of them probably plotted against my mother. It doesn't surprise me if they're at the bottom of our father's killing too. I'll keep an ear out," Astra said.

"Just be careful," I said.

"I can take care of myself." Astra jutted out her chin and stood taller.

"Until you can't." I stared at her. "It's time for supper. May I escort you to the dining hall?"

We took the elevator and the doors opened on the first floor. We walked to the dining room, located on the upper section of the main lounge, and I sat on Mother's right side. Astra sat across from me.

"I understand you're Santurin's best man," Mother said to me.

"Yes." Noticing Grimshaw hadn't joined the table, I took the opportunity. "Mother, did you know Grimshaw offered to court Astra and make her a queen?"

"That sounds like a fanciful notion of the girl. Astra wants to marry anyone of high rank."

"You know I am right here," Astra seethed. She slapped her napkin down and scooted her chair back, leaving the table.

"Why do you treat her so bad?" I asked Mother.

"I will not tolerate her misbehavior in Azure like she did on Volney."

"Are you sure it's not because she reminds you of Dad's affair?"

Mother's lips pinched tight. I knew I overstepped, but I hated all this turmoil over an incident that happened fifteen years ago. *Dad was gone. I felt proud to call Astra my sister. Mother only cared how she looked in public. What about Astra's feelings?*

"Excuse me." I lost my appetite and went searching for Astra. Everyone deserved respect, including my sister, no matter what Mother thought.

Astra stood on the balcony of the third floor, staring up at the stars. "Do you think my mother and our father are together again up there?"

"Possibly." I pointed out a star that blinked. "Maybe she heard you." I smiled.

"Thanks for standing up for me and showing me our ancestors. I appreciate it," Astra said. "Your brother is going to marry that girl from Zavion?"

"Yes, in two days. Mother arranged everything."

"You can't marry for love?" Astra asked.

"Marriages are usually arranged for royalty. Love has nothing to do with it," I said.

"The queen was partly right about me. I do want someone of high rank for a husband. I just didn't like the way she made me feel. Like I was a nobody," Astra said. "Whether she likes it or not, I am the king's daughter. She can't change that." Astra added, "The queen probably hated it when you pointed out that Grimshaw was courting me too."

"I was a bit blunt." I smiled.

"Yes, you were, but you got your point across," Astra said.

Mori had left her box of paints by the balcony door, and I got an idea. "How about we show everyone we matter?" I said.

"How?" Astra looked at me.

I poured some red paint on a saucer and dipped my hand in it. Shaking off the excess paint, I touched my hand on the window. Astra imitated me. Above our handprints, I wrote, *I am somebody*.

"What are you doing?" a voice said from behind us.

Chapter Eleven

THE SUN SHONE THROUGH THE TOWER ROOM WINDOWS on the third floor of the Azure Fortress. Santurin, dressed in a cobalt blue jacket with long tails in the back, and cream breeches draped over the top of his leather boots, wore a corsage of wildflowers on his lapel. I had a matching outfit minus the tails. Tano and Sir Jayel stood on my right, while I stood next to my brother. Santurin hugged me and shock rippled through me.

Was this my brother? He never hugged me. Maybe he felt nervous?

I feared you wouldn't show," Santurin said.

"Why?" I asked.

"Because you hate responsibility and sometimes, I wonder if you hate me too."

My brother wasn't my favorite person, yet he was family. Yes, I hated how he mocked me in front of the men or punched me when the moment struck him. *How do I answer him without causing an argument?* This was his wedding after all.

"I don't hate you, Santurin. No matter how you see me, I wouldn't spoil your wedding on purpose. And before you ask, I have the rings." I patted my pocket.

"Good to know." Santurin nodded to Lady Darshana.

She broke out in song while Tiana strummed her guitar. Lady Darshana and Tiana harmonized, and it sounded sweet. Olivia, Juliana's younger sister skipped down the aisle and tossed rose petals on the floor.

Juliana, dressed in a strapless cream gown and her hair braided atop her head, carried a sunflower, and led the other girls down the aisle. They looked like creamy trumpet flowers in their gowns. The maid of honor was Mori's sister, Pondarosa. She had long reddish hair and was a thinner, younger version of Mori. The bride floated behind her in a sea of green silk and her hair cascaded down to her waist. A coronet of roses and daisies adorned Mori's head. A ruby pendant encircled her throat. Her mother, Sylvia the Chieftain of Zavion, held Mori's arm as they walked towards the groom. Santurin's eyes shone as he smiled at his bride, causing a blush to Mori's cheeks.

"Who gives away the bride?" High Priest Reynard asked.

"I do." Sylvia placed her daughter's hand in Santurin's. She kissed Mori's cheek, then found her seat next to my mother.

I gazed around the room as the ceremony dragged on. Mother, dressed in a cobalt blue gown with a green sash at her waist, tilted her head to me. I nodded back. Sir Edrei and Dad's advisor, Twain conversed in the back of the room. I thought it was rude.

Santurin cleared his throat, and I realized he was waiting for the ring. I handed him the box and Santurin removed the sapphire ring, encrusted with diamonds, and slid it on Mori's finger. I recognized it as Mother's wedding ring. *Didn't she want to keep it as a reminder of Dad? Or perhaps this was her way of keeping the ring in the family?*

Mori placed a gold band, with an emerald and sapphire gem in its center, on Santurin's ring finger.

The high priest said, "You may kiss the bride."

Santurin ran his hand down Mori's cheek and she smiled into his eyes. He dipped her over his arm and kissed her long and passionately. The people whistled and cheered. Santurin pulled Mori back up.

"May I present the married couple," the high priest said.

Everyone clapped. Astra opened the doors, and the couple walked out onto the balcony. Together, Mori and Santurin opened a cage and released the doves, per tradition when a cloud-dweller married, and the birds flew off. Everyone cheered. The wedding couple walked back inside the tower room and Astra closed the balcony doors.

"Dessert served in the banquet room," Astra announced.

Santurin and Mori strolled down the aisle on the way to the banquet room. I linked my arm with Juliana's, and Tano and Sir Jayel hooked their arms with the other bridesmaids. Sylvia and Mother walked behind Pondarosa. The rest of the people followed behind. A line formed in front of the wedding couple. Everyone took their turn to congratulate them.

Afterwards, the wedding couple stood at a small table that held their wedding cake. It was three tiers tall and decorated with birds and ribbons of blue frosting. The couple held the knife together and cut the cake. Each of them ate a small piece, before the servants took it away and sliced cake for everyone. Juliana and I took ours to the table reserved for the wedding party. Cream-colored roses floated in a bowl of water centered on the table.

Mother sat across from me and Sylvia next to her. At the next table, the councilors sat together with Twain and Mother's handmaidens.

Grimshaw's eyes hooded as he glanced my way. Astra took her seat beside him and Grimshaw ignored me. He had discovered us painting our hands on the windows two days ago, but never told Mother. I wondered though if he'd bring it up at some point to spoil things.

A servant poured wine into our goblets. Those of us younger than eighteen drank watered-down wine. Santurin and Mori took their seats. I stood with my glass and tapped it with my spoon.

Getting everyone's attention, I held my goblet in the air. "Congratulations to my brother and his wife. At long last, someone plastered a smile on Santurin's face."

"Here, here!" Sir Edrei shouted.

Everyone cheered and clapped. I sat down.

"Lovely speech, Aidan," Mother said.

"Santurin seems happy, almost giddy in fact. You did a good job selecting his bride," I said.

"Thanks. That means a lot," Mother said. She rang a bell and the servants brought out platters of roasted pork with candied nuts, peas with pearl onions, and sweet yams with apple slices.

I wasn't that hungry after eating cake, but I picked at my food. The candied nuts were sweet, and I mixed them with my yams.

After everyone finished eating, the tables cleared of food. Mori and Santurin opened their gifts. Stacks of boxes piled the table. Councilor Grimshaw eyed the wedding gifts. *Was he envious?*

Twain sidled close to Grimshaw's side and whispered in his ear. Grimshaw wiped his mouth with his napkin, and then stood and left the room with Twain. Curious, I excused myself and followed them. I ducked under a table in the hallway as Grimshaw twirled around. I waited until they left before I stood again. Someone tapped my shoulder and I flinched.

"Lose something?" Juliana asked.

I placed my hand over my chest. "Geez, you scared me. No, I didn't lose anything. I think Twain and Councilor Grimshaw are up to something."

"Let's follow them and see. I was bored anyway," Juliana said.

"Walk ahead of me. They won't suspect you of spying. I'll stay behind you a few paces."

Juliana strolled down the hall. When I caught up with her, the men were gone.

"Which way did they go?" I asked.

"They rode the elevator to the basement. Did you want me to continue following them?"

I was about to answer Juliana, when Astra peered over my shoulder, and I jumped.

"What are you two whispering about?" she asked.

"Geez, Astra. You're too quiet. We were following Grimshaw and Twain. They're up to something. They rode the elevator to the basement," I said.

"What is down there?" Astra asked.

"Storage, pipes, and part of the aqueduct. Not much else," I said.

"Let's check it out," she said.

"What if he puts a spell on us? I'm not ready to face a sorcerer. I haven't learned to control my magic yet," I said. "Simple tricks with fire is basically it."

"What makes you think Councilor Grimshaw is a sorcerer?" Juliana asked.

"Because he vanished from sight after he killed Dad. I've heard rumors that his family is known for dabbling in the dark arts," I said.

"That was his mother and she died. Grimshaw told me," Astra said. "His father is a traveling magician and abandoned Grimshaw as a boy along with his sister. I felt sorry for him. I know what it's like not to have anyone in your corner for support. That doesn't mean he is a bad person."

"You're standing up for him?" I asked.

"I'm just saying we need to know all the facts before we assume the worst," Astra said.

"Okay. Juliana is our lookout. If something happens, she relays the information to the queen. Agreed?"

Juliana and Astra nodded.

"Don't wander too far from me though," Juliana added.

The three of us rode the elevator to the basement. When the doors opened, I peeked out.

"I don't see them," I said.

"Where could they go?" Astra asked.

"Let me try something," I said. Concentrating hard, I imagined a ball of fire. It appeared in my hand. I whispered to my fireball, "Show me the way the sorcerer strayed." I rolled the fireball down the floor.

Footprints appeared on the floor, and we followed them. They ended at a door at the end of the corridor.

"Where does that door lead to?" Juliana asked.

"I don't know. My guess is to Fallow." I turned the knob, but the door was locked.

"Can't you melt the knob or something?" Astra questioned.

"If I did that, we wouldn't be able to open it," I said.

"Try removing the hinges," Juliana said.

"And how do you propose I do that?" I frowned.

"I don't know. Ingenuity?" Juliana smirked.

"How about mind over matter? Remember when our meditation teacher told us about it?" I asked.

I asked. "Hold my hand, Juliana and maybe it will work. Concentrate." I pointed at the lower hinge and wiggled my fingers.

The nails rose, then clattered to the floor. The door leaned to one side.

"It worked!" I said. "Okay, let's try another one." I pointed at the upper hinge.

The nails wiggled up and out. The door slammed to the floor and dust flew up. "Hide," I whispered. "Someone comes. I heard their heavy footsteps."

The girls hid in the storeroom. I squeezed behind a post and peered around it. Grimshaw and Twain ran into the corridor.

Grimshaw grabbed Twain's shirt. "Were you followed? How did that door fall?"

"I don't know. This building is old and liable to fall apart. I've been careful," Twain said.

"Doesn't matter. Soon, I shall rule the kingdom," Grimshaw said.

A burly man, dressed in the queen's guard uniform, stepped from the shadows, and stood in the doorway. I recognized him as my meditation teacher, Dew.

When he wasn't teaching, he worked for my mother. *What was he doing here?*

"Has something addled your brain, Grim? What makes you think the people will accept you as king?" Dew asked. He picked up the nails from the floor. "The hinges lost their nails."

"Watch how you speak to me." Grimshaw glared at Dew. "You struck the young prince with that branch, not me."

Dew flinched. "The prince had no business in those woods. I couldn't chance his recognition of me, or all your fabulous plans gone awry, eh?"

"Pipe down. Your voices carry," Twain said. "I'll not have Santurin aware of my involvement with you two. I like the fellow. He's fair and has a better head on his shoulders than his father."

"I never liked a two-timer. Untrustworthy. You never know when they'll turn on you." Grimshaw plunged his dagger into Twain's throat.

Twain gagged in his own blood and slumped to the floor. Blood pooled around him.

Dew stared at the scene. "Now you've done it."

I turned my head and dry heaved.

"What was that noise?" Grimshaw asked.

My hand trembled as I covered my mouth.

"I don't hear nothing. You're losing it, Grim," Dew said.

I peeked from my hiding place.

"If you know what's good for you, you'll keep mum on this matter." Grimshaw snapped his fingers and vanished.

"You can't blame this on me, Grim," Dew said. He lifted Twain under the arms and dragged his body inside the doorway. Dew heaved the door and placed it across the opening. He twisted the nails into the hinges. He mopped the blood on the floor before he walked away.

I waited a few minutes, then knocked on the storeroom. I informed Juliana and Astra of the circumstances. "We need to tell Santurin."

We rushed to the elevator.

Chapter Twelve

WE RODE THE ELEVATOR TO THE THIRD FLOOR. MUSIC played as we came back inside the banquet room. The tables and chairs had been moved near the walls. Santurin danced with Mori across the floor. I didn't want to spoil his wedding day with news of murder. It wouldn't bring Twain back at any rate. Something had to be done about Grimshaw though, but who would believe me if I accused him of murder? Yes, Juliana and Astra were aware, but they didn't witness it like I had.

"We need to act normal," I whispered to Juliana and Astra. "I'll relay the news to Mother later, than to upset my brother's day. Astra, dance with Tano. Juliana and I will dance too."

"All right," they chorused.

I whirled Juliana around and she giggled. We danced across the white tiled floor and Mother nodded her approval as we passed by her. Tano swept Astra off her feet and danced on the other side of us.

When the music ended, Santurin and Mori sat in some chairs provided for them. I pulled out a chair for Juliana and she sat near her parents. I longed to talk with Santurin about Twain but held my tongue. The music played again and Grimshaw asked Mother to dance. I glared at his backside. Sir Jayel asked Pondarosa to dance and Tano asked Sylvia.

I strolled over to Astra standing near Juliana. "Dance with me." I led her to the dance floor. "I should give Grimshaw a hot seat," I whispered.

"Don't do it. He'll retaliate and you won't be the only one that suffers," Astra said. "This is your brother's special day, remember? Why not tell Juliana's father about the murder? After all he is ahead of security."

I spun Astra around. "He won't listen to me. You're friends with Tano. Maybe he can tell Sir Edrei for us."

"It would sound better coming from Juliana to her father," Astra said.

"True, but she didn't actually see it happen," I said. "If Tano knows the situation, he can take Sir Jayel with him and check it out. Then they report to Sir Edrei."

"Sounds like a plan," Astra said.

The music ended and we walked over to a table with a bowl of punch. A brown-haired maid with an upturned nose, ladled punch in glasses for the guests. Her name tag said, *Elm.* She handed one to Astra. I attempted to grab a glass already poured, but Elm stopped me.

"I have one especially made for you, My Prince." Elm smiled. She handed me a glass of punch and a raspberry tart on a plate. "Fresh from the oven. Sweet for the sweet."

"Thank you. I appreciate it." I bit into the tart and licked the raspberry from my lips. "Delicious."

"I think she likes you," Astra said, as we strode away.

"Why do you say that?" I sipped my drink. "I don't think much of the punch. It tastes bitter."

"Didn't you notice the way she looked at you? You're the only one with a tart." Astra drank her punch. "Mine tasted sweet. Probably the tart and the punch don't taste good together."

"Possibly." I finished the tart and washed it down with the punch. I left the dishes on the table. "Elm seemed nice. Mother would never allow a prince to associate with a scullery maid. Although my brother got away with a lot before Mother brought home a bride for him. Anyway, care to watch the stars together?"

"You're done dancing for the evening?" Astra asked.

"Yes. Unless you want to dance on the balcony?" I wiggled my brows.

"Not a lot of room there." Astra frowned.

"Come on. Where is the fun in that?" I said.

Juliana walked over to us. "I told my father about you know who and what we suspected."

"Oh? And what did he say?" I asked.

"Father told me to quit listening to your fanciful tales."

Frowning, I said, "He's not going to investigate it at least, Juliana? No one respects me and thinks only of my past lies." I shook my head. "Astra, it's up to you. Have Tano meet us on the balcony."

"All right." Astra strode out of the room.

Juliana and I strolled out of the banquet room and over to the tower room across the hall. I opened the balcony doors and we walked onto the balcony, gazing at the stars. I felt a little nauseous and the fresh air felt good.

"Aidan, how are you feeling? You look pale and you're sweating," Juliana said.

"Probably bad punch," I said.

Tano and Astra arrived, and Juliana excused herself. She took Astra by the arm and strolled into the tower room while I talked with Tano on the balcony.

"You wanted to see me, Your Prince-ship?" Tano asked.

"Yes. A situation came up and I thought if you checked it out with Sir Jayel, then Sir Edrei would believe you over me," I said. "Juliana, Astra, and I followed Grimshaw and Twain to the basement because they were acting suspicious. I hid behind a post while the girls hid in the storeroom. Grimshaw got mad at Twain and stabbed him. Dew was there too and dragged the body behind a door at the end of the corridor."

"Twain is dead?" Tano asked. "That isn't good. Why not inform the queen or your brother?"

"They never believe a word I say," I said, "We can't allow him to get away with murder, especially when Grimshaw courts the queen."

"Right-o, Your Prince-ship." Tano saluted me, then rushed out.

I strode inside the tower room and closed the balcony doors.

"Will Tano do it?" Astra asked.

"Yes." I slumped in a chair.

Juliana felt my forehead. "You're burning up."

"I'll fetch the doctor," Astra said. She raced out of the tower room.

"Something isn't right. My lips tingle," I said to Juliana. A bitter taste rose in the back of my throat. A sharp pain doubled me over and I clutched my belly. "Ugh. Juliana, if I don't make it, see that Grimshaw pays for the murder. I fear he may kill Santurin and Mother."

My hands trembled as I said, "Have Astra warn Cosmo too."

"Don't talk like that. Probably something didn't agree with you that you ate or drank," Juliana said. She stared at me.

"You've been a good friend." A cramp wiped the smile off my face. I felt short of breath and tried to stand. My legs were weak, and I collapsed to the floor. I squeezed my eyes shut as another cramp ripped through me. "What is taking the doctor?"

"Aidan it's only been a few minutes. Stay here. I'll notify the queen." Juliana ran to the banquet room.

I pondered my life while I sat on the floor. Was this it? I may never be a king, but it never mattered to me. Santurin was the responsible one where I enjoyed having fun. Too bad I couldn't get to know my twin brother better and I was just getting to know my half-sister, Astra.

What good was magic if I couldn't heal myself? Did Elm poison me? Why? I didn't even know her. I held my head, feeling woozy, when Mother, Sylvia, and Juliana ran in.

"I'm here, son." Mother knelt by me. She felt my forehead. "Juliana, get a wet cloth. My boy has a fever."

Juliana ran to do Mother's bidding.

"What do you think, Sylvia?" Mother asked.

Sylvia looked in my eyes, then smelled my breath. "I believe he's been poisoned, My Queen. She looked at me. "Young Prince, did you eat or drink anything at the dance?"

"A tart and some punch. Tasted bitter," I said.

"Did Astra give you that?" Mother asked.

"No. Elm." I closed my eyes.

Mother slapped my cheeks. "Stay awake, son. It's important."

Sylvia said, "I think the poison derived from some plant by his symptoms and his complaints. I suggest we move the prince to Zavion for his safety after he receives the antidote. I can teach him to control his magic at the same time."

"I agree," Mother said.

"There is something you need to know, Mother," I said. My speech sounded slurred to my ears and I'm not sure she understood me. "Juliana?"

"I'm here, Aidan."

"Tell her." Saliva thickened in my mouth, and I found myself drooling.

"Yes?" Juliana asked.

"Twain," I said.

Doctor Panphilia and Astra rushed into the room. Mother and Sylvia moved aside.

"Your Grace," Juliana said.

"Not now. Let the doctor work her miracle," Mother said.

Sylvia spoke to the doctor, "The young prince complained of a bitter taste. Between the taste, his pupils changing, the drooling, and the nausea, I believe he was poisoned by some derivative of a plant." She glanced at the doctor's medical bag. "Do you carry the antidote?"

"Sounds like Wild Ramp or a Hellebore plant," Doctor Panphilia said. "Poisonous to eat or drink of it." She felt my pulse. "Heart rate irregular." The doctor looked inside my mouth. "See this? He's starting to blister."

Sylvia peeked over the doctor's shoulder. "Yes. Looks irritated too."

My arms and legs shook suddenly.

"Hurry, Doctor. Inject him with the antidote. He's convulsing." Sylvia turned me on my side.

Juliana ran in with the wet rag and halted. "What is happening to Aidan?"

"Don't you die on me, brother," Astra said in my face.

Mother shoved her out of the way. "Give the doctor room." She snatched the wet cloth from Juliana and laid it across my forehead.

"Hold him down," Doctor Panphilia said.

Mother and Sylvia each grabbed an arm. Astra held down my legs. The doctor injected me with an antidote, I presume, and my body relaxed after several minutes.

In the quiet of the moment, Juliana said, "Your Grace, Aidan wanted you to know Twain is dead."

Mother frowned. "Dead? How?"

"Someone stabbed him," Juliana said. "Aidan said it was Councilor Grimshaw."

"Did you see the man do this?" the queen asked her.

"No, Your Grace, but he did talk with Twain in the basement. I saw them together."

"You've done your duty, Juliana. I'll send some men to investigate," the queen said. "Run along and take Astra with you. If Santurin questions you, tell him I handled the situation."

"Yes, Your Grace." Juliana looked at Astra. "You heard the queen."

"One more thing, Juliana. Find your father. I need a pilot to take us to Zavion."

"Yes, Your Grace." Juliana curtsied and left the room.

The doctor bundled me in a blanket. "Need to keep him warm. You should feel better soon, My Prince."

I must have dozed off after that because I don't remember getting inside the airship later. Every bump pained my head as the airship peeled across the track and lifted into the sky. I glanced around, but I didn't see my mother. Lying on the back seat, I noted Sylvia squeezed her eyes shut and gripped the armrests from the passenger seat.

"Fly much, Chieftain?" I asked.

"As little as possible, Young Prince. I believe in a simple life, not filled with machines."

"Where is Mother?"

"She stayed behind," Sylvia said. "We thought it best for you to leave Azure right away."

"What about Elm?" I asked.

"She'll be dealt with. The queen said she will take matters into her hands including the murder of the advisor, Twain," Sylvia said. "You worry about getting well and resting."

Easy to say yet worry plagued me. What about the safety of my family?

Chapter Thirteen

BIRDS TWITTERED. WINDCHIMES TINGLED NEARBY.
Lavender and roses scented the air. My arm and leg muscles felt stiff and
sore as I moved them. A thick coating clung to my tongue. I blinked a
couple of times, until my eyesight focused.

I cleared my throat and sat up. My voice rasped, "Hello."

Sylvia sat on a stool and read from a book. She was a tall, lean woman,
with angular features and a crown of antlers on her long, red hair streaked
with silver. Her misty-green gown held a sash around her waist with several
small leather pouches attached to it. She looked at me and said, "Welcome
back, Young Prince. You were out quite a while."

"Where am I?"

"You are in Zavion for your own safety. Drink. You need to replenish
your fluids." Sylvia handed me a mug of water.

I drank my fill, then wiped my mouth. "How long must I stay here?"

"Don't look at it as a punishment, Young Prince. Consider it a time
of learning new things."

I scowled. "Can't I relax from my studies? That's all I seem to do
on Azure."

"Don't you want to learn to control your magic?" Sylvia asked.

"That's what you are referring to? Of course, I'm interested," I said. "When do we begin?"

"First things first. You need to gain your strength back. I'll call someone to assist you and we'll walk around." Sylvia whistled.

A six-foot tall, muscular man with broad shoulders and a long braid down to his buttocks ducked through the flap of the hut. "Yes, Chieftain?"

"Ash, assist the prince, until he gets his bearings. He needs to exercise his legs, but take it slow," Sylvia said.

"Yes, Chieftain." Ash guided me off the cot.

I grabbed his bulky arm as everything spun. When my vision cleared, I stepped forward.

Ash led me outside the hut. I blinked in the bright light. Sylvia led us down the path.

Everywhere I looked, gigantic trees touched the sky. Yes, we had trees on Azure lands, but never this many in one place. Birds, of various breeds and colors, fluttered from branch to branch. One shot out a long whistle and two toots. I followed the sound and noted the pale grey with silky plumage of a small bird.

Quiet and wraith-like, Sylvia flowed along the path. A doe wandered at her side and licked her hand. A family of quails rustled out of the bushes and followed us. Sylvia circled her finger in the air and a flock of sparrows hovered over our heads. *If only I bore such power.*

Sylvia raised her staff and the birds and animals scattered.

"How do you control your magic?" I asked.

"Curiosity plagues you. Good. I like my students eager for learning." Sylvia said. "Tell me how you discovered your magic."

I relayed the events of Dad's demise and told her of setting Santurin's braid on fire.

"Your brother wasn't amused, I take it?" Sylvia smiled.

"Far from it," I said.

Ash snickered. We hiked down a path cushioned with spongy moss. It was also wrapped around the trees. We rounded the corner and my ears perked at a gurgling noise. A fish statue squirted water from its pursed lips into a small pond. Bright bell-shaped flowers grew around the grounds, and butterflies dipped in and out of them. We walked on and a clear, blue lake sparkled up ahead.

"Any fish in that lake?" I asked.

"Yes, perch and trout. Do you fish, My Prince?" Ash asked.

"I do. Dad and I often fished in the river, but he preferred hunting. He took me to Volney to show me how to hunt, but he died there." A tear drifted down my cheek and I brushed it off.

"I bagged a bear last week." Ash beamed.

"You brought down a bear? How did it taste?" I asked.

"Greasy as a roast yet filling. My wife, Hazel cooked a stew with the rest of the bear meat," Ash said.

"Amazing," I said.

Sylvia sat on a bench near some gardens, and I sat next to her. "Ash, you may leave us for now while I teach the young prince some things."

Ash bowed and walked towards a wooden structure.

"First, I'll go over the elements with you," Sylvia said. "There are four basic cardinal elements incorporated in our practice: air, fire, water, and earth. One or more you'll control as you learn your place in the field of magic. Earth magic determines the spell which shapes and uses iron, stone, earth, and other similar materials."

Sylvia continued, "Each one governed by direction when you chant your spell."

"How do I know which ones I control?" I asked.

"In due time, you'll discover this on your own. Air is east, fire is south, water is west, and earth is north. Remember them," Sylvia said. She drew a circle in the dirt with a stick. Sylvia added a five-pointed star in the middle. "This is a pentagram or magic circle. Stand inside it when you cast your spell."

"Why?" I asked.

"It protects you from bad spirits that seek to harm you. The Goddess Angelique guides me, but also protects Zavion. Believe in her and you shall find peace within you." She scratched out the pentagram with the stick before we walked on.

We stopped at the lake and Sylvia turned to me. "From what you've told me, you control the element of fire. Earth holds magic. Sweep it from the ground and form a fireball."

"With what? I don't have a broom," I said.

"Pretend that you do," she said.

To appease her, I imagined a broom handle in my hand and swept the ground around me. I picked up the make-believe dust and circled my hands. To my surprise I formed a fireball.

"The key to magic is control. It's all in your power. Move your hands out and make it wider," Sylvia said.

I did and stared at the results in awe. "I did that?"

"Yes, Young Prince. Now imagine it larger."

The fireball increased in size. "Wow," I said.

"Make it smaller and throw the fireball into the lake," Sylvia said.

I did it, yet it still surprised me when I heard it plop in the water. "What else can you teach me?" Excitement filled me and my feet bounced up and down.

"The people arranged a feast in celebration of your arrival. They honor you as the son of the forest-dweller Queen Willow. Another time for lessons," Sylvia said.

Disappointed, I plodded along behind her. I wanted to learn more magic, not feed my face. I dare not say anything derogatory and ruin my chances of further lessons. We passed by the lake and as we came into view, the people clapped.

"Hail, Prince Aidan!"

Undervalued at home, the people respected me here. I placed my hand over my heart. "Thank you, one and all for this honor." Walking inside the lodge, I glanced at the sight before me.

Beeswax candles lit the area. The polished cedar floor had a fresh scent. I looked up at the beamed ceiling and enjoyed the open space of the lodge. Plates of watercress, peas, pearl onions, and sliced roasted pig passed around as I sat down at the long, wooden table. I inhaled the wonderful aroma. Ash handed me a steaming mug of herbal tea as he sat next to me.

"Where did Sylvia go?" I asked.

"The chieftain has her duties. You'll see her later," Ash said.

I sipped my tea. "Tasty. What's in it?"

"Mint, rose buds, and some spices. Good for stomach ailments." Ash blew on his tea before sipping it.

Women ladled bear stew in our bowls as everyone took their seats. Sylvia sat across from me and a petite woman, with pretzel braids atop her head, sat across from Ash.

"My Prince, this is my wife, Hazel. She made bear stew and a raspberry pie for dessert. My dear, this is Prince Aidan," Ash said.

"Nice to meet you," I said.

Hazel nodded.

"Ash, do you have any brothers?" I asked.

"Five." Ash beamed.

"Wow, five? Do you get along with all of them?" I asked.

"Sometimes I butt heads with the eldest, Oak. Arm wrestling zaps any anger issues." Ash smiled wide.

"I'm not sure that would work on Santurin." I slurped my tea.

"When you're stronger, I'll teach you to arm wrestle, if you like," Ash said.

I nodded.

Grisly giants, in furred vests over bare, broad chests, and buckskin pants, claimed seats next to Ash. It dawned on me; they were his brothers. A girl, around twelve with pigtails, whispered in Sylvia's ear.

Sylvia turned to me. "This is my youngest daughter, Pondarosa. She wants you to watch the bear dance."

"Yes, I met her at the wedding. Are you the bear?" I asked Pondarosa.

"She's a bit shy, although she observes everything. Already, she knows all the names of the herbs. Healing is her destiny." Sylvia winked at her daughter. "She won't give away the identity of the bear in the dance."

"You're proud of her. I admire that in a parent," I said.

"I am. Dig in, Young Prince, before your food grows cold. The entertainment won't start until everyone has eaten," Sylvia said.

I shoveled the stew in my mouth. It tasted better than beef. "Hazel, you've outdone yourself."

Her cheeks flamed. "Thank you, My Prince. Want some bread with your meal? It's fresh from the oven." Hazel passed the plate.

"A small piece." I slathered butter on the bread, then bit into it, tasting cinnamon and pumpkin. "Scrumptious." When I finished my meal, I rubbed my belly. "Stuffed."

One of Ash's brothers jumped up and Pondarosa tagged behind him. In the center of the lodge floor, Pondarosa plopped on the floor, and pounded on a drum. Someone in a bear costume danced to the rhythm. Ash's brother held a bow and arrow and pretended to shoot the bear.

The animal rolled over and played dead. I stood up and clapped. The entertainers bowed. The person in the bear costume pulled the head piece off and hurried to my table.

"Meet my sister, Yvonne," Ash said. "And that's my brother, Clay with the bow."

Yvonne didn't resemble her brothers, except for her wide shoulders. She was about my age and stood under my arms. She wore a beaded buckskin dress. Her eyes were an unusual blue. Clay resembled Ash, except he stood taller and was older. I guessed around eighteen.

"Nice to meet you," I said to them.

Pondarosa pounded on the drums again and Sylvia strode to the middle of the floor.

A boy, around ten with dark hair, dressed in feathers and wearing an eagle headdress, danced and mimicked the movements of an eagle as Sylvia told a story. The ankle adornments jingled as he danced.

"Long ago, our people left the land of ice," Sylvia said. "We followed brother eagle here.

We promised our spirit guide to care for the forest and not waste its resources. We fished in the lakes and hunted the wildlife. Thank the spirits for this great feast." Sylvia held out her hands.

"Thank you, great spirit," the people said in unison.

I raised my mug. "And thanks to the people for their hard work in my honor."

Sylvia sat down next to me.

"This land of ice you speak of, was it on this planet or another?" I asked.

She looked at me as if I was stupid. "On the other side of this planet, the land is covered in ice. My people passed our story down for generations. You see, my people already lived here, before your great-great-great grandfather called himself king. We compromised." Sylvia continued, "He allowed us to remain on Zavion and we promised to abide his laws if they didn't interfere with our beliefs. It was better than a war between us."

The young dancer sat on his mother's lap, and Sylvia introduced him. "This is my son, Gus. He practiced for weeks learning the steps. I included him in my storytelling."

"Brave soul to dance in front of all these people. Glad to meet you. I'm Aidan."

"I got into the beat and didn't think 'bout the crowd. Did you like it?" Gus asked.

"Wonderful job. Maybe some time you can teach me, huh?" I winked.

"Me, teach a prince? That's a good one." Gus snickered. "Ma, can I get out of this costume?"

Sylvia nodded, and Gus raced out of the lodge. "He's my only boy and a bit wild since his Pa died." She sighed. "Come, I'll show you where to rest."

I stood and my legs felt wobbly, after sitting too long. Sylvia grasped my arm, and we strolled outside. Torches lit the pathway. The evening sky shone with stars. One blinked, and I imagined Dad watching over me.

With the thickness of the trees shading the area, I wondered about predators. An owl darted from a branch and swooped down on a vole scurrying across the path. The owl snatched the vole in its talons and flew off. The poor thing never had a chance. We walked on. After a bit, Sylvia stopped in front of a canvas hut not far from her own.

"This is yours, until you return to Azure. Good night, Young Prince." Sylvia bowed her head and proceeded to her own hut.

I flung the flap over and ducked inside. Pillows and furs covered a cot. A set of buckskins hung from a small hook. I fingered the fabric. Sylvia expected me to dress like the others, I see. On top of a stool, covered with a cloth napkin was a slice of raspberry pie. A stack of books piled in a corner. I removed one from the stack. *Nature's Magic*. I thumbed through the book and a page captured my attention.

I slumped down on the cot and read. After some time, my eyes grew heavy, and soon my chin touched my chest. I snorted awake at fabric ripping.

A huge, brown blur tore the hut apart. I blinked my eyes, trying to focus. Objects flew around and I batted some out of my way. The monstrous bear pushed me down and his claw raked my thigh.

I cried out, "Son of an ugly roach!" Blood poured down my leg and my thigh stung.

The grizzly growled in my face. I picked up the pie and smashed his snout. I crab-crawled backwards and bumped into a kettle. The bear licked the raspberry juice off his face.

I picked up a book and banged it on the kettle. The grizzly stepped back and roared. I tossed a fur over me and picked up the fallen stool. Using it like a shield, I pushed forward.

"Get out of here!" I threw books and anything else, within reach, at the bear.

He ran off. My hands quivered and I dropped the stool. Dizziness claimed me and I collapsed.

Chapter Fourteen

ASH PRESSED A CLOTH OVER MY THIGH AND I HALF-ROSE off the cot. "My Prince, it won't stop bleeding. Relax and trust in the healing powers of our chieftain."

I inhaled a deep breath and blew it out. Nothing looked familiar as I glanced around. "Where am I?"

"My brother, Clay carried you to the healer's tent per the chieftain's instructions. Your hut was demolished." Ash kept pressure over my thigh, but blood oozed around the cloth.

Sylvia and Pondarosa waved incense smoke over me. They chanted together, "We call upon the element of fire to bless this circle. May it grant inspiration and compassion while we perform our work tonight."

Pondarosa handed two sticks to Sylvia.

"Prince Aidan, this will hurt. Bite on this." Sylvia passed me the smaller stick. She heated the other stick in the nearby campfire.

I clenched the stick between my teeth when Sylvia neared me. She nodded to Ash, and he removed the cloth from my thigh. Pondarosa and Ash held my arms down. The tip of the stick, in Sylvia's hand, glowed a bright red. I shook my head and tried to sit up. Ash tightened his grip. I stared at his sinewy muscles as Sylvia touched my wound with the hot stick. My skin sizzled, and burning pain overwhelmed me. I rocked and bucked. Tears sprung to my eyes. I spit the stick out and roared.

My entire leg trembled. The odor of fried flesh drifted to my nose, and I gulped air. Ash released me, and I pounded the cot, while counting to ten. I concentrated on breathing in and out.

Sylvia hovered over me with a bowl. She flicked drops of water from it on me, while she circled around my cot, chanting. "I evoke the element of water. It is a fluid of infinite shapes. A flowing source of adaptability, emotion, and life. I seek the pure spring within that I might drink deep of change, nourishment, and grace. Wash away all the unclean and move like the ocean and river. Water, I call thee hence to heal this wound." Sylvia drank from the bowl and wiped her mouth. She poured the remainder of the water over my wound.

I flinched at the unexpected coldness. Sylvia chewed some herbs and sage together. She removed the substance from her mouth and stuffed it inside my thigh wound. I cried out at the invasion. She covered my thigh with a damp cloth.

"I call upon the element of earth. All aspects of life take place in the earth: birth, life, death, and rebirth. The earth is nurturing, stable, and solid. Full of endurance and strength. Forces of nature, answer my plea. Heal this boy's wound." Sylvia held her arms up.

Moss inched like a long, green worm inside the tent. It wound its way up the cot and wrapped its soft, warmness snug around my thigh.

"I call upon the element of air. For air is the breath of life. It passes through and around all things. It's the glue that binds. Air is the representation of spiritual faith. It reminds us that there is more in this world than what we see. We must grow and change as does the world." Sylvia waved her staff over my injured thigh.

"I call thee to cleanse away the greediness of infection and breathe your life force into his wound." Sylvia blew over my entire leg.

Pondarosa and Sylvia held hands and danced around me. In their shadow, tiny naked beings, with miniature antlers on their heads, danced. They raised their stick-like arms, and a stream of fireflies flew up. They spun around in a ray of colored lights. *Was I hallucinating or were these beings real in this realm?*

Sylvia touched my forehead. "Rest, Young Prince. I have done all I can." She snapped her fingers and my eyes closed.

Chapter Fifteen

ALMOST TWO WEEKS HAVE PASSED SINCE THE BEAR attack. I read the few books Sylvia lent me on magic. Most of it was on the history of it. Restless and bored, I slapped the cot. All because of a bear and I'm a prisoner of my own body.

I rolled on my side and pushed myself up to a sitting position. Taking deep breaths, I blew it out before standing. Blood rushed to my feet. The foot on my injured leg changed to a deep purple and puffed up. I moaned as pain radiated through me.

A long stick stood in the corner of the tent. I hopped over and snatched it. Using the stick like a cane, I stepped forward. "Son of a giant beetle!" Perspiration soaked through my hair and my shirt clung to me.

"My Prince, visitors!" Pondarosa called.

I groaned.

Santurin pushed through the flap. "Good, you're on your feet."

"Come to gloat at my demise, brother?" I hobbled over to my cot and flopped down, propping my leg on a pillow.

"Believe it or not I was concerned about your welfare. Mother informed me of your poisoning. She fired Elm, then sent her to jail," Santurin said.

"That's good," I said. "Did she say why she poisoned me?"

"Said someone paid her, but Elm is too afraid to tell us who," Santurin said.

"What about the murder of Twain?" I asked.

"We couldn't find his body," Santurin said. "When Mother questioned Councilor Grimshaw about it, he denied killing Twain. He told us Dew was responsible for hitting you with that branch in the Lithadora Woods and said if Twain is dead, Dew is probably responsible."

"That's a lie! I saw Grimshaw stab Twain in the throat," I said.

"Without a body, it's hard to prove. Mother sent Dew away though," Santurin said. "Juliana has been worried about you. I brought her along."

"What about Astra?" I asked.

"She'll visit you later. Astra wanted to see Cosmo first."

"All right. Can you send Juliana in, brother?"

Santurin opened the flap and waved Juliana in. She knelt at my bedside and shoved my hair from my forehead.

"I'm thankful you didn't die. First the poisoning, then a bear attacked you. How awful," Juliana said. "How is your leg?"

"Sore, but I survived. I tossed everything within my reach at the bear, before it ran off. Do you think I was set up?" I asked.

"Why do you say that Aidan?" Santurin asked.

"No one here was ever attacked in their hut by a bear. Why me?"

"Beasts are unpredictable. I wouldn't think too much on it."

"Easy for you to say, Santurin. You're not the one suffering, but watch your back," I said. "Grimshaw is power hungry and not trustworthy."

"Thanks for the warning. Heal fast. When you come home, we'll have my coronation."

"Mother retired?" I asked.

"No, but she is considering it since Father died. Mother could marry someone else, but she doesn't feel anyone else is worthy of the title," Santurin said. "She is flattered by the attention of Councilor Wings and Grimshaw, yet she knows they only seek to be king. Mother wants the kingdom stabilized and would rather have me in that position."

"That's good to know," I said. "Thanks for visiting."

Santurin led the way out. As Juliana followed behind, a giant of a man filled the entrance.

"Who is this fetching beauty, My Prince?"

"Clay, this is my friend, Juliana. She paid me a visit. Juliana, meet Clay. He carried me to the chieftain after the bear attacked me," I said.

"Are all the men here, giants like you?" Juliana blurted. She blushed. "I'm sorry. That was rude of me. A pleasure to make your acquaintance."

"No apologies needed. Your beauty outshines the light and welcomes the flowers."

"Are you hitting on my friend or reciting poetry, Clay?" I asked.

"Is it working?" Clay wiggled his brows.

Juliana giggled. "I better hurry, before Prince Santurin leaves me behind."

"I wouldn't mind." Clay pumped his chest muscles.

Juliana rushed past Clay. I imagine most girls considered him handsome with his cleft chin, wide smile, and muscles to boot.

"Did you have something on your mind, Clay or were you only curious about Juliana?"

"The chieftain said it's time you exercised."

"Already?" I asked.

"Her special herbs healed the skin, although you'll carry a scar. Train your muscles or become an invalid from lack of using them." Clay tossed a sleeveless buckskin top and a pair of pants at me. "Put these on."

I groaned.

"Forgive me, My Prince. You're still a boy, yet you grumble like an old man. In our culture, a boy is not a man, until he endures the manhood journey. Stand and face your challenges." Clay handed me a staff.

I gazed at the piece of ash wood. The staff felt solid, buffed, and smoothed with the carved head of a bear on the top knob. "It's a beauty."

"You like it? It's one of my hobbies." Clay smiled.

"A great talent," I said.

"It's my gift to you, My Prince."

"Wow. I shall cherish it." I hopped off the cot and hobbled behind Clay. "Take it slow, I beg you."

"That's a good one. A prince begging a peasant." Clay chuckled.

I didn't find anything funny. My thigh pained me, and my foot swelled, but I continued out the flap. Gritting my teeth, I hobbled behind Clay, using the staff like a cane. Each step radiated up my leg. To take my mind off my pain, I asked, "What about this journey you spoke about? What kind of ordeals do boys face?"

We strolled down the path. I nodded to some villagers we passed by.

"No servants at your beck and call, My Prince. It's a matter of survival on your own in the wild. The elder in charge gives you three tasks to obtain. If you survive and redeem the items, a celebration of your manhood happens on your return. My younger brother, Birch completed his initiation last week." Clay turned and looked at me. "Are you thinking of joining?"

"I like the idea, but I must heal first," I said.

"You won't get stronger if you baby your body." Clay pivoted around and walked on.

I mimicked Clay behind his back.

We trekked the same path Ash and I took a few weeks. ago, but I was weaker. My muscles needed work. When we passed by the lake, I wondered about my safety. *Did I misplace my trust?* We were away from the others. The light filtered through the dark shade of trees. After the past incidents, I found it hard to trust anyone. From the overhanging branches, the crows mocked me. I punched the air, and the birds flew off.

"We're almost there," Clay said.

"Good. My thigh really hurts and look how swollen my foot is," I said.

"You can rest it a bit when we get to our destination," Clay said.

We hiked on. Soon, the area opened into a wide meadow. A wooden enclosure held pulleys with ropes, long chains, and discarded wagon wheels. Off to the side, a bucket held kindling and long, thin poles of wood. Pilings of shaved wood littered the ground. In the back corner of the enclosure, two long benches stood side by side.

A barrel of rainwater propped against a wall of the enclosure. A tin cup hung from a hook on the side of the barrel.

I looked around me. "It looks like a torture center."

Laughter rumbled from Clay.

"I'm glad I amuse you," I said.

"If you join the manhood journey, you won't survive, unless you're fit. I brought you here to build your muscles," Clay said.

"Traveling here was a workout," I grumbled.

"Take a load off and watch." Clay stood under the pulleys. The ends weighed down with metal, clanged as he stretched the pulleys over his shoulders, lifting the weights. "See? Now you try."

I handed my staff to Clay. Yanking on the pulleys, the weights moved only an inch. I tried again, but they moved less. "What's the trick?"

Clay felt my arm muscles. "Puny. Practice and your muscles will get stronger. Try some leg lifts. Lie on the bench and raise your good leg in the air."

I followed his instructions.

"Good. Hold it to the count of ten, then relax." Clay nodded. "Try the other leg but take it easy."

My leg quivered and pain rippled in my thigh muscles. "One, two, three," I gritted through my teeth. I panted the rest of the count and sighed.

Clay frowned. "Weak."

"Try some chest stretches," Clay suggested. "Stand and extend your arms in front of you. Touch your palms together."

I did and flames shot out of my fingers.

Clay backed up. "What in thunder?"

"Uh, sorry. Sylvia neglected to inform you of my magic, I see. Maybe skip touching my palms, okay?" I said.

"Keep your elbows straight and move your arms back," Clay said. "Okay, return your arms in front. Got it?"

I nodded.

"Good. Do it ten times." Clay demonstrated.

I copied his moves.

"Place both your hands on your lower back and point your fingers down. Elbows out.

Move your elbows back and inward as far as you can, and then return to the starting position," Clay said.

"I suppose you want ten of those too?" I said.

"Yes, My Prince." Clay watched me. "Good. You may sit."

"Anybody ever tell you that you're a hard ass? My leg throbs." I sat down on a bench.

"Last exercise, I promise." Clay looked at me. "Place your palms on either side of your seat. Raise yourself up, until your arms are straight, then lower yourself down." Clay demonstrated on the opposite bench.

He made it look easy. When I attempted that exercise, my arms shook. The idea of building my muscles gave me incentive though. I pumped up and down with my arms several times before Clay touched my shoulder.

"Enough for today." Clay strode over to a pail. He grabbed a pair of tongs and lifted a hot brick out. He wrapped it in rags and a towel, before walking back to me. He put it over my thigh. "To soothe your quad muscles. You'll need it before you hike back."

I glanced at Clay's bulging muscles as he practiced on the pulleys. If I developed muscles like him, girls would flock to me. I closed my eyes and smiled. The warmth of the brick lulled me to sleep.

Half an hour later, Clay tapped my arm. "My Prince, it's time."

"Time?" I wiped my eyes.

"Nice nap?" Clay smirked. He handed me my staff. "I'll walk you back."

My stomach rumbled. "Did we miss the midday meal?"

"You've used up your energy source from the workout. You require nourishment." Clay chuckled.

We strolled down the path and approached the lake. I stopped and watched some men fish. Ash reeled in a fat trout. He placed it in his net and the fish wiggled about.

I slapped him on the shoulder. "Nice one."

"Join us, My Prince."

"Some other time, Ash. Your brother wore me out and I'm famished," I said.

"Hazel and my sister-in-law, Twiggy are in the lodge. They'll fix you something," Ash said.

I imagined fried fish in creamy butter as I limped behind Clay.

Sometime later, we strolled inside the lodge. We sat down and a thin girl, with dark braids and an upturned nose, walked towards us.

"Twiggy, this is Prince Aidan. Any rabbit stew left?" Clay rubbed his belly.

"I'll check." Twiggy hastened inside the kitchen.

"She's married to my eldest brother, Oak. I'm surprised he hasn't rolled over in bed and crushed the poor gal," Clay said. "He's thick like his name. Oak's lucky to have a sweet gal like her."

I was too naïve to voice an opinion on married life. "Any future bride in the works for you?" I asked him.

"Me? Nah. All the pretty gals wed, and none of the others appeal to me. Juliana is a pretty thing," Clay said.

"She's out of your league. Juliana is one of the queen's favorite hand-maidens," I said.

"The queen is one of our own and your mother. You speak to her and the queen might consent," Clay said.

"Juliana's father expects her to marry in her station or above."

"I'm good at persuasion," Clay said.

"He's not easily swayed," I countered back.

"We'll see," Clay snapped.

Did I offend him? Silence thickened the room between us.

Twiggy hurried over and set two bowls of rabbit stew and a loaf of grainy bread in front of us. "Anything else?"

"Nah. Thanks." Clay shoveled his food down.

I broke off a piece of bread and dipped it in the stew. I tasted rosemary, sage, and oats. Fork-tender, the rabbit had a rich flavor. I gobbled down my meal in a matter of minutes. "Delicious." I licked my lips.

Clay pushed the empty dishes aside. "How about a lesson in arm wres-tling? Ash told me. you wanted to learn. The more you do; your muscles grow stronger. Give it a whirl or are you chicken?"

"What did you call me?" I stood up. "I won't tolerate insults." *I get enough of that at home. Everyone deserves respect, even me.*

"Forget my insolence, My Prince. I meant no disrespect. Show me what you're made of." Clay egged me on.

I clasped Clay's hand.

Clay's eyes gleamed. "Push your opponent's arm over, before he does the same to you. Always keep your elbow down on the table and hold your opponent's hand. Got it?"

"Yes. I'm not ignorant," I said.

"Twiggy! Come over here and referee," Clay called.

She wiped her hands on her apron and rushed over. "Ready? Go."

Clay slammed my arm down in seconds and tears sprung to my eyes. The man packed power. "Again. This time resist me."

I kept my arm from flopping over by sheer willpower. We fought for control. After many minutes, my arm tired, and Clay won.

"Another round?" Clay wiggled his brows.

With the assistance of my staff, I stood. "Not today. I need to rest."

"Expect me early in the morning," Clay said.

I groaned. "One day of torture wasn't sufficient?" I hobbled out the lodge door and weaved around people, until I found the path back to the healer's tent.

The fresh breeze felt good. Worn out, I took my time traveling down the path. The birds warbled from the trees and bushes. Squirrels collected acorns from under a mighty oak. I liked the peacefulness here and imagined living here the rest of my life. Azure seemed far away.

Rounding the corner, I viewed the tent and hastened the rest of the way. I opened the flap and came face to face with a rail-thin woman with forest-green eyes and scars on her face.

"Who are you and what are you doing in here?" I asked.

Chapter Sixteen

CRICKETS CHIRPED IN THE STILLNESS OF THE EVENING. Not even the wind stirred as we challenged each other. Streaks of gray painted the stranger's dark hair and she bore a diamond-shaped scar across one cheek. A long, jagged scar wrapped her left arm. I refused to back down. I won numerous stare-downs with my friend, Varick and his cousin, Juliana. If I wasn't so blasted tired, I could go on for hours.

Finally, the woman caved. "My name no longer matters. People have long forgotten me.

You must protect my granddaughter at all costs."

"Who is your granddaughter?" I asked.

"Astra, of course."

"Why me?"

"Why not? You are her half-brother, Prince Aidan. I know you care for her."

"And how do you know?" I asked.

"I sense things," the woman said.

"You still haven't told me who you are."

"My name is Valora of the Winged Warrior Society."

"I never heard of you." I frowned.

"Juliana never mentioned me?" Valora gazed at me for confirmation. "No?"

Her shoulders drooped, and pain etched her eyes. "Time has forgotten me." Valora swallowed hard. "My sister, Darshana and I grew up on Meadowlark." She glanced away for a moment. "I taught my daughter how to fly an airship. Skyla maneuvered through tight spots others thought impossible. She attracted the king's eye, your father, and Astra was born from their attraction," Valora said. "Trouble followed Skyla afterwards. Someone in the kingdom ordered her death."

"Skyla's parents died ages ago. Who are you really?" I glared.

"The others assumed I drowned. See these scars? I barely escaped with my life," Valora said." My husband, Robin built an airship with capabilities that glided atop the water and rotated like a fan underneath it. Someone, I don't know who, smashed the side of the ship when we were under water. Glass cut my face. A piece of metal pinned me in place and lacerated my arm. Another stabbed Robin's chest. My love died before my eyes. I dislocated my arm and escaped."

"What about an investigation?" I asked.

"A cover up by the advisory board," Valora spat. "Either one or all conspired against King Arin. Gossip rounded the fortress of the king's weakness for falling in love with a young recruit. I encouraged Skyla to remove Astra from Azure. Darshana must not know of my existence. She can't halt her wagging tongue."

"I don't care about your secrets. I don't even know you," I said. "Someone attempted my life more than once. How do I know it wasn't you?" I folded my arms across my chest and leaned against the tent post.

"Keep your anger for the ones that deserve it. Keep my granddaughter safe. I must go before I'm discovered," Valora said.

I followed the woman outside. She walked over to a field and raised her bubble-like ring. The ring changed many colors. A small disc-shaped airship, the color of the sky, materialized in front of us. It had room only for a single person.

"Impossible," I gasped.

"One of my engineers finished Robin's plans on this beauty. Its lightweight and faster than anything I've encountered." Valora lifted the bell-shaped sleeve of her skin-tight jumpsuit and punched in a code on a device strapped to her wrist.

A set of stairs climbed out of a hidden compartment like a creepy spider. Valora bounded up them and hopped into the pilot seat. The stairs folded up and slid back inside its compartment. The airship shimmered, then shot across the field. The sleek airship ripped across the sky in a matter of seconds and vanished.

"Amazing. I'd love an airship like it." I hobbled back inside the tent.

I lay down on my cot. The details of my conversation with Valora spun around in my mind. It still didn't explain why someone wanted me out of the way. And how can I protect Astra? I can't protect myself.

I wish I could be in two places at once. I leafed through various books Sylvia lent me. I remembered reading about bilocation. Ah, here it is.

The ability to be in two places by projecting one's double or astral self to another location. To others, the double appears as a solid form, but it doesn't behave normally or speak. Bilocation occurs at will or by magical skill. It's acquired through meditation and the channeling of the universal life force.

"If I can't talk, how do I communicate with Astra?" I said aloud. Crossing my legs on the ground, I relaxed my mind, picturing Astra lying in her bed. I whispered her name.

Astra mumbled something. I called her name again. Astra rolled over. I called louder.

Her eyes fluttered open. "What?"

"It's me, Prince Aidan."

"What do you want? I need my beauty sleep." Astra turned over.

"Listen. Don't trust any of the council members. They conspired against our father and your mother. They mean you harm," I said.

Astra wiped her eyes and sat up. "Are you hiding in the dark?"

"No. I'm talking in your mind. I took a chance you might hear me. Your grandmother, Valora yet lives. She visited me. She fears for your life and wants you away from Azure."

"Leave? And go where?" Astra questioned. "I don't even know the woman. And I am not one of those weak girls the queen parades around. I do know fighting skills."

"Go to Meadowlark for your safety. Remember when Tano flew us there?" I said.

Astra punched her pillow. "All right, you said your peace. Now let me sleep." Astra lay back down and pulled the end of her pillow over an ear.

I slipped out of my trance and climbed inside the furs on my cot. "I can't believe the stubbornness of Astra!" I slapped the cot and lay down, closing my eyes.

It seemed minutes since I had fallen asleep when Clay barged into my tent. "Rise and shine, My Prince. It's time for your exercise."

I groaned.

"What? You don't like my looks or something?" Clay pumped his muscles.

"What's on the torture agenda today?" I asked.

Clay chafed his hands together. "I'm glad you asked."

A gleam shone in his eyes, and I knew I wasn't going to like it.

"Here. Put this on," Clay said.

I picked up the canvas backpack and grunted at the unexpected heaviness. I strapped it on. "What do you have in there, a dead pig?"

Clay chortled. "Good one. Wished I thought of it. A pack of rocks. It's to build your muscle strength. Walk with me." He sauntered outside.

I fell over with my first step. "Son of a giant beetle!" I rolled onto my knees and pushed myself up. Concentrating on my balance, I followed behind Clay. We strode down the familiar path.

After a mile of walking, with rocks on my back, I leaned more on my staff. The middle of my back hurt and I had a kink in my neck. I rolled my neck around, trying to get the knot out, and tripped over the blasted staff and hurdled into a tree trunk with my shoulder.

"Here." I thrust the staff at Clay. "I won't rely on special aides."

"Great. Your next torture awaits you." Clay grinned.

"I'm afraid to ask," I said.

We hiked another half mile and clear, blue water came into view.

Clay halted at a secluded part of the lake. "Remove your boots, My Prince."

I pulled them off and scanned my surroundings. The occasional jump of a fish cut the silence. I wiped the perspiration off my forehead with the tail of my shirt.

"Roll up your pants too," Clay said.

I stooped over and the weight of the rocks, inside the knapsack, shifted. I grabbed onto an old stump, before I fell over, glaring at Clay.

"Here, allow my assistance."

I slapped Clay's hands away. Plopping one leg on top of the stump, I rolled up one pant leg, then followed suit with the other. I moaned at the strain on my healing thigh wound.

"Walk in the lake with the pack and follow the water's edge." Clay whistled as he hiked beside me.

I put my feet into the lake and the chill cut me to the bone. "Son of an ugly roach! Are you trying to freeze me to death?"

Clay smirked. "The lake formed from a glacier. You'll get used to it."

With the weight of the rocks on my back, each step in the water slowed like trudging through thick pudding. I fought the urge to push Clay in the water. Instead, I splashed him.

"You don't want to tangle with me, My Prince."

"Threatening me?" I expected a retort, but when it didn't happen, I felt let down. Always on the defense with my brother, but with Clay, he just ignored me and strode on.

At the end of the lake, Clay led me to a lodge constructed of saplings and covered in furs. He removed my pack, and I stretched my back. A great relief.

A younger version of Clay, with short hair and a thinner build, stoked a fire in the campsite. Clay dumped the rocks from the pack into the fire.

"My Prince, meet my younger brother, Birch. He is the fire-keeper." Clay scooped some water with a ladle from a pail. "Drink, before you enter the sweat lodge."

I took a sip.

Clay pushed the ladle back at me. "I said drink. Your body requires it."

"Pushy devil." I drank my fill.

"Remove your clothes and enter the lodge, My Prince," Clay said.

I tugged my shirt off and laid it over a boulder. I wrinkled my nose at my ripeness. I limped to the entrance of the sweat lodge before I dropped my pants. Woven mats covered the dirt floor, except for a circle of rocks in the center. I grasped a towel and concealed my private parts as I sat down.

Birch carried in a basket of hot rocks and placed them in the circle. Clay, in naked glory, strolled inside the lodge and I turned my head away. I felt puny next to him. Birch lit a bundle of sage and sweetgrass. He handed the end of the bundle to Clay before he walked out the flap.

Clay draped the herbs over the hot rocks, and they sizzled, infusing the lodge with steam. "We use them for purification. It cleanses your mind, body, and spirit from impurities." Clay waved the steam over himself. He inhaled deeply, then exhaled.

I copied his behavior. Perspiration rained down me. Birch strode in with a kettle and poured water over the rocks. The water evaporated and a new wave of heat overwhelmed my senses.

Birch tossed me a towel. "Put this over your head and concentrate on your breathing." He walked out.

Drenched in perspiration, yet breathing easier, my body relaxed. A vision of a brown bear appeared before me and called my name. *How was this possible? Was I hallucinating or dreaming?* I saw myself climb his back and I rode the bear to a stream filled with fish. He continued up a winding hill and halted at a hollow tree. The word, *remember* circulated in my head, then the bear vanished.

I rubbed my eyes. "Did you see the bear, Clay?"

"Your totem is strong, My Prince. You had a vision." Clay slapped my shoulder. "It's time for a swim."

I shivered at the difference of temperature from the sweat lodge to outside. I picked up the ladle and quenched my thirst. Clay ran down the hillside and jumped in the lake. Water splashed from the impact.

I took my time down the hill and slipped inside the cool water. Between the warmth from the sweat lodge and the red sun-like star spreading its golden light over me, it felt good in the chilly lake. I raked the water, and a school of minnows swam beside me. I rolled over and floated on my back.

A waterfowl landed on my stomach and floated along. I didn't mind, until he tugged one of my few chest hairs. I turned over and the bird squawked. He pinched my bottom with his beak. I splashed the damn bird, until he flew off. Clay roared with laughter and my face heated. I swam back to shore, then snatched my clothes and my staff.

Clay called my name, but I ignored him. My brother laughed enough at me at home. I didn't need it from Clay. I strode down the path. Mothers covered their daughter's eyes as I stumbled by. Some of the elder women smiled. Young boys pointed and laughed.

I grabbed a boy by his collar. "Why are you laughing?"

"You aren't wearing a stitch of clothing, My Prince."

I released the boy and glanced down at myself. My clothes were still in my hand. I had forgotten in my state of mind to put them on. I hurried away from the people and sought refuge in my tent. Humiliation reddened my cheeks.

I hastened inside my tent. The intrusive warble of the songbirds blended with Clay's obnoxious voice minutes later.

"Go away. No one will respect me again. The clan viewed my nakedness and laughed."

"If that's your wish, My Prince."

I sighed with relief after Clay left.

Moments later, Sylvia barged through my flap, and I covered my nakedness. "I understand you're afraid to show yourself?"

"Don't you believe in knocking or announcing yourself?" I glared.

"You're young. You shouldn't be ashamed of your body. Every person has one."

"It doesn't mean I want everyone to stare," I said.

"They weren't laughing at you. They were surprised," Sylvia said. "Get dressed and meet me at my hut. I want to teach you some more magic."

"All right." I said.

Chapter Seventeen

WALKING FROM THE HEALER'S TENT AND FOLLOWING the path to Sylvia's hut, I spied Clay squatting down near a bush. "What are you doing?"

Clay put his finger over his lips. Apprehension pooled in my stomach. Clay trampled through some thick bushes until I couldn't see him anymore. *Should I follow him?*

A rabbit scampered from the bushes and Clay chased it. He dropped on top of it and grabbed the rabbit by its long ears. The critter scratched Clay's arms with his hind legs. Sylvia's son, Gus, emerged from the bushes with dry leaves in his dark hair. Clay handed him the rabbit.

"The little rascal jumped out of my arms, and I had a devil of a time capturing him again. Thanks for your help, Clay," Gus said. "Pondarosa planned a rabbit stew for dinner." Gus raced down the path with the rabbit.

"What happened to Sylvia's husband?" I asked Clay.

"Lyman died some time ago during a war. The men of the village look out for Gus. You understand what it's like without a father around. Hunting accident, wasn't it?" Clay asked.

Anger simmered within me at the unfairness of it all. "Dad was murdered. I don't have any physical proof."

"Murder?" Clay gasped. "Did the culprit see you?"

"I don't know," I said.

"It's no wonder your mother sent you here. Learn all you can from the chieftain on magic. Between Ash and I, we'll educate you in the art of fighting. You're going to need it."

"Thanks, Clay. I better go. Sylvia's waiting," I said.

The windchimes tinkled as I ducked my head through the flap of Sylvia's hut. Her long, slender fingers arranged a bouquet of wildflowers in a ceramic vase. The scent of mint was refreshing with the other wildflowers.

"Sit, Young Prince." Sylvia pointed to a stool. "I love fresh flowers, don't you?"

"They're nice." I smiled. "Is it safe to talk here?"

"Your secrets are safe, Young Prince."

"I recently found out my father was murdered by Councilor Grimshaw. It worries me how close he's become with Mother."

Sylvia looked up from her flowers. "Are you sure you're not jealous of their relationship? Didn't King Arin die in a hunting accident?"

"Everyone believes that story." I glowered. "Dad placed a special design behind my ear in case something happened to him. When I touched it, I remembered everything clearer."

"Leave the past in the past. The truth won't bring your father back," Sylvia said. "You aren't thinking of revenge, are you?" She stared at me.

"A deep part of me wants Grimshaw to pay for his misdeeds. I informed Santurin, but he believes I made up a story and told me to keep quiet. It's not right," I said.

"It's whether you act on those feelings is the difference between you and Grimshaw. Karma finds a way to repay people like him." Sylvia grasped my shoulders in a firm grip. "Allow your anger to float off you and out the flap. Good." Sylvia pulled a wildflower out of the vase and showed it to me. "This is an herb called Rue. It's distinguished by its small, rounded lobed leaves. It protects one against curses and spells." She put it inside a pouch and handed it to me. "I've put runes and other herbs in this for your protection."

I lifted my wool shirt and tied the pouch to the loop of my breeches.

"People with magic bend the energies of nature to promote healing, growth, and life. Magic rises from harnessing your inner power and from the supernatural forces that change in the physical world," Sylvia said. "A time of great power happens with the light of the full moon. When sorcerers and witches place their arms and legs in a pool of water beneath the full moon, they draw the reflected powers through their fingers and toes." Sylvia peered at me.

"Fascinating. Are you a sorceress or a witch?" I asked.

"I'm more of a shaman or a druid. Yes, I possess magic, but it was a gift. I communicate with the spirits and the goddess," Sylvia said. "The world is a balance between light and dark, and good and evil. You can't have one without the other." Sylvia grabbed a stick of charcoal. "Let's go to your tent and draw your circle."

We strolled outside, but I didn't see my tent anywhere. "Where is it?"

The corners of Sylvia's lips turned up in amusement. "The men built a sturdier hut out of wood. The bear destroyed most of your last hut. You couldn't stay in the healer's tent forever. With the canvas over your hut's doorway, it's easier to come and go. It's not far from my hut. She pointed across the way. "What do you think?"

"I'm honored." I moved aside the flap, and a huge crow flew out.

"Hmm. Either someone wants to frighten you, or they placed a curse." Sylvia frowned.

I showed her the corn scattered on the floor of my hut. Picking up the kernels, I tossed them outside. "That's the reason, the crow wanted a free treat." *I wondered if Grimshaw was responsible.*

We shoved the cot over on its side. Sylvia drew a large circle with a piece of charcoal on the floor. Inside the center of it, she drew a triangle. She added symbols.

"Each cardinal point associates with an element. East represents enlightenment, mysticism, and spiritual consciousness. The element is air," Sylvia said. "The west is the symbol of creative power, and its element is water. The south channels and directs energy forces of nature and the psychic. Fire is its element." Sylvia paused to let it sink in a moment.

"The north associates with darkness, mystery, and the unknown. Earth is its element. A person with magical abilities consecrates the circle with the four elements and invokes the guardian spirit to watch over the four cardinal points of the sky," Sylvia said. "The physical circle matches its duplicate astral counterpart against the invasion of negative forces. Magic is dangerous if you don't know what you are doing."

Sylvia handed me a jeweled dagger. "Stand in the middle of the circle. Trace the air with the dagger and move clockwise. Say these words: I banish unwanted energies and invoke the guardian spirits to protect me. I consecrate the four elements and invoke the guardians to watch over the four quarters of the sky."

I walked inside the circle with the dagger. I repeated her words, moving clockwise, and traced the air with the dagger.

"Repeat these words: clement, loving spirits, send my tears to your gracious advocate and express my mercy. Hear my plea," Sylvia said.

I followed her directions, then gazed at her. "Anything else?"

"Kneel. Hold the dagger up," she said.

I knelt and a bright light reflected off the dagger.

A cluster of voices said, "Rise, young wizard. We shall protect you if you keep the faith."

Power filled me, and I bowed my head. "Thank you, kind spirits." The light vanished, yet the energy remained inside me.

"Step out of the circle, Young Prince," Sylvia said.

We sauntered outside and strode out to an open field.

Sylvia raised a finger in the air. "The wind is blowing North. Face towards the South. Remember the South channels energy and the element is fire. Visualize the object of fire in your mind. See its colors? Smell it?"

I nodded.

"Good. Open your hands and picture the flame inside them. Open your eyes, Young Prince. See your result."

"I did it!" I smiled.

"See, it's all in the matter of control. Throw your fireball in the lake," Sylvia said.

Sylvia gazed at me. "Read some of the books I lent you on magic. Only practice magic when either I'm around to guide you or when standing in your magic circle. It's for your own safety. Let's go inside my hut. I have a gift for you."

"Remain quiet." Sylvia pulled on a long, leather glove. She drew near a large cage and removed the cover. "Come out, my sweet." She opened the cage door and removed a Golden Eagle. "This is Mystic. I keep her hooded, until ready for the hunt. Eagles catch bigger prey, especially the females. Teach her to scan the countryside for you. Whatever she sees, you also see with your gift of sight." Sylvia handed me a leather glove.

After peering at the amber and brown feathered eagle's sharp talons, I felt blessed with the glove.

"Establish a routine and regular conversation with Mystic. You must trust each other," Sylvia said.

"Talk with a bird? How does she understand me?" I asked.

"Don't worry. It happens on its own. Use positive reinforcement and patience. Birds don't understand punishment." Sylvia grasped the tether, hooked to a set of shackles on the eagle's legs, and balanced Mystic on her gloved arm. "Come outside and we'll practice with her."

We strolled to a field of grass. Sylvia passed the eagle to me, and I grasped the tether. I balanced Mystic on my left leather-covered arm. I whispered soothing words to the eagle.

Sylvia said, "I fashioned a lure out of deer hide and tied a small meal of rabbit meat to it. Place it near the end of your hand before I remove the hood. Make Mystic work for it. Ready?"

I nodded. Sylvia removed the hood and Mystic blinked a few times, until her eyesight adjusted to the daylight. I rolled the meat close, and she picked up the scent. I danced the lure across the glove and twirled it at the edge of my fingertips. Her talons grasped the meat. Mystic shredded it with her curved beak, gobbling the meat down.

"Good girl," I said.

"Loosen the tether in your hand, Young Prince," Sylvia said. "Allow her to spread her wings."

Mystic flew ten feet above us and I released my hold. A brown rabbit emerged from a tussock of grass and sprinted across the ground. Mystic spied it, and a contest of hunter versus prey ensued. Mystic swooped down, with her talons extended, but the rabbit dodged her.

The eagle circled back. The rabbit sped across the open field, but Mystic captured it. I whistled long and shrill. Mystic brought me the rabbit.

"You're a magnificent hunter," I whispered to her. "I'll keep this prize and you find another." I handed the rabbit to Sylvia and released my hold on Mystic.

The eagle soared over a fat bush and a rabbit burst from its hiding spot. The game on, Mystic whooshed down and clutched her prey in a matter of seconds.

"Good girl, Mystic!" I jumped up. "Go ahead and eat it. You earned it."

"Well done, Young Prince. She took a liking to you. When she's finished, call her, and place the hood back on. It's her signal the hunt is over," Sylvia said.

"All right." I placed the hood on Mystic's head, when she finished, and grasped her tether. I balanced her on my gloved arm and walked inside Sylvia's hut.

I eased the bird inside her cage. "Thank you, Sylvia. I never had a pet of my own and your gift was generous." I removed the glove and grabbed Mystic's cage. I strode to my hut and placed her cage on a table.

My stomach grumbled as I walked out of my hut and down the trail to the lodge for my meal. I should bring something back for my eagle.

Chapter Eighteen

MEN HUDDLED AROUND A PLATTER OF BARBECUED deer near the lodge. I filled my plate, then ate a piece of meat. It tasted sweet and melted in my mouth.

"Who hunted the deer?" I asked Ash.

"The young buck wandered onto the path. Tender, right?" Ash fanned a bee away from his plate. He sat on a bench inside the lodge.

Yvonne hurried over to us with her full plate. "You don't mind if I sit with you?"

"No." I sat next to Ash. "What are those men doing over there?" I pointed across the way outside.

"They're setting up for the firewalkers. My brother, Birch, performs this evening. Come back later and watch the show," Yvonne said.

"Doesn't he worry about his feet burning?" I asked.

"With the right preparations, trained people prance across the hot coals with barely a blister. Want to try?" Ash's eyes twinkled.

"Are you challenging me?" I asked.

"Are you considering, My Prince?" Ash questioned.

"Why not," I said.

Eagerness shone on Yvonne's face, and she clapped at my announcement.

Ash slapped my shoulder. "Good for you! I'll walk you to the training center after we're done eating."

I don't know if I was brave or plain stupid, but I had Yvonne and Ash's support. Hazel walked over and offered us some salad greens. I took a scoop, and she drizzled some honey-berry sauce over it. I ate it all and wiped my mouth with a cloth napkin.

"Ready?" Ash asked.

"Let's go," I said.

"I'll save you a spot on the grass when you're done walking on the coals," Yvonne called.

I smiled, and Yvonne waved. Ash and I hurried over to the area for the firewalkers.

Inside a huge tent, a bare-chested thin man, with a white goatee, and dressed in a loincloth, demonstrated to a group of people. He glided across a plank of wood like a dancer. His voice rasped, "As long as you move, each step absorbs little heat from the embers. Never run. The lighter the stride, the less chance the cinders will scorch your toes. Each step should last a second or less." He glanced at us and gestured to move in closer. "A safe walk requires the right coals, usually cherry or Maplewood. Hardwoods make great insulators, and they'll protect feet from some of the heat, even though they're aflame. Cherry and Maplewood don't burn as hot as other charcoals, but they're great for illusion purposes with their red- orange embers. Practice walking across the wood." The man crossed his arms and watched each person take their turn.

I pulled off my boots and joined the others, surprised to see women amongst the men. *Aren't their feet more tender?* When my turn came, I pretended the wood was my cloud-board and eased across it.

Ash clapped. "Good show, My Prince!"

The others dropped to their knees at his announcement.

Touched by their respect, this wasn't the time or place for it. I refused different treatment because of my heritage and wanted to blend in. *If I failed at walking on coals, what then?*

"You're too kind. Please rise," I said. "Today, I am one of you, learning a new feat. I'm not superhuman. I make mistakes. Please pretend I'm not here."

"Powerful words, My Prince, but if you burn your feet, the queen might relieve me of my head. I am called Rutland." The teacher nodded.

"Mother never harbored anyone's head. We won't tell her though," I said.

"As you wish. I suggest you toughen your feet, before walking across the hot coals this evening. Go barefoot and walk along the border of the lake. The sand and gravel exposes the soles of your feet to a mild abrasive texture. Come back, before the sun sets," Rutland said.

"All right," I said.

"I'll go with you, My Prince," Ash said.

We ducked out of the tent. I carried my boots and walked across the path. We stepped down into the sand and gravel mix and strolled along the border of the lake. The sand felt warm and squishy between my toes as we strolled. After we walked about half a mile, we turned around, and strode back.

Ash pointed to an open area of grass, not far from the path. "A great area to spar." Ash wiped his wet feet off the grass, and I followed suit.

"My brother learned fighting skills, not me. Can you teach me?" I asked.

"My honor." Ash placed his hand over his heart. "I'll start with some basic tips; in case you're attacked. Keep your back close to a wall, if possible, for your protection. When your attacker punches you, turn to the side to dodge it. Grab their arm and strike the elbow joint.

Another painful area to hit is the nose or the flank."

"What if they hold me in a headlock?" I asked.

"If they grab you from behind, you still have your hands and legs free. Use your elbow and jab them in the stomach," Ash said. "Slam your heel down on their foot. If that doesn't release their hold, tuck your chin in and grab their hands, pulling down. It lessens the pressure on your neck."

"How do you know so much about it?" I asked.

"Easy. I wrestled many of my brothers. When you're one of the smallest, you think fast to escape their torment."

I looked at him. *If he was small, then what am I?*

"Keep your legs bent and apart. This maintains your stability for a counterattack or to free yourself," Ash said. "Prevent an armlock by holding on to something, such as a loop on your breeches. If it occurs, feign a punch to loosen their grip. Punch or kick your attacker the moment the grip releases. The big part of defense strategy is recognizing the move, before it happens."

"How do I know?" I asked.

"Some signs are the formation of a fist, their foot shifts forward, their shoulder drops, and their body turns to the side, away from you. Didn't you ever fight with your brother?" Ash asked.

"Verbally, but not physically. My nursemaid separated us if she saw the slightest inclination. Often, Santurin was sent away. No wonder he hates me. Ash, teach me all you know about fighting," I said.

"Stay unpredictable. Dodge out of the way, duck, jump, or move to the side. The less fear and anger you show, the less your opponent controls you," Ash instructed.

"Like this?" I jumped around in a square.

"Put your arms up and protect your face. Keep your elbows in. Move up and down and side to side," Ash said. "Maintain your balance and move quickly. Avoid placing weight on your heels and stand on your toes. If necessary, pivot and slide on the balls of your feet. Now, keep your left hand near your cheek and your right under your chin." Ash put up his fists. "Give it a whirl."

I jabbed out and Ash blocked my move. Keeping my weight on the balls of my feet, I bounced around him. Ash threw a left jab at my face, but I ducked. I punched the right side of his torso. Taken by surprise, Ash grumbled under his breath, and counterpunched, but I hopped out of his reach.

"You're picking it up fast. After you're adept at delivering a variety of punches, release a flurry of blows to your opponent. You've learned the jab and the cross punch, now try the uppercut," Ash said. "Lower your arm to waist-level, then swing upward. Aim for your opponent's chin." Ash jutted out his lower jaw and tapped his chin. "Hit me."

I struck his chin and Ash fell back. His wife, Hazel glared at me, and ran to Ash's side.

"Sorry, he asked me to punch his chin," I said.

"Men and their stupid games!" Hazel kissed Ash's cheek and his eyes fluttered open. She slapped him. "Don't ever scare me like that again." She stormed back towards the lodge.

"It was worth it to feel your soft lips on my face!" Ash called.

Hazel pivoted around and wagged her finger at him. Ash burst out laughing.

"I never meant to interfere in your love life. I should have asked Clay to teach me."

"Clay assisted the chieftain with a project. The best part of fighting with your spouse is making up." Ash elbowed me. "You know what I mean?"

I hadn't a clue about lovemaking and laughed to cover my naivety. I've heard the ruts and grunts from some of the servants hiding in closets or the alcoves of the fortress, yet I've never seen it or engaged in the practice. Mother told me sex was special when I found the right girl.

"Are we done here?" I asked.

"One more thing, My Prince. Relax your body and keep eye contact with your opponent. It helps you figure out where he'll land his next punch," Ash said. "If he aims at your body, tighten your core muscles, and absorb the blow. I'll meet you at Rutland's near sunset." Ash rushed to the lodge.

I hiked further down the trail. The birds sang from the trees, and I whistled along with them. Soon, Clay's exercise area came into view. I sauntered over to a canvas bag of dirt that hung from a rope on a post.

Donning some gloves, I punched the bag. It swung back and knocked me to the ground. I stood up and brushed myself off.

"Here. I'll hold it for you." Clay said, from behind me.

I flinched. "You scared me."

"Better than laughing at you," Clay said.

"You won't let me forget it, will you?" I whipped my hair off of my face.

"Nope. Unless…you bring Juliana by for a visit." Clay rubbed his hands together.

I arched my brow. "Bribery?"

"Call it what you want. I'd like to see her pretty face again."

"I can't interest you in my sister, Astra? She's in the market for a husband," I said.

"Nah, she's too sassy. I like my women docile and pleasing to the eye." Clay held the bag. "Punch it."

Spreading my legs apart, I balanced on my toes. I struck out, and punched the wall when Clay moved the bag. "Son of a giant beetle!" I shook out my hand. "Why'd you move it? I almost broke my hand."

"I wanted you to take me seriously. Promise you'll bring Juliana by," Clay said. "Didn't anyone ever tell you to wrap your hands or tape them first?" Clay asked.

"No. I'm new at this." I rubbed my hand.

"Rinse your hand in lake water. Stop by tomorrow and we'll practice," Clay said.

I grabbed my boots from the ground and strode across the grass. Walking down to the lake, I knelt at the edge and held my injured hand in the water. The coolness eased my pain. Clay's sense of humor irked me. All because he wanted a look at Juliana. She deserved someone better than an oversized rooster.

The light slipped low behind the mountains as I hastened to Rutland's tent. People gathered round and sat on animal furs on the grounds outside the tent. Rutland raked the bed of coals in the rectangular metal box outside and they glowed red-hot.

What had I gotten myself into?

Rutland sprinkled a fine layer of ash on top of the coals, then dusted off his hands. He lit the torches. I ducked inside the tent. Pondarosa and the other participants dipped their feet in pans of water.

"Why are you getting your feet wet?" I asked her.

"When liquid meets intense heat, it forms an insulating layer of steam. The moisture acts like a protective glove for our feet," Pondarosa explained. "Use my water, My Prince. I'm done."

I dipped my feet in the pan. A few minutes later, a reed played. Pondarosa and the others formed a line. I pulled my feet out of the water and joined the line. Rutland announced us and we walked in formation outside the tent. The people clapped.

"This evening, our guest, Prince Aidan joins us in our festivity. Pondarosa, demonstrate the walk. Our prince will follow behind her. Give them a round of applause," Rutland said.

I gulped. I hadn't expected to be one of the first across the hot coals.

Pondarosa whispered in my ear, "Don't run. Once you step on the coals, walk fast without stopping. Follow my lead."

The drums beat, and she strolled across the coals. When she finished, the people clapped. Pondarosa nodded to me. I held myself erect, and paced across the coals, without glancing down. Hitting the end of the bed, I jumped down. The people stood and roared with applause.

Pondarosa squeezed my hand. "See? You made it."

I smiled, then plopped on the ground, next to Yvonne, and pulled on my boots. The other participants took their turns, and I clapped after each one. Nothing prepared me for the last firewalker though.

Birch, Yvonne's younger brother, strode across the hot coals, flipped backwards, and walked on his hands across the coals. I whistled and clapped. Birch bowed, and the people applauded.

Ash sat down next to me. "He's incredible, right? Mama always said to watch the quiet ones. You never know what they're thinking."

"He's gifted. Which one is your mother?" I asked.

Ash pointed her out. "Next to Sylvia."

"The tiny woman?" I asked. "How did she bare such bruits like you and your brothers?"

Yvonne burst out laughing. "Good one, My Prince. They weren't born huge, but look at Pa. He's the big bruiser arm wrestling with Clay at the table."

I glanced at the bulky man with the wooly red beard. A heavy fur covered his shoulders. Laughter boomed from him after he won the match.

Yvonne plaited her hair into two braids with ribbons that matched her turquoise marble-like eyes. She scooted closer to me. "You were brave walking on the hot coals this evening, My Sweet Prince."

Yvonne had a clean meadow scent with a hint of lavender. It was refreshing, not overly perfumed like Mother's handmaidens. I glanced at her father and flinched. His silver eyes gleamed in the glow of the embers and froze me in place.

"Can you put some distance between us, Yvonne? Your father doesn't look happy."

"Never mind him, My sweet Prince. A little birdie told me you're going on a manhood trip soon." Yvonne flipped one of her braids over her shoulder. "When you become a man and you're looking for a mate, I'm available." Yvonne smiled and dimples showed in each cheek.

Big, hairy hands dug into my shoulders from behind me. "You sit too close to my daughter," a gruff voice snarled.

"You're embarrassing me, Pa." Yvonne jumped up.

Ash touched his father's arm. "Relax, Pa. Yvonne set her claws on our prince. It's not his fault she aims her sights high."

"Daughter, quit harassing the prince. He's too puny for you anyway." Her father grabbed Yvonne's arm, but she yanked out of his grasp. She ran off, and her father stomped off.

Some people snorted. Others muttered, "*Can you believe it? He insulted the prince.*"

I rubbed my temples. "Is your sister always forward?"

"Yvonne wants to settle down. Pa overprotects her," Ash said.

"I've noticed. A prince not good enough for her?" I asked. "My mother was a forest dweller."

Ash's eyes perked up. "Are you interested?"

I wiped my hand down my face. "By law, I can't marry, until I turn sixteen." *Between Ash and Yvonne, I felt pushed into the relationship. What did I know about her or marriage for that matter? I liked my freedom. Yvonne was outspoken, but honest. She'd make a nice wife for someone. I wish my friend, Varick or even Wylie were around to talk things out.*

Ash and I sat on the grass, with the glow of the embers, and the torches giving light to the night. Yvonne stood behind a fir tree and watched us.

She wasn't ugly and had an ample bosom, but her dimpled smile and unusual eyes captivated me.

"Ah, daughter. Come assist your mother," Yvonne's father said, from behind her.

Yvonne jumped. "Don't frighten me." She pushed past him and left her father standing by the fir tree.

I waited for him to leave, before I spoke further with Ash. "I'm not ready to marry, besides my mother picked my brother's bride, and probably will do the same for me."

"Yvonne's tired of Pa interfering in her life. Marriage is an escape for her," Ash said.

"Any recommendations from your father?" I asked.

"Only old men or friends his age. Do you know anyone on Azure looking for a mate?"

"Councilors around Mother's age. No one I'd recommend." *No one good enough for Yvonne anyway. I preferred she stayed mine, but Mother might dash my hopes away.*

Ash interrupted my thoughts. "Wait until you see the feast the women prepared. Hazel made a salad with strips of deer meat. Twiggy baked a gooseberry pie and Hazel outdid her with a blackberry-rhubarb pie. Pa grilled some fish I caught earlier." Ash smacked his lips.

"Sounds delicious." Curious, I asked, "Does Yvonne cook too?"

"Ma has taught her a few things." Ash looked at me. "Oak roasted a wild turkey. I know it's forbidden on Azure to eat any bird, but we live off the land here. How do you get your food on Azure?"

"We trade goods through other villages or some of the servants hunt or fish," I said. "Where did everyone go?"

"They're preparing the evening meal. Come on," Ash said.

We journeyed to the lodge. Candles, in metal tubs, glowed on tables as some of the women brought food over. Everyone took their seats. Sylvia nodded to the reed player. He played a soft melody that drifted on the evening breeze. Ash plopped down on a bench next to his sister and I sat on his right. Yvonne winked at me, and I smiled.

The chieftain strolled to the middle of the floor and raised her arms. "We thank our entertainers for their brave deeds of walking across the hot coals and we offer our celebration feast. We thank the animal spirits for giving their life, so we may eat. We thank our hunters for their great skills, and we thank our marvelous cooks for preparing this feast. Let us eat."

Platters of food passed around. I piled my plate with a little of everything, except the turkey. I tucked some fish in a napkin and put it aside. Mystic deserved a treat. I dug in and surprised myself that I ate everything on my plate. I leaned back and drank my tea.

Ash grabbed a torch and walked me back to my hut. At last, I knew some fighting skills and survived fire walking without burning my feet.

I ducked inside my hut and Mystic stirred in her cage. "You smelled your treat, did you?" I pulled on a glove and opened her cage. Unfolding the napkin, before removing Mystic's hood, I said, "Here you go."

Mystic gobbled her fish in a matter of minutes.

"Good girl. We'll go hunting on the morrow." I placed her hood back on and closed the cage, dropping the glove on the table. Mystic was a well-trained pet, not like Mother's old falcon that tore her cage apart when left unattended. I picked up a book that Sylvia left me and curled up on my cot.

Chapter Nineteen

I LIT A CANDLE AND FLIPPED THROUGH THE BOOK. A page about bewitchment caught my attention. "Listen to this, Mystic. To bewitch a person, collect their nail clippings and hair. Say a spell over them and they must do anything you ask of them. I might use that one someday."

I turned the page. A spell on time- walking caught my attention. I shoved my cot aside and stood in the middle of my protective circle. Closing my eyes, I imagined my bedroom on Azure. I chanted, "Time is the past, the present, and the future. Secure, it passes, flows, and flies, yet time leaves its shadow behind. Connect to my mind and bind time to mine." My body lifted from the floor. I spun in a circle one way, then in the opposite direction. I opened my eyes and found myself inside a giant, metallic bubble. Clocks of various times ticked around me. Between the noise and the spinning, I felt dizzy and nauseous, and closed my eyes.

Moments later, I crashed into something solid.

"Get off me, you worm!" Grimshaw snarled.

"What are you doing in my chambers?" *What was he after?* My dresser drawer was partially open.

"You weren't using it and I sought some peace and quiet. Councilor Wings snores loud enough to wake the dead," Grimshaw said.

I didn't believe him. *He was searching for something, but what?* I'm glad my hairbrush and nail clippers were on Zavion and not here, after reading about the bewitching spell.

"Ask Santurin to show you the guest chambers. My room is not for your convenience. Leave." I pointed to the door. *How did Grimshaw get the code to my room anyway? Did he lift my prints off the numbers?*

"With pleasure." Grimshaw rushed out the door.

I opened my dresser drawer further and peeked inside. Using my handkerchief, I pulled out a blood-stained knife. Was it the same knife that he killed Dad or Twain with? He's trying to blame me for it. I wrapped the handkerchief around the knife and stowed it under some spare blankets on the top shelf in my closet. Grabbing a pouch, hidden in the back of the closet, I dumped salt in front of my bedroom door. Salt kept out evil spirits. I hoped it worked on evil sorcerers too. Grimshaw ruined my idea of visiting my friends and family.

Removing a piece of charcoal from my pocket, I drew a protective circle, with the symbols Sylvia taught me, on the floor. I stood in its center and concentrated on an image of my hut. Chanting the spell on time again, my bedroom disappeared, and I landed, with a thud, on the floor of my hut minutes later. Mystic squawked, and I whispered soothing words, until she settled down.

I scooted the cot back in place and blew out the candle. "Good night, Mystic." I lay down on my cot and smiled. I had time-walked!

The next morning, a horrible odor filled the hut.

"Phew!" I opened Mystic's cage, rolling up the poop-stained rushes, and dumped it in a metal can for refuge outside.

Walking back inside, I washed my hands in a basin of water before placing fresh rushes inside Mystic's cage. I tossed the contents of the basin outside the flap and drenched Yvonne. I hadn't expected her to be there.

Yvonne screeched, and blushed a bright red, before she ran off. I mumbled sorry to her retreating back, then ducked inside my hut and finished dressing. I pulled on the leather glove and removed Mystic from her cage.

Pushing through the flap of my hut, Clay blocked my way out. "What did you do to my sister?"

"I dumped my basin, not expecting anyone outside. If you'll excuse me—" I walked around Clay.

"You owe her an apology."

I trekked on, but Clay stomped behind me.

"Don't walk away from me." Clay grabbed my shoulder.

"Unhand me. You forget your station." I glared.

Mystic raised her wings up, agitated at the change of tone in my voice.

"You're going to apologize to Yvonne if I have to drag you, prince or not," Clay said.

"Lower your voice. You're upsetting my eagle. She's hungry and eager for the hunt."

I considered Clay a friend but felt torn between meeting Mystic's needs and apologizing to Yvonne. *What to do?*

"Forget any more of my time and use of my exercise equipment," Clay said.

I shrugged.

"For a prince, you're naive. Can't you see you hurt Yvonne's feelings?" Clay said. "She likes you, like a man and a woman, you know?"

I stared at Clay.

"Wow, you really don't get it. Go make things right with her. She's washing the stench off in the lake. What was in that basin anyway?" Clay asked.

"You don't want to know, believe me." I wrinkled my nose.

"I'll go with you and make sure my sister is decent," Clay said.

We strode down to the lake. Yvonne sat on a boulder and braided her wet hair. Clay nodded to me. She sniffed and wiped her eyes with the back of her hand.

I squatted down. "Look. I'm sorry. I didn't know you stood outside when I tossed that foul water. Forgive me?"

"You're not going to throw anything else at me, are you?" Yvonne asked.

"Not unless you want me to." I winked.

Yvonne giggled. I held out my free hand and shifted Mystic. Yvonne grasped my hand and stood up.

"Care to join my eagle and I in our daily hunting routine?" I asked.

Yvonne nodded. We strolled down the path, until a clearing appeared in the field. Clay looked around a tree and watched. He gave me the thumbs-up sign. I removed Mystic's hood, and she blinked a few times.

"Your eagle has such lovely colors." Yvonne sighed.

I held onto Mystic's tethers and released her. She flew to the sky and soared around. Mystic spied her prey and swooped down. She captured a rabbit in her talons and brought it to me.

"Good girl." I handed the rabbit to Yvonne, and she placed it in her basket. I sent my eagle out again, but instead of the field, she danced across the lake.

Mystic grasped a large, fat trout and dropped it at my feet, and then she flew off. Yvonne picked up the fish and put it inside her basket. It wiggled around, unlike the rabbit, which lay on its side with a broken neck. I handed Yvonne a cloth to wipe her hands. Mystic skated across the lake and clutched another trout. I allowed her to eat it. Mystic tugged the skin off the fish with her sharp beak, before she plunged into the flesh.

While I waited for my eagle to finish, I gazed at Yvonne. She stood under my chin. Not petite like her mother or a giant like her brood of brothers. Not a speck of fat encircled her, even though she bore wide shoulders. When Yvonne smiled, flecks of silver glistened in her turquoise eyes. No one looked at me the way she did.

My stomach fluttered like butterflies inside. I picked a buttercup and held it under her chin. "Do you like butter?"

A yellow glow beamed under her chin.

"It's true," I said.

Yvonne giggled, then lowered her eyes. "When do you go on your manhood trip?"

"I don't know," I answered.

"Are you proficient with a bow and arrow, My Prince?" Yvonne asked. "My brother, Birch had to learn, before Pa allowed him on his journey."

"Why didn't anyone tell me?" I scratched my head.

"I pestered Pa, until he showed me how to use a bow and arrow. Clay suggested I teach you." Yvonne gazed at me.

Why didn't Ash or Clay teach me? Were they both shoving Yvonne my way? She seemed nice, but I barely knew her.

I cleared my throat. "While I'm on my manhood journey, would you care for Mystic? She requires daily hunting trips."

"Yes, Sweet Prince," Yvonne said.

I leaned down and kissed her cheek. "Thanks."

Yvonne beamed up at me.

I whistled to Mystic, and she flew back to my gloved arm. Placing her hood on, I strolled back to my hut, and ducked through the flap. I put Mystic back inside her cage and shut the door. Yvonne grabbed her bow and a quiver of arrows from behind the tree, as I ran back outside.

She nailed a bullseye on the fir tree, then trekked to my side. "Stand about fifteen feet from the target."

Yvonne stood on my left, and I inhaled her fresh scent as she stood close. She swatted my buttocks. "Pinch them together."

"Hey!" I jumped in surprise at her boldness.

"Keep your back erect. Hold the bow in your left hand," Yvonne said. "Draw an imaginary line from yourself to the target. With your right hand, notch your arrow on the string of the bow." Yvonne nodded as I followed her instructions. "Place your index finger above the arrow and your middle and ring fingers below. Steady. Use your thumb to support the back of the arrow and keep it straight."

"You expect me to hit something like this?" I asked.

"Concentrate and raise your bow," Yvonne said. "Look straight down the shaft of the arrow. Relax your arm and use those back muscles. Try to draw the string as far back as possible." She nodded. "Lift your elbow. Now fire!"

I used my nose as a reference spot. Everything blurred around me, except the target. Silence thickened the air. I released the arrow. It whizzed across and thudded into the target. I stood there with my mouth agape.

"You did it!" Yvonne clapped, jumping up and down.

"You're a great teacher," I said.

"You need much practice. We'll take turns." Yvonne notched an arrow and pulled the string taunt on the bow. She closed one eye and aimed. Yvonne released her arrow and it thundered into mine, splitting the shaft.

"Wow. Amazing," I commented.

Yvonne handed me her bow and another arrow. "Try it again."

Imagining a line from my nose to the target, I closed one eye, and then pulled the string back on the bow. I released my arrow, and it zipped across the air, hitting the target dead-on. "Yes!"

I danced around and Yvonne snickered.

"You got the gist of it, My Sweet Prince. Practice some more. Return my bow when you're finished." Yvonne turned around and rammed into her father's chest.

"Daughter, your mother wants help with the chickens."

"On my way Pa," Yvonne said.

"Forgetting your bow, daughter?"

"Prince Aidan wants to practice with it," she said.

"It's time the prince learned to make his own," her father said. "Run along, Yvonne. Take your bow with you."

"Yes, Pa." Yvonne held out her hand and mouthed sorry to me.

I handed her the bow and the quiver of arrows. When she left, I faced her father.

"Have I done something to displease you, sir? Yvonne offered to show me her archery skills."

"Yvonne doesn't really know what she wants. She takes a fancy to any young male available. It's my job as her father to protect her. Sometimes it's hard for boys to control their urges. Can I trust you?" His silver eyes pierced my soul.

"Trust works both ways," I said.

"Strong words for one so young. Fetch a long straight stick," the man demanded.

"I'm not an animal, sir." My brows furrowed and I crossed my arms.

"For the love of trees! To make a bow, find a stick without knots, and call me, Ulric."

"Why didn't you say what you meant in the first place?" I said, walking away.

I wove through the skirts of trees. Pine burned too quickly. I hiked further and a row of ash trees came into view. I picked through some fallen branches and chose a long, straight one free of knots. I hastened back to Ulric with my prize.

"Fine choice." Ulric slapped my shoulder.

I don't know why it mattered to me about Ulric's opinion, but it did, and I smiled. He pulled a knife from his pocket and slashed a mark in the center of the stick. He placed his hand about two inches from the middle and drew a line around the stick with a piece of charcoal.

Ulric handed the stick back to me. "Peel the bark, where I marked the stick, but not too much off the wood."

I sat down on an old stump and followed his instructions.

"We must determine the bend of the branch." Ulric sat on the ground.

"How?" I asked.

"Stick one end on the ground and push on the handle. It should turn in your hand and reveal which way it wants to flex. Don't force it," Ulric said.

"All right. What's next?" I asked.

"Mark the side that faced you and start shaving off the wood. Don't mess with the side away from you. You want a nice, pointed end tapering up the handle," Ulric said.

After several minutes of working on it, I looked up at him. "Like this?"

"Good work. I brought a roll of nylon string with me," Ulric said. "Tie a loose loop with a secure knot at both ends of your bowstring, before you slip it over the lower and upper limbs of your bow." He continued, "Make your string shorter than the length of your unflexed bow."

Ulric continued, "Both bow and string must stay taunt. If one side is stronger than the other, take off a little more wood. Once it's balanced, string it, and pull back with it. If it's too strong, take more off."

I worked hard on my bow and waited for his approval. Ulric held it up.

"I recommend you wrap cord around it, to increase the power. Do you have your own arrows?" Ulric asked.

I shook my head.

"It's better to know how to make your own anyway. Arrows form from the straightest, dry sticks. Make each one as long as your bow," Ulric said.

"Why are you helping me, sir?" I asked.

"For some reason, my daughter likes you and this gives me the opportunity to see your worth. I'm not one for titles. It's the person that matters. You earn respect to be respected," Ulric said.

I left his side in search of sticks. His words played on my mind. The people of Azure respected Santurin, yet he complained of all his responsibilities. Are the people of Zavion only pacifying me because of my mother? I hope not, I like it here.

I hiked through the trees and picked up branches of ash and maple. With a bundle of sticks in my arms, I walked back. Someone plowed into me, and the sticks flew out of my arms.

Gus held his left arm and sat on the ground. His lips trembled. "I think I broke my arm. It hurts bunches. That root stuck up and tripped me." His arm hung at an odd angle.

"Can you walk?" I asked.

Gus emptied his hands of turkey and chicken feathers into mine. "Yvonne told me to give you these. I didn't want to miss you. They're for the fletching."

Guilt knotted my stomach. The boy injured himself on my account. I shoved the feathers in my pocket, then assisted Gus up and he paled. "Whoa. Don't pass out on me, kid."

Gus sniffed. "I want my mom."

I picked him up and carried Gus to Sylvia's hut. The boy weighed next to nothing, but it was awkward balancing his hurt arm and his stork-like legs. I pushed through the flap. "Sylvia! Gus is hurt."

Chapter Twenty

SYLVIA PUSHED EVERYTHING OFF HER TABLE. "PUT GUS here. What happened?"

"He tripped over a tree root in his haste to give me some feathers. Gus broke his arm."

I placed the boy on the large table. "Can you forgive me, Gus? I didn't see you."

"Don't blame yourself, My Prince. In my hurry, I didn't watch where I went," Gus said. "Can I tell you a secret?"

"Of course, little guy," I said.

"I'm scared. Can you stay with me?" Gus asked.

I squatted and rubbed Gus' head. "If it's all right with your mother."

"Yes. I can use your assistance." Sylvia examined the boy's arm. "Bring some flat wood for a splint, Young Prince."

"I'll be right back, Gus. Don't you worry." I rushed out of the hut.

As I neared Ulric, he flagged me down. "Where are the sticks for the arrows?"

I informed him of Gus' accident. "Sylvia wants flat pieces of wood for a splint."

Ulric said, "I tore down my shed. She can take the wood for the boy. Follow me."

We strode west and the trees parted into an open area. A wooden house, with a large wraparound porch, filled the middle of the grassy lot. Cedar boxes of vegetables lined one side of the house. On the opposite side, a water wheel spun and dumped its contents into a small lake. A couple of swans glided across the placid water.

A herd of horses grazed in the pasture. To the right, Yvonne chased a headless chicken around the yard. Her mother held a bloody axe.

How did a petite woman yield a heavy axe? I swallowed hard. *Best to keep on her good side. How could a chicken run around without a head?* I turned away from the gruesome scene.

"Ulric, did you build your own house?" I asked.

"Yes. It kept me busy when Flora was first pregnant. I've added things to the property over the years with the help of my lads." Ulric walked behind the chicken coop and picked two long flat pieces of wood from a pile sprawled on the ground. "Take these to the chieftain. Return here, and we'll finish your arrows."

I nodded and ran with the wood in my arms. Ducking through the flap of Sylvia's hut, I brought in the wood, and she took them from me.

"Grasp Gus' arm and pull it straight," Sylvia said. She put the wood aside.

"But--won't it hurt?" I grimaced.

"He'll feel some pain, but his arm won't heal right without the deed. I already massaged some willow bark cream over his arm. Ready?" Sylvia asked.

"Gus?" I smoothed his dark hair back from his forehead. "Stay brave a little longer.

Tears welled in Gus' eyes. "All right."

I pulled Gus' arm straight and he cried out. "Shh, it's almost over. You're doing great, little guy."

Sylvia applied the boards on each side of her son's arm, then wrapped long strips of cloth around the splint. She positioned his arm on a pillow. "Rest, love." Sylvia hummed a song.

Gus closed his eyes, and Sylvia pulled me aside, whispering, "I appreciate your help, Young Prince. Don't fret over this. This won't be the last of his injuries. My son is quite clumsy."

When Gus' breathing eased, I felt satisfied he slept in peace. I left Sylvia's hut and trekked back through the forest. Finding the sticks that I had dropped when Gus hurt himself, I gathered them in my arms and hastened to Ulric's place.

Ulric fed wood into a small campfire. I dropped the sticks on the ground and sat down. Ulric picked a stick and peeled the bark from it.

"Don't cut deep into the wood." Ulric handed me one of the sticks.

I stripped off the bark.

"Good. Sand it down to avoid any big bumps or jagged pieces." Ulric tossed me a piece of sandpaper.

I burnished the wood until it smoothed out. Ulric passed me a pair of leather gloves. He pulled on his own pair.

"Grasp the shaft and hold it above the heat source, but don't allow it to catch fire.

Start at one end. Several cycles of heating, bending, and cooling straightens each segment." Ulric demonstrated. "If some minor discoloration happens, sand the shaft again."

After many minutes of holding the shaft over the heat, I allowed it to cool on the ground.

"The next step depends on the type of tip you want. Either you sharpen the narrow end to a point and the wide end the nock side or you attach a point," Ulric said.

"If you choose the latter, it's easier to attach the point to the wide end and the narrow side for the nock. Which do you prefer?" Ulric glanced at me.

"What are the points made from?" I asked.

"Either stone, bone, or metal. Plenty of animal bones here," he said.

"I'll attach a bone point on the wide end and use the narrow side for the nock."

"Good choice." Ulric held a tree-shaped bone piece in his palm. "From a deer femur. Two thirds of the base thickens the shaft and where we attach it to the arrow. First, notch the end of the shaft."

"How deep do I cut?" I gazed at it.

"No deeper than one-eighth of an inch but center the notch. When you complete it, trim the point by whittling or sanding. I'll demonstrate, then you work on your own." Ulric formed a u-shaped notch in the shaft. He rubbed a strip of sandpaper around the area. He held it up for my inspection.

I copied his movements and Ulric nodded his approval.

"It's time to secure the point." Ulric dipped a small stick into a can of pitch and painted the concoction into the notch. He added the bone point and pushed it into the base. "Smear the excess pitch around the top of the shaft. I'd wet your fingers first, before you touch the arrow again. Less pitch sticks to your fingers." Ulric watched me. "Next, cut some sinew, about twelve inches long, and wrap it around the shaft. Secure the end with a blob of pitch."

"What about the feathers?" I pulled out the ones Gus gave me from my pocket. Some of them stuck to my fingers. I tried to shake them off, yet they refused to budge.

Ulric laughed. "Rinse your hands in the bucket. We'll use the feathers later. Fletching improves the flight of the arrow. They act like a rudder on a ship."

I soaked my hands in the bucket and the feathers loosened from my fingers. I grasped a sharp rock and chipped away a few bits off my arrowhead.

"Two ways to attach the feathers. One, split the back of the arrow, slide the feather in, and wrap a thin thread around the fletching. The second way, hold three feathers at the end of the arrow with pitch, then wrap sinew around the shaft," Ulric said. "The first feather goes on the nock, and the other two around the shaft. Apply a thin layer of pitch over the top of the sinew. At this point, trim the feathers about one-half inch. The last step, mark your arrow to distinguish it from others."

I ripped a purple thread off my shirt and wound it tight around the fletching, after I split the back of the arrow. I held it up for Ulric's approval.

Ulric slapped my back. "Good work. Make some more arrows, then put out the fire. The manhood initiation test is in three days. Bring your bow and arrows and meet me in front of the lodge in the morning. I'll give you further instructions at that time."

Why didn't Ash or Clay inform me their father was the elder and oversaw the manhood journey? Could I trust anyone?

Chapter Twenty- One

Three days later

CLOUDS HUNG LOW OVER ZAVION AND CHILLED THE air. The village men sang and pounded their drums. I wore loincloth and goosebumps riddled my arms. I bit my lip to stop my teeth from chattering. Birch painted the lower half of my face in black, a combination of ash and dark earth. It felt cold and wet. When he finished, Birch handed the pot to Clay, then wiped his fingers on a cloth.

Birch held out his hand. "You are a shadow of a man. A boy. We paint your naivety, so all may see you walk the line of severance from childhood. To become a man, and thus a warrior, you must detach yourself from your mother and women around you. You can live without them and prove your masculinity. The rites of passage involve emotional and physical pain. It begins with an ending and ends with a beginning. Aidan of Azure, are you ready for your journey?"

I grabbed his hand and turned toward the men, staring at each one's face. Some I considered friends. Others I didn't know. Fear of the unknown and my impulsive nature begged me to run. "Yes!" I blurted out, surprising myself.

The men whooped and jumped up and down. They shook wooden rattles around me. His face painted in black with white globs of tears, Ulric strode to the center of the men.

Ulric raised his arms. "We mourn the boy known as Aidan. We send him out, so that he may become acquainted with the goddess of nature and sense his true place in his body and spirit. Aidan must leave the comfort of the placenta and deny the support of others."

Ulric added, "Forced to deal with outward circumstances, he'll discover his inner resources of strength and resolve. The closed door of his heart opens him to the beauty and mystery of the natural world around him."

Oak, Ulric's eldest son, with his face painted green, resembled a stocky fir tree. He entered the center of the circle. "The boy, restricted of food for three days as part of his ordeal among us, his physical strength wanes, yet another kind of strength gathers within him. All young men listen to your inner voice and clarify your values. Above all else, confront and ponder the meaning of death and survival. Boy, are you ready for your endurance test?"

I stepped forward. "Yes."

Oak led me to a crude wooden tower. The others crowded behind us. Oak tied a long vine around my ankles. I glanced up and estimated the tower stood a hundred feet tall. The other half of the vine tied the platform.

"Scale the tower and dive headfirst off the platform. Touch the ground with a part of your body," Oak said.

I swallowed hard. "You're jesting?" *What had I gotten myself into?*

Ash sidled close and whispered, "Don't look down and free fall."

I scurried up the wooden structure like a long-legged spider. As a child, I climbed trees and rock ledges numerous times. I stood on the edge of the platform and panic whipped through me. My legs trembled. I've done worse things in my life. I closed my eyes and dropped. I plummeted down and adrenaline rushed in my veins. "Wahoo!" my voice echoed.

The vine halted and squeezed my ankles while I dangled above the ground. I opened my eyes and raised my arm over my head, touching the ground. The men cheered.

"You passed and lived." Clay cut the vine and hoisted me to my feet.

Oak handed me a mug of water. "Drink. This is your only nourishment. You must hunt for food on your journey. Your knife and your bow with arrows are your only weapons."

I guzzled the water, and it sloshed in my empty belly. It didn't quench my thirst but made me nauseous.

Ash gave me a mint leaf. "Chew on this. It relieves the nausea."

"How did you know?" I asked.

"We've all been through it, My Prince. I gift you with these arrows," Ash said. "Yvonne helped."

Purple ribbons braided through the fletching.

"They're marvelous. Thank her for me," I said.

Ash walked away as his father stepped forward.

"I give you three tasks to accomplish," Ulric said. "Bring them back as proof. It doesn't matter the order you obtain them. One: a purple trillium flower. It only grows on top of Fang Mountain." Ulric paused and let it sink in. He held up two fat fingers. "Bring a tail feather from the Tankini bird. Her tail feathers are purple, and her body is bluish black. She makes her nest on the rock ledges of the cliff overlooking the sea." Ulric raised three fingers. "Your last task: bring back a tooth. Not any tooth, but from a ferocious beast. I'll give you two weeks. If we don't hear from you, we'll assume you're dead." Ulric waved Birch over. "My son leads you to your destination. Good luck."

Birch placed my weapons in my hands. I pulled on my boots and shoved the knife inside the side pocket. Over my shoulder, I hung my quiver of arrows and bow. Ash held the reins of two beige horses. Birch climbed on one and I hopped on the other.

"I assumed we were walking," I said.

"No, too far. I'll lead you to the right path, then you're on your own. If you survive the journey, you lead the next candidate." Birch kicked the sides of his horse and galloped down the path.

I forgot the freedom of riding a horse and kicked its sides, catching up with Birch, and reined my horse close to him. We slowed the horses to a trot.

"How do you walk on the hot coals without burning your hands?" I asked him.

Birch smiled wide. "Easy. I wet my palms before I danced across. Did you enjoy my performance?"

"Magnificent. Can you teach me when I return?"

"We'll see."

Was he afraid I'd take the attention away from him? I tried another tactic to get him to talk. "Did you marry after your manhood test?"

"Not yet. Pa promised me a trip to find some suitable girls in the other villages. Do you know any eligible ones?" Hope shone in his warm, brown eyes.

"What are you looking for in a woman?" I asked.

"Fair in face, but not conceited. Not lazy either. She must do her share of the work." Birch rubbed the back of his neck. "Do you know of such a girl?"

"Possibly," I said.

"Put in a good word for me," Birch said. "What was I thinking? You're on your manhood journey. Forgive my eagerness."

"It's okay." I smirked.

We rode in silence. A smile lit Birch's face. He seemed miles away, probably conjuring an image of wedding bliss.

We traveled a distance, and soon the purple Fang Mountains loomed ahead. Birch guided his horse to a small creek. He climbed off and allowed his mare to drink her fill. I jumped off and pulled the reins of my horse to the creek.

Birch gave me a canteen. "Fill it for your drinking water. The trail is over there and leads up the side of the mountain. I'm taking the horses back with me. Good luck."

Chapter Twenty-Two

I KNELT NEAR THE CREEK AND CUPPED MY HANDS, sipping the water, and then filled the empty canteen. Watercress grew nearby and I yanked some of it for a salad later. I rinsed it in the creek, then rolled the watercress in a ball, and tucked it inside my arrow container. Peering up at my destination, I figured it was a long way up.

A family of quails paraded in a line in front of me. I debated with myself whether to eat them and go against my upbringing of not eating birds. Anything looked good right now. A rustle in the bushes snapped my attention. I readied my bow and waited. A brown rabbit hopped onto the path. Its ears twitched as if it sensed danger. I waited for the rabbit to move, and it didn't disappoint me.

I released my arrow and hit my mark. Skinning the rabbit, I kept some of the fur. I removed the intestines and spread them out on a rock. Not much into organ meats, I left them for the wild animals to feast on.

I jabbed a stick through the body and carried the rabbit with me, until I found a place to make a fire. Hiking farther up the trail, a chicory plant grew alongside the gravelly road. The young leaves and flowers tasted best, but the older plants tasted bitter. I broke off a light, blue flower and popped it in my mouth. Not too bad. It tasted like almonds. I snapped off a few more and ate them, while I searched for an area to build a fire.

To the right of the road, the trees parted, and opened in a clearing. A circle of rocks outlined an old campfire.

I gathered small branches from the ground and piled them inside the circle, adding dry grass and some rabbit fur on top of the twigs. Holding my palm out, I imagined a flame. I dropped it onto the grass and twigs and a fire sparked. The stick, holding the rabbit, I stuck in the ground facing the campfire.

Bright pink fireweed grew along the edges of the path. I raced over and plucked some. I sprinkled the petals over the cooking rabbit. The fireweed had a peppery taste and added flavor to the meat. Between my old nursemaid and Mother, I learned a few things about herbs. My mouth watered at the site of the roasting meat.

A rustle in the leaves startled me. My eyes darted about, sensing someone nearby. I flipped the meat around and some critter jumped on my back. I twirled around and it bit the back of my neck.

"Son of a giant beetle!" I flung the ugly rat off, picking it up by its wiry tail, and stared at the face of Grimshaw on it. Tossing the rodent away, a cougar, I hadn't seen watching me, pounced on the critter. The rat curled its claw into a small fist and punched the cougar's snout. The cougar snarled and reached for the rodent. *Poof*: the rat vanished.

"Good kitty. You deserve a treat for getting rid of that pest." I cut off a chunk of rabbit meat and tossed it to the cougar.

The rabbit was a tease to a big creature like the cougar and I kept my bow close by. I didn't plan on being her next meal. The cat carried its share to a tree and climbed up it. The cougar devoured its meal, and I ate the rest of the rabbit meat.

Grimshaw must want me out of the way since I witnessed Dad's murder at his hands. I poured water, from my canteen, over the bite on my neck. Shaking the canteen, I figured the remainder of the water wouldn't last long and trekked back to the creek.

I filled my canteen again, but also picked some reeds and cedar branches along the way back. I peeled the green needles off the cedar, until they were bare sticks. Mother taught me as a child how to weave a basket. With the reeds, I formed six together, then twisted six more around the center, then wove the cedar into the mix. Grasping the sinew from the rabbit, I formed a handle with it and the cedar. It wasn't the best basket, but it fit my purposes.

I strode past the tree, where the cougar napped, and walked towards a blackberry bush. I filled my basket, halfway with sweet berries, when a black bear lumbered towards me from the other side. The bear growled and swept his big paw at me. I jumped back. I tossed blackberries at the bear's face. The cougar had woken and leapt over me, swatting the bear's face. I crept out of their way and rushed back to my campfire.

I dipped a branch into the fire, until I had a torch. Most animals feared fire. The bear weighed more than the cougar, but they both had sharp teeth and claws. The bear stood on his hind legs and hugged the big cat around the waist. The cougar fought back and clawed the bear's sides. The bear roared. With one swat of his enormous paw, the cougar flew into the tree trunk. Her head hung at an odd angle and her chest didn't budge. She wore a vacant stare. Blood wept from her wounds, and she released her bodily fluids.

The bear waddled over, and I shoved the torch in his face. I yelled, and he backed up. The cougar died saving my ass and I refused the bear's access to her. I continued shouting and throwing rocks, while pushing the torch at him. Finally, he lumbered off. I sighed with relief.

He would probably come back later for the meat. I set to work.

The cougar had a beautiful tawny fur with a creamy chest. I skinned her and kept the pelt, laying it over some rocks to dry out. I cut the meat into sections, keeping the best parts, because I couldn't carry it all, and the smell of fresh meat would draw other beasts. The rest I left by the berry bush for other animals to feast on and tossed a few berries in my mouth.

I cut some ivy vines, then gathered two long branches, tying the tops together with them. A discarded wooden box stuck out of a spiky bush. I used it as a platform and wove the vines through the slates of the box and tied it. The travois sturdy now, I placed the cougar meat, twigs, and my basket on it, and crisscrossed vines over it to hold the contents. I raced over and snatched the pelt, covering everything with it.

I dragged the travois behind me and trudged up the path, peering over the side of the mountain road. Miles and miles of greenery and trees met my eyes. Sweat irritated the bite on the back of my neck and it itched. I fought the urge to scratch it. Also, I felt a little light-headed, but the air thinned the higher I climbed, yet I wondered if Grimshaw infected me with something. I pulled some woundwort plant and rubbed some on the bite before pushing on. The herb was good for healing wounds and stopping the itch.

After several miles of hiking, a small waterfall trickled over some boulders to the right of me. I dropped the travois and climbed up some rocks for a better view. A stream threaded through the shade of some tall, white trees, until the water tumbled over the boulders.

The area seemed a great place for camping. I jumped down and retrieved my travois, pulling it up. I dragged it to an area of fallen trees. The ground, covered in moss, provided a snug shelter. Young maples grew nearby. I rigged a long branch through the notch of maples and hung the cougar pelt over it. Removing the basket first, I flipped the travois on its side, blocking the wind. I cut a steak of cougar meat for my meal and left the rest of the meat in the basket.

Some distance away from the travois, I dug a hole in the soft dirt with a stick. I encircled the hole with rocks, then tossed twigs and dry grass inside. Producing a flame in my palm, I lit a campfire. I sat cross-legged in front of it and added branches. The wood crackled as it burned. Sage grew nearby. I ran over and cut a stalk of leaves and rolled them together.

I placed the sage bundle on top of the fire and waved the cleansing smoke over me, concentrating on breathing slowly in and out. A vision appeared before me. Juliana and the other handmaidens sewed seeds of pearls and beads onto a cream-colored gown. Tiana styled my mother's hair atop her head. Another handmaiden admired the garnet ring on Mother's left hand. *Who had proposed?*

Grimshaw can't become king unless he killed Santurin and me. Did Grimshaw already harm my brother? How do I save my family from him? Grimshaw had years of experience with magic. The vision clouded over. I hope Mother is okay. Not like I could do anything right now about it.

I picked up a forked branch and slid the cougar steak on it and cooked the meat over the fire. Basil grew along a sunny hillside, and I ran over to it, grabbing a handful and crumbled the herb onto the meat as it cooked. The fire crackled as juices splattered.

After some time, the meat finished cooking, and I peeled off a hunk. A bit gamey, but the basil flavored it. It might taste better in a stew, but I didn't carry any pots. I made a salad from the watercress and berries and ate them with the meat.

By the time I finished my meal, the sky had set in orange, purple, and pink stripes. The trees silhouetted against the background. It was breathtaking and worthy of any artist. I watched, until the light descended behind the curtain of night and the sky filled with twinkling stars. My old nursemaid, Damira told me the stars were the energy left behind of those who had died.

"Dad, I'm sorry Grimshaw killed you, but he's after Mother and possibly Santurin. Please guide me." A star blinked in answer. I smiled and climbed inside my shelter.

Sniffing and snarling outside my shelter woke me. I peeked through the logs of my shelter.

Eyes glowed red near the embers of my campfire. I snatched my bow and notched an arrow. Wolves fought over the cougar meat I left out in my basket. I had forgotten to haul it up a tree. Wolves usually stayed in packs, but these two were young. Howls rang in the night and the wolves left with meat hanging from their mouths. My arms trembled from holding the bow in my grip. I laid it down and stifled a yawn. I napped on and off but kept my ears open for any danger.

Dawn broke, and I crawled out of my shelter. A young buck wandered into my campsite and nibbled the tops of new fir trees. I raised my bow and the deer's ears perked.

I closed one eye and aimed. The buck moved his front leg forward and I released my arrow. It thudded into the deer's broadside, four inches above the pit of his front leg. Bright red blood poured from his wound, and I knew my arrow pierced his heart. The buck keeled over and died within minutes.

"Thank you, spirit of the deer for feeding me," I whispered. Building up the campfire, I waited for the blood to empty from the buck. Using a bone needle, I sewed a pouch out of the rest of the rabbit fur.

Half an hour later, I pushed down and twisted the arrow to break the seal from the deer. I splayed my hand above the point and yanked the arrow out. Gutting the deer, I removed the intestines and its head. The bitter taste of bile rose in the back of my throat, and I swallowed it back. To keep my mind focused on my chore, I hummed a tune, and skinned the buck. I laid the pelt aside. The meat, I sliced into hunks, and rolled it in some cedar leaves.

I raced over and detached my travois from my shelter, piling the deer meat on the platform, then covered it with the pelt. The wind's chill blew under my loincloth, and I shivered. Cutting holes in the cougar fur, I wore it like a coat, with the head draped over my back. Time to move on. I dragged the travois to the stream and washed my hands and chest from the blood, then refilled my canteen.

I trod up the hill and the clouds darkened the farther I climbed. Crows cawed and gathered in the treetops. Smaller birds hid in bushes. I tasted rain in the air. Rounding the corner, thunder rumbled overhead. Lightning flashed and outlined a hollow tree. The clouds emptied and rain beat down my head and my back. The wind hurtled pinecones and twigs my way.

I sought shelter in the hollow tree and pulled my travois close, covering the opening of the tree like a shield. Worrying about frying if lightning struck the tree, I huddled like a scared mouse, ready to flee if necessary. The rain pelted the tree, and I wrapped the cougar pelt tighter around me.

It seemed like hours before the storm passed. My fingers tingled with pin pricks, and I wiggled them around. I shoved the travois on the ground and walked around puddles. I glanced up at the sky. A rainbow shimmered near the mountain top and illuminated a small field of wildflowers and purple flowers. Were those trilliums?

I scaled the rest of the way and halted at the patch of flowers. Picking a couple of trilliums, I dropped them in my pouch. My second task was accomplished, and I stood on a flat rock and gazed around. The view of the fortress of Azure rose through the fluffy clouds in the distance. The Harmony Waterfalls and the adjoining rivers carved into the valley. All the other lands spread out like the spokes of a wheel with Azure at its center. My ancestors glimpsed this on their arrival. No wonder they considered themselves rich and royal. I sucked in the beauty.

Juliana's voice popped into my head. "*Aidan, do you hear me?*"

"*Something wrong?*" I asked.

"*It's your mother. I think Grimshaw did something to her.*"

"*What do you mean?*" I raked my hand through my hair.

"*She stares into space and complies with Grimshaw's wishes. It's not like her. Also, Santurin has taken ill. Mori suspects someone poisoned him. She doesn't trust the staff and makes his valet taste his food before she handfeeds her husband,*" Juliana said.

"*Elicit Mori's help. Check under Santurin's bed and under the floorboards for a charm or an animal heart,*" I said. "*I've read that someone can control and sicken another person by piercing a heart, usually a pig's heart, with nails. If you find it, remove the nails, and burn some sage over the heart and the room. Don't allow anyone to cut Santurin's hair or fingernails. If things worsen, I'll drop everything here."*

"All right, Aidan. Thanks for the advice and hurry back," Juliana said.

The connection broke, and I took a swig of water from my canteen before I hiked further. My stomach grumbled and reminded me I hadn't eaten in a while.

Juliana's words played on my mind as I walked. Grimshaw killed Dad and Twain. I know he's behind Santurin's illness and Mother's strange behavior. I must get stronger at my magic if I'm to beat the sorcerer, but I hadn't practiced much.

I want to finish this manhood journey, but how can I when my family suffers? If I achieve the last task, the sooner I return home. I pulled the travois along. Light filtered through the arches of trees. A squirrel, with a pinecone in its mouth, scampered down a fir tree, and scurried across the path in front of me. In my haste to avoid the rodent, I tripped over a rock, and skinned my knee. I dribbled a small amount of water on my abrasion, then applied some woundwort on it. Picking up the travois again, I limped down the trail.

After some time on the road, I pulled the travois behind some boulders, and made camp. The rocks blocked the wind, and I dug a hole, and then arranged a campfire. I removed the deer meat from my supplies and poked a stick through it, jabbing the end of the stick in the ground near the fire.

While the meat cooked, I put the rest of the meat in my cedar basket and hauled it up a tree. I sat in front of the fire and the colors changed from yellow to orange with a blue center.

With a stick, I drew a magic circle around me and applied the necessary symbols. I mumbled a protection prayer to the goddess. Pouring a small amount of water on my hands, I reached for the flame, while muttering an incantation. I stretched the flame out, then shrunk it.

I rotated my finger and the flame circled above my head. Splitting the flame in two, I divided it again. The fire danced around my arms and my legs like lassos. Clapping my hands, the flames dropped back inside the campfire. I checked the meat and turned it around to cook the other side. I sat back down and looked at the deer pelt.

I raised my hand and concentrated on the air under the pelt. "I command you to rise!"

A gush of wind lifted me from the ground. I spread my arms out to gather some balance, and then the deer pelt slid beneath me. I waved my hand in front of me and the pelt flew forward. Raising my hand, the deer pelt rose above the trees. I glimpsed a view of the ocean further west and tasted salt in the air. Pointing down, the deer pelt zoomed to the ground. I covered my face with my arms, as the fur dumped me into some ferns. Dusting myself off, I walked back to my campfire.

I prodded the meat and the juices dribbled clear. Cutting off a slice, I plopped a piece in my mouth. The deer tasted sweet and tender and melted in my mouth. I ate my fill and guzzled half my water. Shivering from the chilly wind, I rolled inside the cougar pelt. I closed my eyes and listened to the sounds in the woods, the hoot of an owl, the cawing of the crows, the chittering of a rodent, the rustling of the trees, and the whistle of the wind. It lulled me to sleep.

I awoke to a misty morning. Kicking dirt over the embers of the campfire, I packed the travois again. The ocean lied ahead, but the heavy mist blocked my view. Pulling my travois, I walked on.

After some miles, seabirds circled above me. A Madrone tree leaned over the cliffs. Its sides blistered and peeled like butter on a knife. I rushed the last few steps, dropping the travois by the tree, and peered at the ocean below. Its waves crashed against the bottom of the cliffs. The crisp air chaffed my cheeks. Where were the Tankini birds?

I inclined on the grass and leaned over the edge of the cliffs. This was my hardest task. How do I get anywhere near the birds and pluck a feather, without falling to my death?

I climbed up the Madrone tree and gawked at the birds. Blue bodies, with black bars on their wings, the Tankinis formed a V-shape as they flew. Their tail feathers fanned out in a deep purplish- blue, and two long paddles protruded from the fan. They had sharp-pointed beaks and almond-shaped eyes, with black bands around them. Their nests were inside holes and crevices eroded from the soft limestone of the coastal cliffs. The birds tucked the end of their paddled tails around them as they landed. Tankinis ate squid and fish. The male and female birds shared the responsibility of nesting. One hunted, while the other parent guarded the eggs. The holes where they nested reminded me of stairs. If I stepped down, perhaps I'd snag a bird?

I lay on my belly and stretched my arm to the closest nest. A bird pecked my hand, and I drew it back. Not too bright of an idea. I glanced around and spotted ivy growing around the base of some short bushes. I cut lengths of it and wrapped it around the Madrone's trunk, knotting it.

With the other half of the ivy, I tied it around my waist.

I emptied my cedar basket and wore it like a hat, easing myself over the cliff, and placed my feet in the empty crevices of limestone. The Tankinis squawked at my intrusion. Some flew around me and pecked my arms and my back.

I hummed a song about pretty birds. A Tankini cocked his head. With the gentlest motion, I removed the basket from my head and scooped up the bird. I plucked two tail feathers, and the Tankini screeched. I released it and shoved the feathers in my pouch. Quickly, I plopped the basket back on my head.

Inch by inch, I pulled myself back up the cliffside, when a crack ripped through the tree. The roots loosened from the ground and tipped the tree further on its side. I scrambled for a hold on the edge of the cliff. The tree snapped and pulled me down with its weight.

Chapter Twenty-Three

THE MADRONE SPLASHED IN THE SEA AND FLOATED ATOP the water. My face planted the side of the tree and knocked the breath out of me. My face ached, and a couple of my teeth broke, but I lived. I paddled with my hands. The waves tossed the tree closer to shore. I reached for my knife, from my boot, and sliced through the ivy bounding me to the tree. I trudged through the icy water and collapsed on the beach, spitting out the shards of my teeth. The rush of cold air on the empty sockets stung. Every bruise hurt and my face swelled. Would Yvonne still like me with missing teeth?

I stood up, holding my cheek. My supplies remained up on the cliff. How would I ever get them? I broke off branches from the tree and dragged them across the beach to an old campfire. Imagining warmth, flames burst from my fingers and lit the wood on fire. I warmed myself, before seeking food.

A crab crawled across the sand, and I smacked it with a rock. My ribs bruised, I held my side, as I hurried back to the campfire, and tossed the crab on the fire. The crab shell cracked and sizzled. A few minutes later, I removed it from the fire, and peeled away the shell, feasting on the meat. With a full belly, I placed my head on my arm and dozed.

Snarls and growls alerted me, and I jumped up. A pack of wolves, above me, thrashed my travois and kicked my supplies over the side of the cliff amidst their scuffles. The cougar pelt landed on my head, along with my bow and quiver of arrows. I pulled the coat on.

Did the sorcerer control them? Everywhere I've gone, wolves appeared. They sniffed the cliffside, debating whether to come after me or not. One of the wolves snatched the deer meat from the platform and ran off. The others followed.

I traipsed through the sand and rocks, searching for the rest of my things. Remnants of the cedar basket scattered the sand. My canteen snagged a piece of kelp and I unwound the strap from it. The deer pelt draped over a large rock. I tossed it over my shoulders and walked along the beach.

I had fulfilled all my tasks, but how was I going to get back to Zavion? Was this place near Waverly? My friend, Varick, had moved there. Perhaps his father might give me a ride, or would it be cheating? I didn't know all the rules of this manhood journey, but my family problems weighed on my shoulders as I walked. A run-off stream jutted from the ocean. I followed it to a cave and peeked inside.

A sandbar divided the cave in half. Beyond it, a large chamber opened. A musty odor emitted from the wet walls. Shelves of stalagmites rose along the sides of the cave like different sizes of stools. Up above, a blow hole opened in the roof. Mist crept along the bottom of the cave, but the chamber extended further in and stretched all the way back. Water dripped and echoed off the walls. It lured me on.

In the back of the cave, a waterfall plummeted down a wall, from a tall chamber, and crashed into a pool. I cupped a handful of water and drank its sweet nectar. I filled my canteen.

Something shimmered on the floor, but sand covered it. I brushed it off.

An axe lay atop the lid of an old truck, bound by ropes and chains, and submerged halfway in the ground. Curiosity nagged me to open it, but something held me back. Why would its owner leave it behind?

The cave was a good place to camp for the night. I strode to a rock bridge and flung the deer pelt on top of it. I lay down and wrapped the cougar pelt around me. The waterfall bounced off the walls in the back chamber and reminded me of home. I slept soundly.

I woke in darkness and choking on water. I stood up and the water rose to my chest. The tide must have come in. I had to get out of here or drown, but I couldn't see a blasted thing. Too wet to ignite a flame, my mind raced to find a solution. I was a fair swimmer, but in the darkness, I might swim farther out to sea.

Looking around, I remembered the blow hole. I waded back to the bridge and hauled my canteen, bow, and quiver over my shoulder. I wrapped the deer pelt around my neck. Closing my eyes, I chanted, "Element of air, let's play fair. Pave the way to the roof of this cave." It wasn't the best chant, but it worked.

The wind whistled through the chambers and circled around me. My body lifted. Up, up, I flew, until I touched the roof of the cave. I opened my eyes and clutched the edges of the blow hole, pulling myself through. Mist covered the beach below and haloed the crescent moon above.

"Dear goddess, once again you saved me. I've made some foolish mistakes on this journey. Thanks for watching over me." Wolves howled and startled me.

I had nothing to fear though. The wolves were too far away. I crawled over the spikes of rock and away from the blow hole. The chance of getting wet again when the sea sprayed wasn't appealing. I wrung out the deer pelt and punched it into a pillow, lying down on some moss-covered rocks.

My mind wandered back to the trunk. What was in it? Maybe the owner left it because the trunk got stuck in the sand and the sea rolled in? At any rate, I planned on investigating the trunk's contents in the morning when the tide washed out.

I tossed and turned. Every rock poked me in the side or in the back. And a bothersome cricket chirped half the night. I listened to the wildlife prowl and the flow of the ocean. The wind whirled around me and chilled my face. I huddled in my damp cougar pelt.

By dawn, the ocean mellowed, and the mist cleared. Orange and pink colored the morning sky. My imagination conjured pictures of delicacies and fruit inside the trunk. My stomach growled. Whether the trunk contained anything useful or not, I wanted food. I cast about my surroundings.

I trekked across the craggy roof, and it led up a limestone hill. By the time I reached the top, my dry throat burned. I tipped my canteen up and quenched my thirst. A rustle in the bushes drew my attention. I pulled an arrow from my quiver and notched my bow.

A brown rabbit hopped onto the path, and I released my arrow. It plowed into the side of the animal, and he flopped over. I picked him up by his long ears, and crossed a small, wooden bridge over a weed-infested creek.

A skeleton, in tatters of clothes and a bandana over his skull, hung by a railing. I snapped the string that held a key around his neck and shoved it in my pouch. If I'm lucky, it fit the trunk's lock. I trod on.

A board collapsed from the bridge and my boot slid into the muck of the creek. My foot stuck like quicksand, the more I moved, the stronger it held me prisoner. A snake slithered up my thigh, and I grimaced. Was it poisonous? He skirted up my loincloth and I swallowed hard. I prayed he bypassed my family jewels. How could I father my future children if he bit me?

The snake peeked his head from my waistband. "S-S-Stubborn fool. Your mother and your brother are under my s-s-spell. Die and get out of my way. The Kingdom belongs to me."

Was I hearing things? The snake sounded like Grimshaw. I grasped the snake around the neck, but he wrapped his tail around my arm and squeezed. The rabbit fell and hung on the railing. I pulled an arrow, from my quiver with my other hand, and stabbed the snake through his eyes. His tail uncoiled from my wrist, and he dropped on the bridge. Grabbing another arrow, I jabbed it around my boot until it freed from the muck.

I hurried across the bridge and wiped the mud off my boot on the grass. A rope of ivy circled the trunk of a tree, and I sliced a piece off. I eased my way back across the bridge and grasped my rabbit, carrying it over my shoulder.

By the time I reached the cave again, the tide flowed out. I lassoed a rock with the vine and eased myself down the blow hole. My feet bounced along the side walls, until I hit the floor. I released the ivy and hustled to the trunk.

I removed the deer pelt from my shoulders, along with the canteen, bow, and quiver, placing them on a rock. I picked up the axe and sliced through the ropes and chains that bound the trunk. Inserting the key in the lock, it clicked open, and I lifted the lid. The hinges squealed. A damp, musty smell permeated the contents inside, and I covered my nose with my arm.

On the inside of the lid, written in big letters, were the words: *Belongs to Grimshaw, the Almighty Sorcerer of Fallow.*

Why was it here? Did the dead fellow steal it from Grimshaw and the sorcerer took his revenge on him? I prayed nothing happened to me from disturbing his things. The top layer held a hairbrush on top of a white shirt. I yanked some hair from the brush and put it inside my pouch. It might come in handy for a spell against my foe someday. Underneath the shirt, I found some beaded necklaces and bracelets. I chose three from the lot. Coins didn't interest me, and I left them. In the bottom of the trunk, I found a small shovel. Clams whetted my appetite and I vowed to use the shovel for them.

The rest of the contents held books, dried herbs, and unspeakable things in jars of liquid. Nothing of importance. I walked out of the cave, with the few items I selected, and inhaled the fresh, salty air.

A rusty bucket lay in a stream, and I carried it to my old campfire. I sat on a log and skinned and gutted the rabbit. When I finished, I skewered the meat on a stick and stuck it on the side of the campfire. I found some wood and lit a new fire. While it was cooking, I took the shovel and the bucket in search of clams. I searched for little dimples in the sand. A razor clam digs a foot every 30 seconds! One squirted water up my loincloth and I shuddered.

I inserted my shovel around six inches from the "show" and dug down. After two scoops of sand, I reached my hand in, and felt for the clam. Close. I shoveled some more and found my prize. My arms and legs covered in sand; I dropped the clam in my bucket. I dug further down and found a few more clams. I carried the bucket to the ocean and filled it with water. This allowed the clams to spit up grit before I cooked them. I heaved the bucket back to the campfire and plopped it down on the sand.

I tore off a piece of rabbit meat and checked it for doneness. No longer pink, I removed it from the fire. While I ate, I wondered how to get home. Too long to go back through the mountains. I had the tools to build a raft, yet that took time. I dumped the old water from the bucket out and poured fresh, from my canteen, into the bucket and cooked the clams in it over the fire. After five minutes, the shells opened, and I ate the clams.

A familiar figure strolled along the beach. I rinsed my hands off with the canteen water before I walked over to the lad. As I got closer, I realized it was my friend, Varick. I waved to get his attention.

"Aidan?" he asked. "What are you doing here?"

"It's a long story. Come over to my campsite and we'll talk."

We sat down on the log, and I told him about my manhood journey.

"Did they break your teeth too?" Varick asked.

I flushed. "No. A tree I climbed, fell over the cliff, and my face planted into the trunk on the way down. Does it look that bad?"

"Whoa! That must have hurt. You'll gain sympathy of the girls, I bet."

"I only care about one girl, Varick. Yvonne isn't empty-headed like those gossipy girls that Mother parades around." I paused. "I was disappointed you didn't come to Santurin's wedding."

"You haven't heard the news?" Varick asked.

"About your mother's endeavors?" I asked.

"In a way. Mom took her new ship out to sea. One of her men got it in his thick skull that he was the captain. Mom and he argued. He shoved Mom overboard and she drowned." Varick swiped at a tear that streamed down his cheek.

"I'm so sorry for your loss. That's terrible news. Was the man punished?" I asked.

"He stole Mom's ship. Father plans a trip to Azure to relay the news to the queen. I don't know if he'll allow me to go with him. When are you back?" Varick asked.

"In a week. Sooner if I can enlist Astra's help."

"Good to know. I better get back home before Father worries." Varick waved as he walked down the beach.

I sat down and concentrated on Astra's face. *"Do you hear me? It's Aidan."*

It seemed forever, before she responded to my telepathic message.

"Better be important. I'm in the middle of something," Astra said.

"Sorry to interrupt you, but can you fly to the ocean and pick me up?" I asked.

"How did you get over there?" she asked.

"I've been on a manhood journey organized by the elders on Zavion. I wouldn't beg you if it wasn't important."

"All right, Aidan, but leave me a sign, so I can find you."

"And Astra?"

"What?"

"Thanks." My eyes lit on the white shirt I took from the trunk. I grabbed a long stick and pulled the shirt over it. I waited until I heard the airship.

About a half an hour later, I waved the shirt back and forth as Astra flew by me. I guess she didn't see it. I thrust the shirt in the fire, until it burned bright, and swung it about. The airship turned around. Astra came straight at me. I dove behind a log.

Chapter Twenty-Four

SAND SPRAYED OVER ME AS THE AIRSHIP DREW NEAR. Astra stopped within a few feet and opened the safety hatch of her airship. "Sorry." She grinned. "I'm new at piloting these airships. The soft sand surprised me."

I shook sand from my hair and my cougar pelt. I picked up my things and tossed them in the back seat of the airship. Removing one of the bracelets from my bundle, I handed it to Astra. "Here, I found this."

. Astra held the bracelet up to the light and the turquoise gems sparkled. She pulled it over her wrist.

"Juliana told me telepathically that Mother isn't acting right, and Santurin is ill. I suspect Grimshaw put a spell on them," I said. "Grimshaw wants those in line for the throne out of his way. The man lives for power and won't stop until he's king. I must halt his progress before he kills my brother," I said.

"What do you propose?" Astra asked.

"I don't know yet." I pouted.

"You better think of something," she said.

The ground vibrated, and something huge tunneled under the sand straight for us. Rocks and sand flew up.

I jumped inside the airship. "Astra, take off!"

"All right. Why all the fuss?"

I pointed and Astra's eyes widened. An armored-shelled, gigantic sand flea, with sword-like mouthparts and front claws, emerged from the sand. Astra engaged the airship, and it zipped across the beach, before it lifted into the air. We flew over the water, and the ocean rose like a huge arm and swiped at us.

"What are these crazy things?" Astra shrilled.

"Grimshaw's trickery. Get us out of here!" I shouted.

Astra pressed a button on the dash and cloaked the airship. She punched another and the ship sped ahead. "How did he know we were here?"

"I found a trunk of his inside a cave," I said. Opening a book in my bundle, I found a small, black square that blinked a bright red light. I showed it to Astra.

She opened the safety hatch, and the wind tousled my hair. Astra grasped the book and tossed it out. "Anything else you stole from him, throw it out too."

I kept the jewelry but handed her the bundle. Astra hurled it out, then shut the safety hatch.

"Why not ask Sylvia for a talisman?" Astra suggested.

"Brilliant idea! Stop at Zavion. I need to give Ulric some things anyway," I said.

Astra changed directions. "What happened to your teeth, by the way?"

"It's a long story. A tree broke two of them. Do I look bad?" I asked.

"Negative. More warrior-like," Astra said.

I kissed her cheek. "Great compliment, sis."

"Don't get all mushy on me." Astra wiped her cheek.

Sometime later, we landed on Zavion. Astra stayed inside the airship, while I hopped out, and strode to Sylvia's hut. I rang a bell outside her entrance.

Sylvia called out, "Come in, Young Prince. Tea?"

"How did you know it was me?"

"I sensed you, before you rang the bell," Sylvia said.

I shook my head to the offer of tea. "May I borrow a talisman? Grimshaw put a spell on my brother and he's quite ill."

"What about my daughter? Has the sorcerer harmed Mori?" Sylvia clutched my arm.

"Fine as far as I know. On the manhood journey, some strange critter tunneled under the sand towards me, then the ocean rose in the shape of an arm. Creepy," I said.

Sylvia paced around the hut. "Grimshaw holds the elements of earth and water." She grabbed my arms. "Believe in yourself and use the other elements against him."

"Yes, I control fire, but I'm new learning the other elements. I've learned some magic using the element air, but the sorcerer is far advanced in magic." I raked my hand through my hair.

Sylvia pulled a porcelain inverted triangle, with symbols carved into it, on a silver chain, from her pocket. She shoved it in my hands. "Place this over Santurin's head. He must wear it always. Magic calls within you. You're stronger than you think."

I stuffed the talisman in my pouch.

"One last thing, Young Prince. Tell Mori to light sage around their bed chamber and line the door with salt. Pound iron pins or nails around the wood frame of their bed and give her my love," Sylvia said.

"I'll relay your message. The sorcerer won't survive with our powers joined. Don't you want to save the kingdom?" I searched her face.

"I lost my husband and my eldest boy in the last war. I gave my daughter in marriage to your brother. What else do you expect from me?" Sylvia lifted her hands. "My place belongs with my own people."

"I expect your loyalty. The kingdom protects all the people, not a choice few." I strode out of her hut and down the trail towards Ulric's place.

Clay and Ulric chopped wood in the field. Perspiration rolled down their muscular chests. I raised my arm in greeting, and they paused in their work.

Clay swatted my shoulder. "Hey, you made it. Good for you."

"Not easy," I said. "Wolves stole my food. I fell off a cliff, and I almost drowned, yet I survived."

"You look like shit. Lost a few teeth too," Clay said.

"Better than dead." I bumped elbows with him. "Do you know anything about a dead man on a bridge near the ocean?"

Clay and Ulric exchanged a look.

"What? Did I say something odd?" I asked.

"My brother, Echo never returned from his manhood journey. We'll give him a decent burial. Thanks for telling us," Clay said.

"Did you finish the tasks I instructed?" Ulric asked.

I opened my pouch and handed him the Tankini bird tail feathers and the purple trilliums. I whipped off the cougar pelt coat. "You required a tooth from a ferocious beast. Choose one of these or keep the whole pelt if you like. Where's Yvonne?"

"Great work. I love the pelt," Ulric said. "Yvonne exercises the horses with my wife. Here they come."

Yvonne jumped off a bay mare and raced towards me. She ran into my arms, and I swung her around. She giggled, and I put her back on her feet.

"You survived. I knew you were strong." Yvonne smiled and her dimples showed.

"I brought you something." I slipped the necklace over her head.

"It's lovely." Yvonne kissed me.

"Daughter, too forward." Ulric's brows furrowed.

I wrapped the deer pelt over Yvonne's shoulders. "It's your gift in appreciation for teaching me how to use a bow and arrow. I shot this young buck." I smiled.

"What happened to your teeth?" she asked.

"I lost a few in a fall. I'll tell you about my journey another time," I said.

"Is it painful?" Yvonne stroked my cheek.

"It's tolerable. I must return to Azure. The sorcerer caused problems in my absence."

"I shall cherish your gifts, My Sweet Prince." A pink blush painted her cheeks. Yvonne's smile lit her eyes.

I kissed her hand, then hastened down the path to the airship. Jumping inside the passenger seat, Astra flew us back to Azure.

She turned to me. "What took you so long?"

I pulled the talisman from my pouch. "Sylvia gave me this to protect Santurin from Grimshaw. I hope we aren't too late to save him."

"We better hurry then." Astra sped faster and I held onto the armrest.

It took us four hours to get through a thick fog that seemed to appear out of nowhere on our way back to Azure. Normally by airship it took two hours. Two days by horseback. And close to four days by foot.

Astra parked her airship in the meadow behind the Harmony Waterfalls. We raced to the fortress. A plan formed in my head on the way.

"Let's go to Grimshaw's chambers. I'm curious to see if he has Mother's fingernails or her hair in some charm bag. That's the only reason I can see her agreeing to marry him," I said.

"All right, I'll stand guard outside and distract him if he nears his chambers," Astra said.

"Did Santurin have his coronation while I was gone?" I asked.

"He wanted to wait until you returned."

"No wonder Grimshaw took the opportunity to control Mother." I shook my head.

Astra guarded Grimshaw's chambers, while I sneaked inside. I opened a drawer and found a charm bag marked, *Willow*. I opened it and removed Mother's nail clippings and hair. I circled my hand over the items. "Dwindle dee, hear my plea, and set my mother free." I wrapped my hanky around Mother's things, then deposited some broken razor clams along with Grimshaw's hair into the charm bag. Closing it, I tucked the bag back inside the drawer. I stuffed my hanky inside my pouch, then tip-toed into the hall.

"Done?" Astra asked.

I nodded.

"Good. I'm out of here. Bring Juliana with you, before you speak to your mother. You'll need a witness if anything goes wrong." Astra hurried down the hall.

I wanted a shower and out of this loincloth. My greasy hair had grown long enough to pull into a ponytail, and I reeked. I hastened to my chambers.

The door opened at my touch. My eyes darted around the room, but nothing seemed out of place. I crawled under the bed and inspected the under carriage. No fruit with spikes or any other surprises. I stood up. Something wiggled under my bed covers.

I yanked the bedspread off. A snake coiled in the center of my bed. I opened the lid of the pneumo-vac canister and placed it upright on my bed. I twisted a hanger into a rod and pointed it at the snake. It rolled around the metal. I dropped the snake inside the canister and shut the lid. I propped the canister in the vac station and pressed the button, sending the snake to the kitchen. *Perhaps the cook will serve it to Grimshaw?* I smirked.

I removed the loincloth and walked inside the shower stall. Hot water eased the tension from my shoulders and my back. I scrubbed the filth off me with sandalwood soap. Refreshed, I dried off, and pulled on clean clothes. I braided my long hair and tied the end with a piece of rawhide before I strolled down the long hallway. I took the stairs, two at a time, to the second floor and strode to Mother's chambers.

Juliana carried a tray of cookies and a cup of tea. Her eyes lit up. "Aidan, you've returned. Why didn't you tell me?"

"And spoil my surprise?" I winked. Taking the tray from her, I placed it on the hall table. I slipped an almond-colored bracelet, with amber stones, over her wrist.

"What's the occasion?" Juliana admired the jewelry.

"None. I found the bracelet on my trip. It goes with your reddish hair. Is Mother inside her chambers?" I asked.

"Yes. I brought her a snack. Come in. Maybe she'll respond to you." Juliana carried the tray inside the room.

I followed Juliana inside and gasped. Mother lost about twenty pounds and her dark hair streaked with gray. She stared into space.

I knelt in front of her and grasped her hands. "Mother?"

She blinked her eyes several times, before she focused on my face. "Aidan?"

"Yes, I've returned from Zavion."

Mother gazed at her reflection in the mirror and touched her hair. "What happened? Am I ill?" She glanced at her garnet ring. "Where did I get this?"

Grimshaw barged into the room. He grabbed Mother's hand and kissed it. "Care for a stroll, wife?"

"Wife?" she asked.

"Forgotten our wedding already?" Grimshaw arched a brow.

Mother turned to Juliana for confirmation.

"Yes, My Queen. You married the fiend."

"What did you call me?" Grimshaw glared at Juliana. "Careful, girl how you speak to your future king."

"Ha! Santurin's the rightful king," Mother said.

"Not for long, my sweet. He's quite ill." Grimshaw patted her hand.

"Why was I not informed?" Mother, the queen asked.

"You've known, but forgot, my dear," Grimshaw said.

"If Santurin dies, Aidan is next in line. Where do you get such fancy notions?" Mother scowled.

"We'll see." Grimshaw yanked the charm bag from his cloak pocket and squished it. He grimaced and clutched his head. "I don't understand. Why isn't Willow affected?"

"What are you rambling about, Grim?" Mother stared at him like he had lost his mind.

Grimshaw opened the charm bag. "What's this?" He whipped around and glared at me. Then he noticed Juliana's wrist. "Where did you get that bracelet?"

"From a friend." Juliana jerked her arm free.

The sorcerer whirled on me. "You stole it from my trunk."

"You left it behind in the cave. Free for all," I said.

"You're a fool, Prince Aidan. You don't know what you've done. I chained and roped that trunk, but you've released her." Grimshaw stroked his chin.

"You're touched in the head." I circled my finger around.

"Keep the damn bracelet, Miss Juliana," Grimshaw sneered. "It's far painless than what Prince Aidan caused."

"What do you mean?" I asked.

Chapter Twenty-Five

GRIMSHAW LOOKED FAR AWAY AS HE SPOKE, "WHEN THE scientists wanted test subjects for their latest experiment and promised a good amount of coin; my sister, Twyla volunteered. She felt guilty about me earning all the income for us. They injected her with a bat virus. Her craving for blood disgusted me. First, small mammals, but when she attacked a lab tech, I took matters into my own hands." The sorcerer turned to me. "Did you open any of the jars at the bottom of the trunk?"

"No. I grabbed a few trinkets and supplies." I stared him down. "Afraid Twyla's ghost coming for you?"

"That doesn't deserve an answer." Grimshaw frowned. "As your new stepfather, I'll teach you great feats of magic. Think about it. The magnificent magicians of the galaxy." Grimshaw grinned.

I crinkled my face. "You're full of fancy notions. You're a terrible person. You stabbed my father in the back like a coward because of your jealousy and took Twain's life. Why would I allow you to teach me anything?" *Why was he telling me his life story with his sister? Did he think I would feel sympathy for him?*

"Skyla belonged to me. Arin had a wife. He didn't need Skyla too. He ruined my life," Grimshaw said.

"Are you responsible for Skyla's death too?" I asked.

"I didn't shoot her airship down." Grimshaw pulled on his ear. "If any of my followers shot her airship down, it's not my fault. I offered her marriage, but Skyla refused. She'd rather raise a bastard child on her own, yet she claimed she loved Arin and me. Unbelievable."

"The people saw their future in my father's reign, and you stole it from them. You stole him from my life too." I glared.

"Arin taught me, if you're capable of taking something, then you deserve it. Given a chance, I'd make a great king too." Grimshaw held out his hands.

"No one wants a murderer for their ruler. You probably chopped your sister into pieces and her spirit nags you. I never saw a body in that trunk. Only a bunch of jars with weird parts floating inside some liquid. You're one sick person." I curled my lip.

Juliana tore the bracelet off her thin wrist and threw it in Grimshaw's face. "Keep it."

"You've tried my patience." Grimshaw circled his hands around and mumbled some incantation. The bracelet changed into a small python. Grimshaw flipped his hand, and the snake wound around Juliana's throat.

Her eyes bulged and her face turned a purplish-red. Juliana pounded her fists on the python. Her lips tinged blue, and she struggled for air.

The sorcerer must love snakes in the number of times he used the reptiles. I called upon my strongest element: fire. With a flame in my hand, I touched the python and it withered into a black mess. Juliana brushed the remnants of dead skin off her neck and gulped bursts of air.

"Run," I whispered in Juliana's ear. "Go to Mori."

Juliana protested in between coughs. "I must protect your mother."

"Go!" I shouted.

Juliana grasped Mother's arm and they raced out of the queen's chambers. I produced a barrier of fire around me.

"Fire won't stop me," Grimshaw sneered.

"It slows you down though." I concentrated like Sylvia taught me and conjured an illusion of an angry Twyla in front of Grimshaw and said, "You tried to destroy me, brother. I should drain you dry."

"Please forgive me." Grimshaw covered his face and knelt before the illusion.

"Release me," the illusion said.

"I'm sorry, but I can't." Grimshaw touched the tiled floor and the fortress trembled. "You think I'm a simpleton, Prince Aidan? I saw through your illusion. Feel my power!"

The servants screamed as the floor swayed. The windows shattered. Tables fell and dishes crashed to the floor. A rumble rippled through the walls. Water rushed through the glass-less windows and into the room. The barrier of fire blew out.

"Get to safety!" I yelled at the people. Raising my arms, I invoked the element of air.

A cyclone burst through the room and spun around Grimshaw. He clawed at the furniture, yet the cyclone picked him up and flung him out the window. "This isn't over, Prince Aidan!" his voice carried on the wind.

"We'll see." I sloshed through the watery mess to the stairwell and climbed the steps to the third floor. I hurried to the balcony and gazed below.

The cyclone carried Grimshaw towards Fallow. Satisfied, I left the tower room and hastened to Santurin's chambers down the hall.

I rapped on the door. "It's Aidan."

Juliana opened the door and hugged me. "Are you all, right?"

"I'm fine. I sent Grimshaw back to Fallow. How is Santurin?"

Mother moved aside from the bed. "See for yourself."

Santurin sat up in bed and Mori spoon-fed him a chunky stew.

"You were right, Aidan. An apple, with nails poked through it, was under our bed. When I removed the nails, Santurin perked up. Still weak, but his fever broke." Mori flipped her hair over her shoulder.

Santurin cleared his throat. "I never expected heroics from you, my little brother—"

"Any side effects from Grimshaw's magic?" I asked.

"Magic? Mere trickery, I say. He probably slipped me some poison. Nothing time and exercise won't fix," Santurin said.

"I know we differ, brother, but I never wanted you dead," I said.

"I'm sorry I've treated you harshly. I was jealous of your freedom," Santurin admitted.

"I tired of your seriousness and wanted you to enjoy life," I said. "If you'll excuse me, brother, I'll see to the cleaning and the damage of the fortress. Grimshaw made a mess.".

"How bad?" Mother asked.

"I suggest you find other accommodations, Mother. The whole second floor is chaos. Do you plan to divorce Grimshaw?" I asked.

"I was not in my right mind when I married him. My handmaidens will vouch for me." Mother patted Juliana's hand. "Councilor Wings may draw up the paperwork. I'll file an annulment."

"Grimshaw won't like it." I chuckled. I pulled the talisman from my pocket. "Sylvia told me to give you this, brother. It protects you from evil magic."

"I shall wear it with pride." Santurin pulled the chain over his head. He examined the inverted triangle and rubbed his fingers over the engraving of strange letters. "We should prepare for Grimshaw's next move."

"I'll think on a plan later. The battle of wits and magic zapped my energy." I turned to Juliana. "Want an escort to your unit?"

"No, I'll see to your mother's comfort first."

"I bid you all a good day." I strolled out of the room. I leaned against the door and wondered where to start first.

Chapter Twenty-Six

The next day

SUNFLOWERS STRETCHED THEIR FLOPPY HEADS TO THE sky and the birds feasted on their seeds. The roses climbed up a trellis, behind Mother, as she sat on a wrought iron bench. Hedges formed a spoked wheel affect with different colored pansies, daisies, and violets inside. The air smelled sweet with their scent. The gardener planted a young dogwood tree this morning, not far from the hedge, and close to a marble fountain. Already, birds warbled and twittered from the branches. I picked a dandelion from the grass and twirled it around.

"Thank the goddess that Grimshaw never learned of my secret," Mother said.

"Secret?" I queried.

Mother tapped the bench seat. "Sit. I don't want to yell. Prying ears may hear."

My curiosity was piqued; and I plunked down on the bench next to her.

"I waited, until you matured, to bring up this subject." Mother pointed. "See that spire? Inside the sunroom, a pool of scrying waters exists. Ask it a question and the waters reveal your answer. I'll program the computer to give you free access."

"How does it know who I am?" I asked.

"Security verifies, before you are allowed inside. Because of Santurin's illness, I expect you to pick up some of his responsibilities." Mother searched my face.

I didn't respond right away. I vowed since Dad's death, and the way Santurin and Mother acted afterwards to never take on responsibilities. Mother refused to show emotions around the public. The two of them expected me to wear a mask and lie to our subjects to save face.

"I don't mind helping Santurin, and I'm honored you trust me to fulfill those needs, but I won't mask my emotions for the people. They deserve the truth, Mother," I said.

"Sometimes the truth hurts and it's better to sugar coat it."

"No, Mother. I've learned that honesty builds trust."

"You're young. Someday, you'll see things my way." Mother sighed. "I planned to retire from the humdrum of royal life, once Santurin is crowned king, and live out my days on Zavion. Two suitors offered me marriage, but they cared nothing for me. I was a pawn in their game. You tried to warn me."

"Why go to Zavion when Mori might carry your grandchild?" I asked.

"I may lend a hand when the time comes. What about you? Any girls interest you?" Mother looked at me.

"Ulric's daughter, Yvonne. I'd like to court her with your permission, Mother."

"Wonderful news! Tell me all about her." Mother's face brightened.

"Yvonne likes me for myself, not because I'm a prince. She doesn't get frightened easily. Her eyes shine like blue marbles, and she has the cutest dimples when she smiles. Yvonne is excellent with a bow and taught me how to shoot. I get along with her many brothers."

"Sounds like a perfect match, son. When the time comes, I'd love to plan your ceremony."

"Mother, give me some time to know her better." I kissed Mother's hands. "I'm curious to visit the scrying waters."

"Wait!" Mother gazed around, before she spoke. "Our planet's power source centers in those waters. Only a select few know of this for security purposes. The special waters show the past, present, and future. I was entrusted as guardian, by your grandfather many years ago, until you reached maturity. He saw your future as our savior."

"Savior? Me?" I shook my head. "Perhaps Grandfather confused Santurin and me."

"No. He knew of your magical powers and voiced his concern about an evil presence lurking among us," she said.

"I assume he meant Grimshaw," I said.

"One more thing, Aidan. You know our ancestral history. A portal exists behind the Harmony WaterFalls. I am telling you this in case you need to escape this planet. Tell no one unless it's necessary. Your grandfather blocked the entrance with a boulder," Mother said.

"The histories spoke of danger to the planet our ancestors came from." I frowned.

"Yes, but that was hundreds of years ago and perhaps it healed over time, if it still exists." Mother stared at me. "The future of our people depend on you."

"I promise not to tell anyone unless it's necessary. Thank you for trusting me with your secrets." I held her hand. "You may not want to hear this, but it's best I told you, then to hear a rumor."

"What, son?"

"My twin brother lives. Damira raised him as her own son. She called him, Cosmo."

"May the goddess forgive me," Mother murmured. "I was in a bad state of mind back then. I heard the rumors of Arin and his young recruit. I wished for Skyla's death."

Mother paused a moment. "I thought the goddess punished me when I saw the deformed face of my baby son." She brushed away her tears. "I called in Twain, your father's advisor. He informed me of Skyla's pregnancy. I told him to get rid of her. I never meant for him to kill her.

I expected Twain to banish her somewhere far away. Twain tried to talk some sense into Arin breaking off with the girl. But he was infatuated with her and delighted she was with child." Mother sipped from her water glass.

"I bare Skyla's death on my shoulders." She glanced up at the sky a moment. "When Lady Darshana brought Astra here, I saw the resemblance of Arin in her. When I look upon her, I face my husband's infidelity. Sorry I lied to you, Aidan."

"I understand, Mother. Didn't Dad question Skyla's death?"

"Arin assumed it was an accident. He spent more time hunting afterwards. If he had other affairs, they were silenced."

"Did you want me to escort you inside?" I asked.

"No, I like the warmth out here," Mother said.

"If you'll excuse me…" I rushed inside the fortress.

The heat plowed into me, after the fresh air from outside. I pulled off my cloak and charged to the elevator. "Third floor," I told the call box.

The elevator zoomed up. The doors slid open on the third floor. I strode to the backside of the tower region and climbed the four steps to the sunroom, located under the fortress' spire. I inserted my palm on the security panel outside the glass door.

Blue lights flashed, and a computer voice said, "*Step forward. Ready for pupil identification.*"

I peered into the sensor, and the computer announced, "*Welcome, Prince Aidan.*"

The door clicked, and I walked inside. I trekked over to a large, black marble basin of aquamarine water, and sat on the edge of the pool. I dipped my hand inside and the waters throbbed to life. I swirled them around. "Crystal waters of Azure, hear my cry. Show me the sorcerer, Grimshaw and where he lies."

The pool frothed and bubbled. As I watched, a picture formed. My brother, Cosmo tied to a chair in some underground structure, and a woman, with red hair and round spectacles on her nose, pricked one of his fingers.

She smeared his blood on a glass slide. "I'll get started on the cloning process." The woman hurried down the hallway.

Grimshaw stooped over Cosmo. "Prince Aidan refused my advice on magic. Perhaps I'll make you my apprentice, hmm?"

Cosmo spit in his face.

"Bold move, brother," I said. *How did the sorcerer capture Cosmo? Didn't Damira keep him on Meadowlark? What makes Grimshaw believe Cosmo harbors magic?*

Grimshaw wiped his face with a cloth. "You'll regret that." He snapped his fingers.

One of his flunkies brought Damira into the room and shoved her to the floor. Her face, puffy and bruised, and her hands tied behind her, Damira couldn't stop her fall, and scraped the side of her face across the stone floor. I gasped.

Grimshaw opened several jars with organs floating around in some liquid. He grasped some forceps and placed the organs inside a human-sized clay figure. His scarecrow of an assistant sewed the 'skin' shut. Grimshaw wrote something on a scrap of paper and stuffed the clay figure's mouth with it. He wrote the word, *Emet* on the figure's forehead.

"I command you to follow my orders. Rise, Twyla." Grimshaw raised his hand.

The clay figure's arms lifted, and she sat up. Twyla moved her legs over the side of the gurney. She stood up and walked like a stiff doll towards the sorcerer.

"Kill her." Grimshaw pointed to Damira.

Damira rolled onto her knees and scooted backwards. Twyla marched over to her and wrapped her massive clay hands around Damira's throat and squeezed. Damira gasped for air.

"Stop!" Cosmo cried. "What do you want?"

Twyla dropped Damira on the floor when she quit moving and stared into space.

"No!" Cosmo cried. He struggled with the ropes that bound him.

She had been like a second mother to me, but Damira was the only mother Cosmo knew. Tears rained down my face. I should have destroyed those jars in Grimshaw's trunk in the ocean cave. How can I fight a golem brought to life by magic?

Something unexpected happened to Cosmo. His eyes changed to white orbs and his body glowed. His ropes snapped from his wrists and his ankles. His voice blended with others locked inside him. "You killed an innocent and shall pay for your evil deeds."

I sensed energy building inside Cosmo, seeking release. The shock of Damira's death manifested into magic within him. The deities protected him.

The vision vanished and disappointment filled me. I wanted to witness the battle between Cosmo and Grimshaw. Walking out of the sunroom, the door locked behind me. I strode down the hall to the elevator and strolled inside.

"First floor," I said into the intercom.

The elevator rushed down, and I grasped the railing. The door opened on the first floor. I hurried to the main lounge and strode to the upper level. I existed out the glass doors that led to the courtyard. Soldiers practiced their fighting skills with Sir Edrei's guidance. The men teased and jeered each other. Sweat gleamed off their bare chests. Axes and swords clanged. Others sparred in the far corner. The kingdom owned technology, yet we only resorted to firearms if necessary. *What good was any of it against magic?*

Astra leaned against a wall and watched Tano lift weights. I think she had a thing for the pilot but refused to admit it. Her eyes lit up at my approach.

I pointed at Tano. "Did you dare him to lift weights?"

"Negative. Tano wants to impress me. I should stop him before he hurts himself."

I touched Astra's arm. "Don't. You'll hurt his ego. It's a guy thing."

"I'm bored." Astra tossed a long pike at me. "Let me see how you handle yourself."

I gave her a lop-sided grin and smacked her stick.

"Weak shot." Astra hit my pike and sent it flying across the courtyard. "Pick it up and come at me." She stood with her legs apart and her pike held in front of her. She clucked like a hen.

We whacked each other's pikes a couple of times, before Astra twirled around, and smacked down. My hand stung from the unexpected blow, and I shook it out.

"Gonna cry? Boo-hoo," Astra teased.

She slapped my pike, but I blocked her next move. She thwacked my sides. I squelched the pain and hammered back. Astra leapt in the air and whirled. Her long legs kicked me in the chest. I fell back and slid across the ground. Rocks and gravel bit into my back. I stood up and brushed the grit from my hands. Astra swung down, and I jumped up, striking her pike.

"Good one!" Astra said. "I'd practice more, but my grandmother called a meeting."

"Tell Valora the kingdom expects her winged warriors to assist us in the upcoming war."

"War? With whom?" Astra stared at me.

"Grimshaw and his cronies' prepare for war as we speak. They captured Cosmo and Damira."

"Why not rescue them?" she asked.

"Grimshaw made a golem, a magical creature. I'll contact Sylvia because I don't know how to defeat something like it." I wiped the sweat from my face with the end of my shirt.

Sir Jayel, the husky friend of Sir Edrei, wheeled a squeaky target into the courtyard. Numerous men lined up for a chance to hit the bullseye. I joined the line and Astra stood in the corner. The other men pushed me ahead of them. I picked up a bow and notched an arrow. The men snickered and talked behind their hands. I raised the bow level to my nose and pulled the string taut. Closing one eye, I aimed. Everyone hushed. I released my arrow. It thudded into the center of the bullseye and the men cheered. Others clapped my shoulder.

"I bet he can't do it again!" Astra called.

The men placed bets amongst themselves. Sir Jayel nodded. I notched another arrow, raised my bow level again, and pulled back on the string. My arrow sped across the distance and split the shaft of my last arrow. The men jumped up and shouted.

Astra ran over and hugged me. "Nice." She left my side as the others congratulated me.

"Since I have everyone's attention, Grimshaw plans a war against us. Santurin remains weak and I've taken on some of his responsibilities. We must prepare and fortify the kingdom."

I scanned the men and waited for a response.

"Yes!" the men shouted.

Sir Edrei strode over to me. "Natural skill at the bow, Prince Aidan. Care to wield a sword?"

Was this all it took to gain his respect? Why did Mother keep me away from the courtyard?

Sir Edrei handed me a vest. "Put this on for protection. The material is cut resistant."

I pulled the vest over my woolen shirt.

Sir Edrei said, "Keep aware of your environment. Look for advantages and disadvantages. Maneuver to protect yourself and attack with effect. Don't stand still. You want to avoid openings for attack." Sir Edrei placed a lightweight sword in my hand. "Hold the sword with your right hand, at the top end of the grip, and the other hand close to the pommel. Keep your elbows bent and close to your body."

I followed his instructions.

Sir Edrei demonstrated. "Open your body at a forty-five-degree angle, with your left foot ahead of your right. Face your hips towards your opponent."

I copied his moves.

"Good. Avoid stabbing movements. It makes you vulnerable. Perform the basic attack, bring your sword forward, then step towards your opponent slightly to the right," Sir Edrei said. "Bring your sword down in a straight line and hit your opponent. Step away from his attack. When he swipes at you, lift your blade to block his attack. Push his weapon out of the way with yours. Then move in for the attack."

I followed his example. It felt like a dance. One step forward, one step back. Attack, defend, counterattack.

After an hour of practice, I finally got the hang of it. Every muscle in my body ached. Sir Edrei called a halt. I touched my forehead with the sword like the other men.

"The men see you as one of them now, instead of a spoiled brat. You impressed them."

I frowned. *Was it what the men thought or only Sir Edrei?*

"I suggest you plan our battle strategy." I left Sir Edrei standing there. *Bet he didn't expect me to stand up for myself.* I hurried back inside the fortress and sought my chambers.

The warm water flowed over my aching shoulders, while I stood in the shower. Every muscle screamed from the exercises in the courtyard. My valet pestered me, outside the door, about a meeting with the advisory board. I wrapped a towel around my waist and existed the shower.

Jarvis strutted around like a flustered peacock.

"I've laid out your cloak and your royal garb, My Prince. Precious time wasting."

If the beak of a nose got any higher, Jarvis might fall over, worrying over such nonsense.

"What is this meeting about anyway?" I asked.

"I don't know, but it's important," Jarvis said.

"What else is on the agenda?" I asked.

The valet glanced at his clipboard. "Your brother expects an update and lunch in his chambers."

"Find some time on my schedule for a trip to Zavion. I require advice from the Chieftain. I don't know how Santurin does this day in and day out," I said.

"The Chieftains of Volney and Zavion are already in the conference room," Jarvis said.

"Why wasn't I informed?" I ran my hand through my hair.

Jarvis scratched his head. "Did you not understand? I told you about the meeting."

Groaning, I slipped into my royal blue jumpsuit with winged shoulders. The chest of the garment resembled an armored shell. I chose not to wear the offered cloak by my valet because I was already perspiring in the outfit. Jarvis opened the door, and I hastened down the hall.

I took the stairs, two at a time, until I reached the second-floor conference room and walked through the open door. Mother, Chieftain Yewande, Chieftain Sylvia, Councilor Wings, Sir Edrei, and Sir Jayel sat around a long table.

"Excuse me for my tardiness." I sat in Santurin's high-backed chair.

"Since you told us of the impeding war with Fallow, we the advisory board, decided the immediacy of the queen's annulment. Grimshaw shall not gain the crown," Sir Edrei stated.

"I agree. All in favor, raise your right hand," I said.

Everyone raised their hands, and the papers were signed.

"I suggest we crown Santurin king before we go to war. The formalities of the coronation can wait until later. All in favor, raise your right hand," I said.

Everyone raised their hands.

"Good. Next on the agenda?" I asked.

"Prince Aidan, any plans to stop Councilor Grimshaw?" Councilor Wings asked. "I suggest we strip him of his position as councilor."

"Agreed but allow me to fill you in on what I know." I stared at each person, before I continued. "Grimshaw made a golem, using clay and his sister's organs. His scientists are in the process of cloning soldiers from DNA of the late King Arin."

The advisors gasped.

"Grimshaw thinks the people of the Kingdom will be confused at the sight of their old king and not fight back. Clones die like any normal human." I turned to Sylvia. "Any ideas to stop the golem?"

"Any writing on the creature?" she asked.

"Yes. Grimshaw wrote *Emet* on her forehead. Do you know what it means?" I asked.

"It's an old language, Young Prince. It means truth. Remove the first letter, E and it becomes *met*, which means death. The clay dissolves into dust and the golem dies," Sylvia said. "You must get close to the creature and remove the letter, before she harms anyone."

"Leave that to me," I said. "Chieftains, send some of your people to Sir Edrei for the battle. Can I count on you?"

Chieftain Yewande nodded. "I shall send our best." She stomped her staff on the floor.

"You ask a lot of me, Young Prince. My eldest son and my husband died in the last war. My brother, Ulric sent his son, Dew, here as a guard, yet you've caged him like an animal," Chieftain Sylvia said.

"Dew joined forces with Grimshaw against the kingdom." I dared her to deny it. "He is responsible for smacking my face with a heavy limb."

The advisors gasped.

"He stood by while Grimshaw stabbed Twain. Dew is not innocent as you believe, Chieftain. He also talked his friend, Elm, into poisoning me. If anything, your people owe us."

I stared at her.

"I won't promise anything, but I'll ask for volunteers." Sylvia adjusted her antler crown.

"You should all hear this news. I have an identical twin brother named Cosmo. It's a long story, but hear this, the scientists on Fallow created clones of King Arin and of Cosmo. The sorcerer plans to use them as soldiers against us," I said. "My father 's children possess birth marks shaped like birds, usually on their arms. The clones won't have them. I'm open to any advice." I gazed around the room.

Silence thickened in the air.

"This meeting is adjourned." I pushed the chair back and stood. "Excuse me. I have another meeting." I rushed out of the room.

Chapter Twenty-Seven

JULIANA BROUGHT IN A CART TO SANTURIN'S CHAMBERS. She ladled squash soup into mugs for us and added a slice of buttered nut bread on a cloth napkin. She curtsied and left the room.

"How was your meeting?" Santurin blew on his soup. "Any issues?"

"I have a signed document that makes you King of Azure. The formalities will happen later when you're feeling better." I handed him the document. "It was deemed necessary due to an impeding war with Grimshaw and the people of Fallow." I sipped my soup. "Yewande and Sylvia agreed to send us help to fight against Grimshaw and his soldiers. Sylvia brought the girl Elm back home with her. She believed it was her responsibility to punish the girl for poisoning me." I nibbled on my bread. "Mother's annulment papers were signed. I don't know what to do about her."

"What do you mean?" Santurin arched his brows.

"Mother confessed she ordered Twain to get rid of Skyla. Since you're officially king, should we punish her?" I asked.

"Fifteen or sixteen years ago, Skyla died. Mother did not physically kill her, and Twain is dead. Why bother with a punishment this late?" Santurin gulped the rest of his soup. "Do you really want to see our mother hung for a crime she did not commit?"

"No. Still, what about justice? If it happened to a regular citizen, would you hesitate to punish them?" I held out my hands.

"Aidan, every case is different like every person. Mother feels guilty without me adding on to her misery." Santurin swallowed the last piece of bread. "I feel restless lying here. Tell Sir Jayel to come to my chambers. I'd like to build my strength and won't show weakness to my people in time of war."

"That's the spirit!" I placed the dirty dishes on the cart and pushed it outside the door.

"One other thing, Aidan."

"Yes?" I pivoted around.

"You're going to be an uncle," Santurin announced.

"Terrific news, brother!" I smiled. On the inside though, I cringed. *If Grimshaw found out, Mori's life would be in danger.* I left his chambers.

Mori stopped me in the hallway. Her ruby pendant sparkled in the light. "Prince Aidan, glad I caught you. Your mother and mine await you in the garden."

"I hear congratulations are in order. How are you feeling?" I asked.

"Santurin told you; I take it. A little nauseated in the mornings, otherwise I'm fine. Excited about becoming an uncle?" Mori smiled.

"Delighted. A warning though. Grimshaw seeks the kingdom for himself. I'd hate something to befall you because he found out you're pregnant," I said.

"He doesn't want to mess with me. I know my herbs and won't hesitate to use them to protect my family." Mori stood taller and jutted out her chin.

"I believe you, still…extreme caution advised." I hastened to the gardens.

Mother and Sylvia sat on a bench with a covered cage between them. Yvonne jumped up from her stool as I approached.

"Yvonne insisted on bringing your pet eagle here," Sylvia said.

Was this a set-up on Mother's part? Probably curious about Yvonne. With Grimshaw to attack soon, I really hated Yvonne here.

I kissed Yvonne's hand. "Thanks for caring for Mystic, but it wasn't necessary to bring her here. We're on the verge of war."

"I know. I volunteered, along with my brothers. Auntie Sylvia said you requested our assistance," Yvonne said.

"Your father allowed your participation?" I questioned. "That's a surprise."

"I asked for volunteers. Yvonne raised her hand first. Upset because she's female, Young Prince?" Sylvia's eyes twinkled with mischief.

"If something happened to her, I'd never forgive myself." I raked my hand through my hair. *How to concentrate on my magic and watch her back at the same time sounded impossible.*

"Noble of you, but I can defend myself." Yvonne pouted. "I taught Mystic a few tricks too. Nothing clever, really. Mystic retrieves things. Also, she attacks on a signal. I'll show you." Yvonne pulled off the cover of the cage. She slipped on a leather glove and brought Mystic out. "Watch the scarecrow in the field." Yvonne removed Mystic's hood and pointed at the scarecrow. "Attack!" She clicked the roof of her mouth.

The eagle soared across the distance and shredded the scarecrow's face. Straw and cotton littered the field.

Yvonne snapped her fingers with her ungloved hand. Mystic flew back to her. Yvonne fed the eagle a treat.

"What did you give her?" I asked.

"Part of a mouse," Yvonne said.

"Beautiful bird. Remember my falcon, son?" Mother beamed.

"Yes, but your falcon only responded to you. Since Yvonne trained Mystic, she might not listen to me." Jealously gnawed at my stomach.

"Why don't you find out?" Sylvia handed me a glove.

I pulled it on and lifted my arm out.to the side. Whistling to her, Mystic flew to me. "Good girl." I stared into her eyes, and pictured Grimshaw in my mind, and sent it to Mystic. "Find him and see what mischief he plans."

Mystic flew towards Fallow. A vision formed in my head of what Mystic saw. Grimshaw circled his hands over the border walls of Fallow. Each section fell and the iron gates vanished.

Grimshaw stood on a metal ramp with his blood-red robes flapping in the breeze. He wore a cone-shaped hat and clutched a staff in his hand. Power sizzled from him.

Soldiers, in long, mesh vests down to their knees and marked with a red 'F' on their chests, marched down the metal ramps. Rows of clones, resembling my father, raised goosebumps on my arms. I knew Dad died, yet it was freaky none-the-less. Another set of clones, in Cosmo's image, paraded behind them. I whistled, and Mystic cried, startling Grimshaw.

He aimed his staff at her, but Mystic dodged his magic, and flew higher.

She circled overhead, before Mystic landed on my outstretched arm.

"You're such a good girl. Yes, you are." I fed her the other half of the mouse. When she finished, I whispered, "Go hunt."

Mystic sailed over the river. She swooped down and caught a fat trout in her talons. She feasted on her prize in the garden field.

"Any visions, Young Prince?" Sylvia asked.

"The sorcerer comes. I must ready the troops." I called Mystic back and pulled her hood on. I returned her to her cage. "Mother, please care for my eagle, while I inform Sir Edrei."

"Of course, dear."

I grasped Yvonne's hand. "Come on."

We raced to the courtyard, where Sir Edrei practiced swordplay with his men. A shadow overhead caught my eye, and I glanced up. Mystic flew towards Fallow.

"Why is Mystic airborne again? I put her in her cage." I stood on the courtyard wall and whistled.

Grimshaw mimicked my voice and Mystic flew to him. I punched the air. My eagle clung onto Grimshaw's arm. I called her, but the sorcerer distracted her with a treat. While she ate, he raised his staff and zapped her. Feathers scattered, and a burned husk of Mystic crumpled apart.

"No!" I cried. My heart sank.

"A pet of yours, Prince Aidan?" Grimshaw called. "Pity." His laughter echoed in the air.

I wanted to beat his face in and clenched my hands into fists at my side.

Yvonne sensed my anger and touched my arm. "He's not worth it. The men await your orders."

I gained strength from her and shoved my sadness over Mystic aside. "Let's not disappoint them." I climbed off the wall and strode over to Sir Edrei and his men. "Grimshaw wants a fight. Let's beat him at his own game. For the kingdom!"

The men raised their weapons in the air. "To arms!"

We hustled out the back gate of the courtyard and crossed the bridge over the river. We ran down the hillside. The road to Fallow was longer this way, than through the corridor in the basement of Azure, but it also gave us a chance of cover and surprise.

Sir Edrei took me aside. "Chieftain Yewande sent her men ahead to set traps. Ulric and his men wait for us near the border. I made our battle plans, after you told me of the sorcerer's intentions." He handed me a sword.

"Good show." I buckled the scabbard, baring the sword, around my waist.

We marched down the road. A young recruit held the Azure banner, and it fluttered in the breeze, while another lad beat a drum. The men wore cut-resistant vests over their royal blue uniforms. They carried their shields in front of them, swords at their sides, metal armlets donned their wrists, and hatchets and daggers looped in their belts. The more experienced soldiers carried metal firearms strapped over their shoulders that shot lasers with one touch of a trigger.

Normally, we didn't resort to such weapons, but the clones weren't ordinary men. Santurin believed in the old ways of combat as a fair way to fight. A bit old-fashioned, but he was king, not me.

Santurin stayed at the fortress, guarding it with two hundred men, and trusted me with the responsibility of defending the borderland. I believe he really stayed because of Mori's pregnancy. Better to let Grimshaw think the king died.

I strode behind the men, with Yvonne at my side. She wore her bow and her quiver of arrows over her shoulder. The wind blew at our backs. Birds and squirrels scattered from the road in our haste.

After almost two hours on the road, the sun-like star started to set. I slapped a mosquito that buzzed near my ear. Crickets chirped and bull frogs croaked in the evening air. The river, close by, swished. An occasional trout leapt and dove back in the water. As the men neared Fallow, they divided into groups. Sir Edrei led one group and Sir Jayel the other.

Sir Jayel paced back and forth in front of his men. "Today, we fight a battle against a devil that walked among us. Don't underestimate him. Grimshaw is not our friend. He cares only for himself. We shall beat him and his cronies. He will not take what is rightfully ours."

His men shouted, "For the kingdom!"

"Apply your contacts," Sir Jayel ordered. He placed the night vision contacts in his eyes also and they illuminated a bright green. He hid some of his men among the trees of the border and the rest he marched across the battleground. Our men had the advantage over the clones; years of experience and fighting skills.

Sir Edrei's group followed the lower region of the river, camouflaged by rows of sunflowers. Yvonne and I raced up a hill for a better view. I looked at the city of Fallow in the distance and whispered an incantation, blowing a thick fog towards Grimshaw's soldiers.

His clones turned in circles in their search for the correct path through the mist. Grimshaw placed swords in the clones' hands, but they swung them around like they didn't know what to do with them. Sir Jayel took advantage and sent his first troops in. At first, his men hesitated, not sure what to do.

"King Arin died. Those clones are imposters. Don't twiddle your thumbs. Knock them on their asses!" Sir Jayel shouted.

His men skewered the clones with their swords. Losing his patience, Grimshaw grasped one of the swords from a clone and sliced off his arm. The clone picked up the body part and tried to stick it back on. He looked at Grimshaw for help. The sorcerer tossed the arm into the field and stabbed the clone to death. With the next set of clones, Grimshaw demonstrated how to fight with a sword and the clones imitated him.

I sensed Yvonne's eagerness to join the others, yet I stalled her a little longer. "You mean a lot to me." I placed an enameled barrette in her hair. "To remember me, in case something happens."

Tears shone in her eyes. Yvonne kissed my cheek, and then ran down the hillside, and joined the other archers. I directed my attention to the war at hand and quelched my fear for her safety.

What transpired since I last saw Cosmo with the sorcerer? Was he still alive? I focused my mind on my twin.

A voice whispered on the wind. "Do not fret, brother. I merely transformed. Grimshaw assumed I died. When the time's right, I shall appear."

"Thank the spirits," I said.

The archers released their arrows and they thudded into a group of clones marching on Sir Jayel's men. An arrow pierced Grimshaw's shoulder, and he cursed.

Ulric swung his mace and pulverized many clones near him, until they were a bloody mess. His sons followed his lead. Ash jabbed his sword into one clone and whirled around stabbing another. Oak sliced his axe into the bellies of the next row of clone soldiers, and then cut off their heads. They rolled down the battleground. Blood splattered Oak's beard, face, and arms. I shuddered and turned my head, emptying my stomach.

Clay charged ahead and rammed his shield into a clone's face, while he hammered another with a mallet. As strong as our men fought, more clones advanced.

How long had the scientists produced the clones and where were the cowards?

The Volney men's dark skin blended in the shadows of the night. They hid in the brush. Only the white war paint on their faces showed in the moonlight. They covered pits with leaves and grass. They peered around the brush and waited for the enemy. As the clones fell in the pits, spikes pinned them in place like a common animal. The Volney men poked their spears into the sides of the clones as an added measure.

Sir Edrei's men advanced on the clones and fired their weapons. The clones fell in a heap. Out of the sky, the Azure fleet flew over the crowd and fired on the next bunch of clones.

Grimshaw released his golem and Twyla charged down the ramps. She plowed into our men like stacks of blocks.

"Retreat!" Sir Edrei called.

His men scattered out of the golem's way. Sir Jayel blasted the golem with his laser gun, but it had little effect on her. The holes in her clay figure healed over in minutes. She stepped over the pits. The bat virus retained in her organs, Twyla bared her fangs and hissed.

She stomped forward and the ground quaked with her weight. Her small, rubbery wings fluttered, but she didn't lift off the ground. Twyla roared with her frustration and whirled around, ripping her wings off.

The archers positioned themselves and discharged numerous arrows at the golem, but they bent and fell to the ground. Twyla kept coming. The archers soaked their arrows in oil and lit them. They released an arc of arrows, and they caught the golem's head on fire. The odor of fried hair reeked. The fire burned further down her body. Twyla's body half melted, she resembled a wax monster, but Grimshaw's magic healed her wounds.

I had to get close enough to erase that first letter, *E* off her forehead, before she killed all our soldiers. Placing the EEG headset on my forehead, I commanded my cloud-board, and it locked my ankles in place. I flew over the battleground and squatted down as I neared the golem. I raised my hand over her forehead with my hanky, but Grimshaw froze me in place. Blocks of ice numbed my arms and legs. My teeth chattered, but I couldn't move my body.

"Watch my next move, Prince Aidan." Grimshaw rolled his hands in circles. "Rise before me!" He summoned the river and the water rose twice its size. Grimshaw pushed his hands out and the river flooded the borderland.

Sir Edrei's men floundered in the water. The Volney and Zavion men climbed the trees. Sir Jayel and his men raced to the Fallow building. Grimshaw laughed at all the chaos.

A moment of panic churned my stomach. *Where was Yvonne?* I couldn't move my body, but I was able to turn my head slightly. Yvonne scrambled up a rock formation, in the shape of a large lizard, sitting in the river.

Twyla swatted me like a pesky fly, and I flew across the air. Looking at my hands, I conjured flames. The ice melted from my body. I pivoted around on my cloud-board and flew straight for the golem. I wiped away the first letter, *E*, from Twyla's forehead and she crumbled to dust.

"No!" Grimshaw cried.

I zoomed down and picked up the wadded paper dropped from the golem's mouth. Opening the paper, one word was written: *Twyla*. I ripped it into pieces and set them on fire.

"You'll pay for that." Grimshaw pressed a small remote.

Half animal and half machine, strange creatures rolled out from the Fallow building. The scientists had been busy over the years. First the clones, and now these monstrosities. A coyote's head propped atop a metal box-like body, with wheels for legs, clambered down the ramp. Another creature bore a wolf's head with a mechanical body. Its teeth gnashed together. I shot flames at them, but the creatures kept coming.

Ulric and Clay snuck behind them. Ulric smashed the body of the wolf with his mace. It reared up and snapped at him, but Clay pounded in the wolf's teeth with his mallet. Oak chopped off the head of the coyote, then twirled around, cutting off the wolf's head. I grimaced at the bloody mess.

"A little help over here!" Ash called.

A wildcat, with steel claws and daggers for fangs, jumped on his back. Ash swung around, but the wildcat machine clawed his arm. Dripping with blood, Ash staggered. His sword arm looked like ground beef.

A battle cry rent the air. Yvonne fired arrow after arrow into the soft sides of the wildcat machine. One arrow pierced its eye and dripped yellow goo. Oak ran over and chopped off the creature's head and waved his trophy around. Blood splattered his face and chest. Yvonne assisted Ash over to a tree stump and sat him down. She pulled off her shawl and wrapped it around Ash's arm.

Yvonne turned and gazed at me. "Are you all right, My Prince?"

"My, you're fast. First, you're climbing a rock over there—" I pointed at the river, but the rock formation disappeared. I rubbed my eyes. "Where did it go?"

Yvonne shrugged.

"The men need our help. They're drowning in the flood—" My eyes widened. "Look out!" I pushed Yvonne down.

A rooster with mechanical hands launched a grenade at us. Ulric batted the grenade with his sword, and it struck the side of the Fallow building. A deep hole hollowed it and the stone crumbled. The rooster shot a missile, from its tail, at us next.

"Take cover!" I shouted.

Grimshaw laughed. I scrambled to get out of the way, but the missile followed my cloud-board as I sped higher in the air. Grimshaw controlled the missile, and I soared closer to the building, then released my hold on the cloud-board.

The missile exploded into my board and took out half the building. I somersaulted in the air and landed in stinging nettles. My legs and buttocks burned from the contact of the hairy, spiky things. I pulled the needle-like hairs out, but the stinging sensation irritated my skin. Racing to the river, I jumped in, washing the plant's chemicals from my skin.

Sir Edrei floated on his back. "Give me a hand, My Prince. One of the clones stabbed my side."

Shoving bloated, dead bodies away, I guided Sir Edrei to safety. Something bumped into my backside. I turned and faced a lizard-like beast. My mind did a double take. *Wasn't it the same rock formation Yvonne climbed?*

"Brother, it's Cosmo. I've come to help," The blue-scaled lizard-like creature said.

I pulled Sir Edrei to shore, and then removed my shirt, pressing it to his wound. Calling out to the other men in the floodwaters, I yelled, "Climb on the lizard-like beast's back! He'll bring you to safety."

"You're joshing me. He'd eat me than spare my life." A soldier, treading water, said.

"Have faith," I said.

Cosmo floated atop the water and the men scrambled for a hold on him. The lizard-like creature swam close to shore, and the men climbed off, wading the rest of the way. Cosmo returned for more survivors. I dove back in and grabbed another man struggling in the water.

"Get me outta here. I don't wanna be fish food." The man kicked and splashed.

"Calm down or you'll drown us both." I hooked him around the neck and propped his head up before I swam to shore with my burden.

My brother dropped several men and women soldiers off as I dumped my man on the shoreline. Cosmo descended under the water. Grimshaw clapped and a huge wave rolled towards my brother. I twisted my hand and the wave switched directions, slamming into the sorcerer.

Soaking wet, Grimshaw raised his staff and pointed at some stone blocks. He mumbled an incantation and the stone wobbled as it rose. Grimshaw swung his arm, and the stone flew at me.

I held out my palm and stopped time. Stepping aside, I restarted it. Grimshaw stomped his foot as the stone missed me. I formed a fireball and pitched it at the sorcerer. Not expecting the blow, Grimshaw fell back. I struck him again before he stood. His hair singed, and holes marked his robes. The sorcerer staggered inside the remnants of the building. I started to follow him, but something held me back.

A six-foot tall mechanical being, with the head of my old nursemaid, Damira rolled towards me with pincer hands. Sharp blades rotated from her stomach like a fan. Her exposed brain, hooked up to a light system, blinked and dinged with each movement. The bottom half rolled on a conveyer belt.

"What's the matter, Prince Aidan? Don't you recognize me?" a computer voice said. "Come to Damira, honey and I'll soothe away your fears."

I shook my head. "Get away from me, you freak of nature!" I backed up.

"Is that any way to speak to your nursemaid?" She edged closer.

"Duck!" Yvonne shouted.

I dropped to the ground and somersaulted out of the way. Yvonne shot arrows into the brain of the robotic Damira.

"What have you...*click, whir*, done to me-e-e...?" Her voice died and the blades stopped rotating. Oil dripped onto the ground and smoke puffed from Damira's brain.

A boat-shaped machine, with headlights on its bow, lurched from the bowels of the stone building. Grimshaw and a redhead sat up front and steered the thing. The other scientists sat on benches in the back. The machine mowed down anyone in its way. I jumped to the side and the machine plunged into the river.

The Volney soldiers tossed mud at the sorcerer. Grimshaw cursed as mud splat his face. Oak and Clay raced to the water and grasped the stern. They flipped inside and punched the scientists, until they fell overboard. Grimshaw vanished. Everyone scanned around for his where-abouts. Cosmo reared up from the water and the scientists screeched. They attempted to swim back to shore, but Cosmo nabbed them with their breeches. He shook them around. The Azure soldiers rounded the scientists together, after Cosmo spit them out on shore. Sir Jayel tied their hands behind them and pushed them forward.

The boat- shaped contraption floated down the river. I flung a fireball inside it and burned the damn thing. A red- orange sea serpent rose from the water and sunk his fangs into Cosmo's back. My brother yelped and whipped around, clawing the serpent's face. They rolled in the water, each trying to best the other. The sea serpent dove down, and Cosmo followed. Anxiety pestered my gut, until Cosmo popped up with Grimshaw hanging upside down with his foot inside Cosmo's mouth.

"Put me down, you pathetic beast!" Grimshaw swung around and punched Cosmo's snout, but he missed contact. My brother spit him out on the shore.

I hustled over and yanked the sorcerer's hands behind him. Sir Jayel bound Grimshaw's hands with iron handcuffs. Iron stings anyone with magic. I was grateful Sir Jayel handled them.

I stretched my arms over the river and said, "Hear me, goddess. Recede the waters back to their natural habitat."

The floodwaters shrunk back, and the river returned to its natural form. Cosmo had disappeared.

The men sang songs of victory as we marched back to Azure. We had lost some men, but many survived. Grimshaw glared at me. Sir Jayel pushed him along. Yvonne hooked her arm in mine and for a moment, I forgot about the sorcerer.

"The scientists survived, all these years, living underground in the stone building of Fallow. They had plenty of time to rid the land of their poisons, but they cared nothing for the environment. If left to me, I'd make them clean the land of their toxins," I said.

"I say they hang," Sir Jayel said. "It's the king's decision though."

I peeked at Grimshaw. He didn't seem concerned. His mind probably planned his next move. With his experience in the dark arts, he'd survive somehow.

Our men removed their night vision contacts as the sun-like star rose. We marched back to Azure. Grimshaw slipped the grasp of one of the soldiers and attempted to run off. I lassoed him with my binding rope, I kept around my waist. He slipped in the muck and spit out mud. I yanked him to his feet.

"You, Azurins, think you're almighty with your aristocratic noses high in the air. You stole my sister from me. Nothing hurts me worse than what you've done." Grimshaw glared.

I pointed at a soldier. "Gag him. Tie his ankles together too. If he flees again, truss him like a pig."

The men snickered. Tired and hungry, I cared less about the sorcerer's comfort.

We strode home.

Chapter Twenty-Eight

WE'D BEEN ON THE ROAD A WHILE, WHEN WE ROUNDED the corner, and faced the back side of the fortress of Azure. Smoke filled the air and my stomach lurched. *What happened in our absence?*

We raced up the hillside and stared in silence at the destruction. Trees uprooted and deep holes grooved into the hill. The smell of death lingered, and flies landed on bodies strewn about the land. A buzzing nagged me. I peered up.

Small drones, resembling bumblebees, fired on the kingdom's people. They screamed and ran for cover. I glanced at the scientists corralled together. They smiled like they had a big secret.

"You think this is funny?" I poked the chest of a bald man with a large mole on his cheek.

"Yes. My master's plan worked. You had no clue." He chuckled.

"I'll see you're the first one hung for treason." I scowled at him.

The scientist's smile left his face.

A drone charged at us. *Who controlled them?*

Oak tossed a rock at it, and it crashed into pieces. We walked past the gallows and our prisoners stared at their fate. From the balcony of one of the towers, a shadow hovered.

"Tiana? What has gotten into you?" I called.

My mother's personal handmaiden held the control box and sent further drones towards our soldiers. "I'm sorry, My Prince, but I had no choice," she called.

Ulric batted a drone away with his sword. "Yvonne, archers to the front. The king needs your help. We'll handle this mess."

"All right, Pa." Yvonne hustled to the frontlines and her archers tagged behind.

"Tiana, come down and we'll talk about it!" I yelled.

She shook her head. "You don't understand. Grimshaw kidnapped my mother. He said he'd kill her if I didn't do this."

"I hate to break it to you, but Grimshaw did something far worse than kill her."

"What! But he promised not to harm her if I followed his orders. I even sent him your eagle." Tiana smashed the control box. She raced down the stairs.

It hurt to hear her news of Mystic, but it also fueled my anger. I ripped the gag from Grimshaw as Tiana rushed over to us. "Tell her the truth."

"I don't know what you're talking about." Grimshaw grinned.

"Liar!" I drew a magic circle on the ground with a stick and stood in its center. "To see the truth, to know the way, I cast a spell in every way. I conjure thee, to speak the truth to me." I blew thyme in Grimshaw's face.

The sorcerer opened his mouth and relayed Damira's destruction to Tiana.

She gasped. "You'll pay for your misdeeds." Tiana pulled a small dagger from the pocket of her long skirt and dug it into the bend of Grimshaw's leg.

With his hands handcuffed and his legs tied, the sorcerer cried out and squatted down. Blood poured between his fingers as he held his leg. He lowered himself to the ground and touched it with a hand, while mumbling some incantation. The ground trembled.

Ulric arched a bushy brow. "How can this happen? I broke the magic man's stick."

"My magic isn't controlled by my staff, fool." Grimshaw sneered. "I use it for theatrics. Magic runs in my family."

"Get his hands away from the ground," I said.

Ulric and his son, Oak wrestled with the sorcerer, until they got him to his feet. Oak shoved him forward.

"Clay, bring Tiana to Santurin. He's up front with his men," I said.

Clay ran to her side and grasped the handmaiden's elbow.

Tiana raised her chin in defiance. "I'm not sorry. Grimshaw deserved what he got."

"Brazen lass," Clay said. He led her to the bridge.

I ripped fabric from Grimshaw's cloak and staunched his wound.

"Hey, that's the only decent cloak I own," Grimshaw said.

"It's either that or let you bleed to death." I tied the cloth a little tighter than necessary. "You're enjoying this way too much," Grimshaw muttered.

We walked the prisoners to the jailhouse. An old barn sufficed for the purpose, yet the

smell of old horse manure lingered in the walls. The bars allowed some fresh air in. Each of the scientists had their own cell with a locked door and straw to relieve themselves. I removed a leather collar, from a nail on a post, and placed it around Grimshaw's neck.

I stuck a finger under it. Snug, but room enough for him to breathe. "Try to escape and the collar shocks you." It was a ruse to make Grimshaw cooperate. I nodded to Sir Jayel, and he locked Grimshaw inside his cell. I handpicked two muscular soldiers to guard the prisoners, while the rest of us rushed outside to assist in the battle.

I aimed my hands at mechanical squirrels that carried grenades and flames ignited them. As I gazed upon the Hope River, metal crabs crawled up the bridge from the water. I struck them with my fire power, and they fell apart.

Grimshaw had saved the best of the clones and attacked the kingdom. Santurin battled a clone, which resembled Dad, at the end of the bridge. They matched blow by blow. Grimshaw trained only a select few to fight. Tiana sat on the landing of the stairs, with the waterfall background behind her. Clay stood with his hand on her shoulder. His eyes glanced my way.

I tiptoed behind the clone and held my sword against his throat. Santurin stabbed the clone in the chest and the thing collapsed. My brother picked him up and tossed the clone over the railing.

Santurin said to me, "Did you defeat Grimshaw?"

"He's locked in his cell with the others," I said.

"Good" Santurin turned to Tiana. "Treason against the Crown is a serious matter."

"Brother, Grimshaw coerced her into the deed. He threatened her mother's life if she didn't follow his instructions."

"Is this true?" Santurin asked her.

"Yes, Your Highness." Tiana looked down at her feet.

"And where is Damira?" Santurin asked.

I told him of the circumstances and Santurin paled. He stroked his chin. "Tiana, it's regrettable what happened to your mother, but I can't trust you. I shall ask Lady Darshana to escort you to Meadowlark. In the meantime, Clay assist Tiana to the jailhouse."

The handmaiden dropped to her knees. "I beg for mercy."

Clay pulled her up and led her away.

On the opposite side of the river, our men fought the rest of the clones. Robotic scorpions scurried across the other bridge and into the garden area. I hastened over as some girls screamed. The scorpions raised their tails and shot lasers at anyone near them. I winced as a laser zapped my exposed shoulder. My vest only covered my chest and back.

"My Prince, you're injured," Rashida, one of Mother's handmaidens, said. "Allow me to assist you."

"No. Join the other handmaidens inside." I admired the bravery and concern of this Volney girl. I smirked at her bare, grass-stained feet. "Still refusing to wear boots?"

Rashida covered her feet with her caftan. "They pinch my toes. It feels natural to touch the grass without shoes."

"Ah, the little rebel." I chuckled. "Where's Mori?"

Rashida pointed up. "In the west tower room with Astra per the King's instructions."

"Why? Did he think to distract Mori with her artwork?" I asked.

"Yes, but it's not working," Rashida said. "See. The queen paces."

"Hurry inside and relieve Astra. Never mind my minor injury." I raked my hand through my hair and flinched from the strain on my burn. Tapping and clicking alerted me to mechanical scorpions drawing near me. I whipped around and burst them apart with flames from my hands.

Potholes and scorched grass from the explosions and charred fruit trees leaned on their sides. Fallen soldiers were strewn on the land. The coppery taste of blood filled my nostrils and I gagged. The clanging of swords drew me away from the destruction. Several clones charged at Santurin, and I hastened to his aid. Sir Jayel and the other men joined us, and we slaughtered many clones.

My shoulder ached, but I whacked the head of one clone and twirled around, striking another's legs. I butted my head into the stomach of a clone that raised his sword. Yvonne's arrow pierced another's throat and the clone fell over a rock, gurgling in his own blood. I saluted her and she ran off, firing more arrows into the advancing enemy.

After hours of war with the strange creatures, we finally beat them. Crows and other scavengers pecked at the dead. I grimaced as one of the blackbirds snacked on a man's eyeball.

Weariness etched our men's faces and blood smeared their uniforms and weapons. Bodies floated in the river. Grimshaw had fooled us. He wanted us to leave Azure, so he could attack the kingdom. I shook my head at all the damage.

Santurin slapped my shoulder and I winced. "We made a good team. Get that shoulder looked at. I'll have the men round up the bodies."

"All right. You sure you don't want my help?" I asked.

"You've done enough, Aidan. Do me a favor and check on the ladies," my brother said.

I strolled across the lawn and walked inside the fortress. I strode up the stairs to Mother's chambers and knocked on the door. "It's Aidan."

Juliana opened the door and rushed into my arms. "Thank the goddess you're safe. What about the King?"

"Santurin survived," I said.

"Monica died saving the Queen. The other handmaidens are fine." Juliana paused. "Your arm is bleeding. Sit on the stool and I'll clean it."

I sat down and exhaustion seeped in. Juliana grabbed her supplies, and I closed my eyes. A ripping noise startled me. Juliana tore my shirt and washed my burned shoulder. I sucked in a breath. The skin pulled away and fresh blood beaded. She washed away the blood that ran down my arm. Juliana smeared an antibiotic cream over my shoulder.

Rolling gauze around my wound, she said, "Come see me once a day for dressing changes, until your burn heals."

"Thanks. I better check on Mori." I left Mother's chambers and sauntered up the stairs to the third floor. Opening the west tower room door, I walked inside.

Astra sat on a stool as Mori painted her portrait. Astra turned around as I walked inside the tower room.

"Poo, you moved." Mori pouted. She held her paintbrush in the air. "Prince Aidan, is the battle over?"

"Yes. Santurin survived. The men are exhausted and hungry." I looked at Astra. "I sent Rashida to replace you. Why are you still here?"

"I wanted to finish Astra's portrait and sent Rashida away. I'll speak with the cook. If you'll excuse me." Mori set her brush down and wiped her hands on a cloth. She lifted her skirts and left the room.

I glanced at the painting. "A good likeness. Mori has talent." I turned to Astra. "Why didn't you join us in the fight?"

"Believe me, I wanted in on the action. The King insisted I stay with Mori. How was the battle?" An eagerness brightened Astra's eyes.

I informed her what happened on Fallow and the battle on Azure lands.

"Poor Damira. I liked her. What happened to Cosmo?" Astra queried.

I told her about Cosmo's transformation. "He said he'll explain everything later."

"And the sorcerer?" Astra questioned.

"Locked in his prison cell. A good place for him," I said.

"What happened to your shoulder?" Astra touched it and I winced.

"You wouldn't believe the weird, mechanical critters the scientists created. A scorpion shot a laser from its tail and burned my shoulder. Juliana cleansed and dressed it. It's sore, but I'd rather not think about it." I informed her about Tiana's involvement in the war and Santurin's plan to send her to Meadowlark.

"Maybe Tiana and Cosmo will get along? Damira was like a mother to Cosmo too. I'd like to escort her to Meadowlark," Astra said.

"I thought you didn't like Tiana. Santurin asked Lady Darshana to escort her," I said.

"Tiana defended me when your mother treated me harshly when Grimshaw wooed her. The sorcerer told some lies about me to the queen and she refused me as her chaperone," Astra said. "It's best he's locked away or I might kill him myself."

"I'm sorry you were treated that way. You should live in Meadowlark where you're happier. I'll speak to Santurin on your behalf." I strode out of the west tower room. Food and sleep called me.

Chapter Twenty-Nine

THE AROMA OF FOOD DREW ME TO THE MAIN DINING hall. Mori stood next to Santurin at the head of the table and addressed the soldiers.

"I only have one rule. Please wash the dirt and blood from your hands and face, before you eat, gentlemen." Mori gazed at Santurin, "That includes you, husband."

The men laughed and teased him. My brother withheld any harsh words to his wife, but everyone knew Mori shrieked about him leaving her in the west tower room, while the battle ranged. The men rushed to do her bidding.

Mori smiled as they returned with clean faces. The men hurried to their seats and awaited their meal. Mori snapped her fingers, and the servants filled their goblets with honey mead. The men perked up.

I raised my glass. "For the kingdom and the brave souls that fought alongside us."

"For the kingdom!" everyone shouted.

"And for this delicious meal that my beautiful wife arranged." Santurin kissed her cheek.

Everyone tapped their glasses. "For Mori!"

Her cheeks pinkened. The servants brought the food to the table, and I licked my lips. Platters of trout passed around. Another dish contained a tender deer roast. Acorn squash, drizzled with butter and brown sugar, and green beans, covered in pearl onions and strips of bacon, made the rounds. I filled my plate with a little of each.

When we finished the main course, the servants removed the dirty dishes. Rashida served slices of saffron cake with blackberries for dessert.

Imani, another handmaiden of Mori's and friend of Rashida, held a pot. "Anyone desire coffee?"

Santurin pointed to his cup. He loved the rich flavor of Volney's special brand. I personally couldn't stomach its bitter taste. What was the point of drinking it, if you piled sugar and cream into it to make it palatable? I'll stick to the mead. I wasn't the only one.

Clay elbowed me. "Did you notice Mori didn't press the women soldiers to wash?"

"They cleaned beforehand. Blood bothers sensitive souls. It puts reality to war," I said.

"How'd you get smart?" he asked.

"It's not a matter of brains. I'm more observant." I sipped my drink. The mead a bit strong, I felt a little woozy. When Dad lived, he allowed me one glass, but he diluted it. Today, I drank full strength mead since I fought in the battle like the others.

Santurin cleared his throat, and everyone stopped talking. "I propose a memorial service on the morrow for our comrades that died in battle and for my old nursemaid, Damira. After everyone has rested, of course. Any suggestions for punishment of the scientists?"

"Hang 'em high, I say," Sir Jayel said.

"Yes!" Most of the men agreed.

"Brother, I suggest we keep one or two of them to clean up Fallow," I said.

Santurin peered over the table. "The scientists had plenty of time to fix the problem. Instead of cleaning the toxic waste, they hid underground and plotted against the kingdom."

My brother paused for emphasis. "I don't trust them. They'll hang for treason in two days." He turned back to Mori. "Find out all you can on plants that remove contaminants from the soil. It's your special project."

Mori glanced at the people. "Any volunteers to assist with the planting?"

"I'd love to help." I volunteered.

"Anyone else?" Mori asked.

With a full belly and the honey mead, the men sagged in their chairs. They nodded off. Ulric's chin touched his chest, and he snored like a bear.

"Sorry, Mori. They're too battle-weary. Ask them later," I suggested.

Santurin kissed the top of Mori's head. "I'm seeking my own bed. Join me when you're able." He stood up.

"Gentlemen." Mori clapped her hands. "Please find your own units. Those from Volney and Zavion that want to spend the night, let me know, and I'll arrange something. If you'd rather go home, transportation is available."

The servants rushed in and removed the dishes. Chairs scooted back as everyone stood. Santurin departed. I escorted Yvonne, Ash, and Ulric out of the fortress. Sir Edrei and Tano waited to transfer guests at the airship hangar. Clay stayed behind. I assumed he wanted time with Juliana.

Yvonne blew me a kiss, climbing inside the airship, and I pretended to catch it. I waved, then strolled back inside the fortress.

Exhaustion tugged at me, and my burn stung. I strode down the long hallway to my chambers. The door opened, after I put in my code, then I took a few steps, and flopped on my bed.

Chapter Thirty

THE MORNING LIGHT PEEKED AROUND THE SHADES AND reflected off the crystal top of my staff, piercing my eyes. I squinted and staggered across the room, putting my staff inside the closet. Stripping out of yesterday's clothes, I hopped in the shower. The warm water felt good over my achy muscles. After several long minutes, I stepped out of the shower.

My blue tunic and matching breeches lay on my bed, and I pulled them on. Jarvis, my valet, held my hairbrush and gestured for me to sit. He brushed my hair back and tied it with a piece of rawhide. I pulled on my leather boots, then journeyed down the long hall.

Familiar voices chattered in the lounge, and I stepped into the upper half. Santurin concentrated on his next move at the chess table, while Clay waited his turn. Juliana poured coffee into the players' cups.

She smiled at me as I strolled over. "Good morning, Prince Aidan. Coffee?"

I scrunched my face. "No way. What's on the morning menu?"

"The cook set out pastries. He's busy with the memorial feast. If you'll excuse me, I promised the queen some tea." Juliana rushed off with a tray.

I leaned over Clay's shoulder. "Who's winning?"

"The king won the last two games, but he's met his match." Clay snickered. "He promised to introduce me to Sir Edrei if I win this round."

Clay already had Santurin's queen and bishop. In a matter of minutes, the game ended, and Clay won. "You owe me."

"Why do you want an introduction?" Santurin asked.

"Your brother said Sir Edrei won't bother talking to anyone not in high standards for his daughter. I plan to sway him in my favor," Clay said.

I frowned. "You've taken what I said out of context."

"It's not Sir Edrei, it's my mother you must persuade in your favor, Clay. She dotes on her handmaidens and Juliana is one of her favorites. Please her and she'll put in a good word to Sir Edrei. But I promised you an introduction. This way." Santurin led Clay out of the main lounge and out the back door to the courtyard.

I strolled inside the dining room. A plate contained pastries on top of a table. I bit into one and raspberry jelly oozed out. Licking the jelly from my mouth, I gobbled the rest of the pastry. I walked inside the kitchen. Mori and the cook argued over the menu. I fixed myself a bowl of oats with milk and carried it out to the dining room. Juliana had returned and sat at a table sipping tea.

"Are you interested in Clay?" I sat next to her. "He plans to speak with your father."

Juliana groaned. "Clay follows me around like a pet. It's embarrassing. I know he's your friend, but I'm not ready for marriage."

"I told him Sir Edrei probably won't approve of him, but Clay believes he can talk your father into it." I spooned some oatmeal into my mouth.

"He doesn't know my father. He's not persuaded easily." Juliana drank more of her tea. "I hoped we could cloud-board together today."

"A missile exploded into my cloud-board during the battle. Sorry," I said.

"Shame." Juliana pouted. "A rumor said you like Clay's sister."

"Yes. Don't tell me you're jealous." I leaned in.

Juliana pushed me away. "Maybe a little. I'm bored with the gossip of the other handmaidens. With my cousin, Varick away, I have no one to banter with or play games." She bit into a pastry. "Mm, blackberry." She licked her lips. "Mori hates me, yet your mother expects me to hold the nursery position for your brother's baby-to-be. If I get close to Santurin, Mori glowers. Tiana had the position, but lost favor. Who do you think is suited for the job?"

"Imani smiles a lot and has a sweet nature, but Rashida might feel left out without her friend. Maybe both for the position?" I smirked.

"Aidan, don't you think they'll fight for control? I'd hate their friendship ruined over it."

"No, I think they'll share the burden. Are you going to the memorial service?"

"It depends on how your mother feels. She has sniffles. Speaking of her, I should get back." Juliana stood. "Nice talking with you." She rushed out of the room.

A young page blew a horn, from the top stair of the main lounge. "The memorial service is under way."

Everyone herded out the back doors to the courtyard. I followed behind them. The high priest, in his gold robes and tall cone hat over his bald head, roamed across the courtyard, waving incense from a brass pot. He set it down, below a pulpit, while everyone grabbed a seat.

His voice rang out, "We've come to pay our last respects to our fallen comrades. May they find peace in the afterlife. Anyone like to say a few words?"

The people clapped as Santurin strode to the pulpit. "Thank you, High Priest Reynard. Today, we remember the good of those that gave their lives for our kingdom. May they rest in peace, but let us not forget, we were all victims of Grimshaw and his cohorts. I thank all of you that fought beside us." Santurin's eyes fell on me. "Aidan, anything to add?"

I strode to the pulpit. "As my brother said, we were all victims. Damira, my old nursemaid, didn't deserve what Grimshaw did to her. She was sweet and kind. Our men fought hard to rid us of the evil sorcerer and his cohorts. When I read the names of the deceased, the priest rings a bell, and you answer, we'll remember you." I pulled out the list.

When I finished calling out the names, the priest waved incense over the list. He nodded and placed the brass incense container behind the pulpit again.

"A buffet awaits in the main dining room. All are welcome." I strode back to my seat.

The people lined up and moved inside the fortress. I didn't see Mother in the crowd nor Juliana. Something nagged at me to check on them. I pushed through the people and hurried inside the fortress.

I took two stairs at a time up the staircase to Mother's chambers. I rapped at her door, but no one answered. "Computer, override. Prince Aidan. Code B12. Open the chamber door," I uttered into the intercom.

The door slid open. Tied to a chair, a scarf tied around her mouth, Juliana squirmed. I untied the scarf, and she took a breath.

"Where's Mother?" I asked.

"Tiana blamed the queen for Damira's death. She said if the queen hadn't annulled her marriage to Grimshaw, he wouldn't have killed her mother. Tiana plans to burn the queen and the sorcerer together," Juliana said.

"I thought your mother delivered Tiana to Meadowlark?" I asked.

"Mother postponed the trip until after the memorial service," Juliana said.

"Do you believe Tiana capable of killing the queen?" I frowned.

Juliana sighed. "You didn't see the crazed look in her eyes."

We raced out of the fortress and down the hillside to the jailhouse. I probably should have notified Santurin, but time was running out. I covered my nose from the acrid smoke fueling the air. My heart thundered. People yelled and pounded on the walls from inside the jailhouse. Flames licked the side of the building.

"Run and tell your father. He has a key. Go! I'll try to put out the fire," I said to Juliana.

She lifted her uniform skirt and ran to the security building. I turned on the facet and stretched out the hose, aiming the nozzle at the inflamed building, and it sprayed at full force. Servants hauled buckets of water down the hill and sloshed some on the way. They tossed the rest of the water on the flames. I peered up as Sir Edrei, Juliana, and Sir Jayel hurried over.

Sir Edrei stroked his pockets. "I can't find my keys. Juliana run and inform the king."

"We don't have time to waste." Sir Jayel grabbed an axe and chopped through the wood of the jailhouse.

My mother lay on the floor at the feet of Grimshaw. I picked her up and carried her away from the building, placing her on the grass. I wiped the soot from her face with my hanky. Mother roused and deep, retching coughs issued from her.

"Thank the spirits you heard me, son." Mother coughed more. "Where is Tiana?"

"Good question." I glanced around, yet I didn't spy her anywhere.

"Get me out of here!" Grimshaw called.

"I should let you burn." Sir Jayel grasped the sorcerer's arm and yanked him out.

"Remove this damn collar." Grimshaw wheezed, then coughed up black sputum.

"Disgusting." I turned my head, and spotted Juliana and Santurin running towards us. "We'll wait for the king."

Grimshaw kicked my shin. I bent over to rub my leg and he kneed me in the chin.

"Feel my pain, little prince," he snarled.

"You prick. I ought to rip your throat out," I said. "Sir Jayel, get a better hold on him." My chin felt like one huge bruise.

Sir Jayel wrestled the sorcerer to the ground and sat on him.

"Get your fat ass off me. I can't breathe," Grimshaw said.

"Hmm, sounds like a personal problem." Sir Jayel laughed.

Santurin squatted down by Mother. "Are you all, right?"

"Yes, thanks to Aidan." Mother coughed. "See to those people locked in their cells."

Santurin handed his keys to Sir Edrei. "Keep the scientists shackled but get them out of their cells. Anyone know how the fire started?"

"Yes, Sire. It was Tiana." Juliana explained the circumstances.

"Where is she?" Santurin asked.

"I don't know, Sire," Juliana said.

"I expected your mother to guard the girl. Rules must be followed, or chaos runs afoot." Santurin's brows furrowed as he scanned the area.

"I imagine my mother is with Olivia, Sire. May I escort the queen to her chambers? She hasn't been well," Juliana said.

Santurin nodded. Juliana wrapped her arm around the queen's waist and Mother leaned her head on Juliana's shoulder. They strolled back inside the fortress.

"Sir Edrei, scout the territory for the wayward girl, Tiana. She had a chance at a normal life, yet she forsake it for revenge." Santurin punched his palm.

Sir Edrei bowed, then strode off.

"Both Mother and Grimshaw suffered smoke inhalation from the fire. They're lucky I got to them in time," I said to my brother. "Tiana had tied Juliana to a chair when she kidnapped Mother. It's not like Lady Darshana abandoning her duty. Perhaps Tiana did something to her?"

"What about my collar?" Grimshaw interrupted us.

"Until things are under control, it stays on," I said.

"You'll pay for my mistreatment, little prince," Grimshaw spat. "I promise you; I'll do more than strike you next time." Grimshaw mumbled something unclear.

Out of the cracks in the dirt, hundreds of red ants swarmed my legs. Painful, stinging bites burned and itched. I grabbed the hose and doused them.

"What's the matter? Don't like my games? Poor Aidan. Always your brother's underling and never a king." Grimshaw's eyes glimmered.

I turned the hose on him and watched the sorcerer sputter.

"Hey! You're getting me wet too." Sir Jayel frowned.

"Get off the sorcerer, Sir Jayel. No time to spare on building another jailhouse. Line the prisoners to the gallows," Santurin announced.

Sir Jayel stood and pulled the sorcerer to his feet. Grimshaw gulped in air. Sir Jayel strode off to do the king's bidding, while Santurin and I grasped Grimshaw's arms, leading him to the gallows.

I understood my brother's position, but his decision seemed hasty. We couldn't chance the prisoners escaping though. The scientists were too smart for their own good. Who knows what else they'd throw at the kingdom? Their hatred had grown for years.

Sir Jayel and his men paraded the prisoners to the gallows. Their chains rattled as they duck-walked to their doom. We steered the sorcerer in front of the gallows and halted.

"See the fate of your comrades?" Santurin said.

"Am I supposed to fear it?" Grimshaw asked.

"Do something!" one of the scientists called to the sorcerer.

"It's out of my hands." Grimshaw shrugged.

Santurin signaled the executioner. One by one, the scientists walked up the stairs of the wooden platform across from the infirmary. They climbed atop a wooden box in front of their nooses.

The high priest stood next to the executioner. "Anyone care to confess?"

The prisoners refused to answer.

"May the goddess have mercy on your wicked souls." The high priest nodded to the executioner.

Nooses flung around the prisoners' necks. The boxes kicked from their feet, the scientists dangled by their ropes, gasping for air, and their faces purple. I whipped my head away and Grimshaw laughed.

I leaned in his face. "You don't want to mess with me, or I'll tighten that collar."

"Not a wuss after all." Grimshaw smirked.

Santurin and I dragged the sorcerer to the infirmary. Grimshaw never shed an ounce of remorse over the fate of his cohorts. Pity the man that befriends him.

The infirmary stood downwind from the gallows and not far from the jailhouse. A set of healers ran the place for injured and sick soldiers and prisoners. Groans and cries emanated from inside.

"You're not leaving me here with these wimps, are you?" Grimshaw asked.

"Shut up." I shoved him inside the stark-white building. The odor of bleach and antiseptic irritated my nose.

Dressed in white robes and a winged cap, a healer ushered us to a spare room.

Santurin told her the circumstances. I pushed the sorcerer onto the empty bed and strapped his ankles in leather restraints. I rolled him over and Santurin removed the handcuffs. The sorcerer rubbed his wrists. I placed a leather waist restraint around him.

Santurin snatched one arm and moved it above Grimshaw's head. He snapped a leather strap on the sorcerer's arm and locked it in place through the headboard. I strapped his other arm to the bed rail.

I raised my palm over Grimshaw and wove a spell. "Not a word of magic may he speak, nor matter if he's weak. Grimshaw can't be trusted, this we found, and my choice is to keep him bound." I released the collar.

Grimshaw jerked his restraints, yet they held. A deep cough was issued from him. One of the healers offered him some water. He drank it and swirled the water around his mouth. He spit the contents in my face.

"Real adult of you." I grabbed a towel off the nightstand and dabbed my face.

"Let the sorcerer stew a while," Santurin said. "I'll post a guard near him."

We walked outside and Sir Edrei strode over.

"What do you want me to do with her, Sire?" Sir Edrei held on to Tiana's arm as she struggled.

"Take her to the executioner," Santurin said.

Sir Edrei stiffened. "But, but Your Majesty… she's so young."

"It doesn't matter her age. Tiana attempted murder on the queen, my mother. Do you dare usurp my authority?"

"No, Sire." Sir Edrei shook his head.

"You mean the queen still lives?" Tiana asked.

"Barely. No thanks to you," I blurted.

Tiana twisted her arm as Sir Edrei clutched her tighter. He pulled her towards the gallows.

"I'll haunt you all!" she seethed.

"Leave Aidan. I'll bear witness to her execution," Santurin said.

I rushed inside the fortress. It was hard enough to watch the hanging of the scientists. My stomach flip- flopped, thinking of someone I knew hanging from a noose. Circumstances might differ if Grimshaw hadn't harmed Damira. *Where was Lady Darshana anyway?*

I rushed upstairs to Mother's chambers and rapped on the door. The door slid open, and Juliana stood in the entrance way.

"I've sent for the doctor. The Queen's cough worsened," Juliana said.

I followed behind Juliana to my mother's bed. Her face flushed, perspiration beaded on Mother's upper lip and forehead. Her cough rattled in her chest. I knelt by her bedside and held Mother's hand.

She turned glazed eyes on me. "My boy, you were meant for something great. Santurin needs your intellect and powers to guide him as king. He may not see it yet, but he will. I'm afraid my time is limited." Mother wheezed and coughed. "Forgive me for sending your twin brother away. At the time, I couldn't fathom raising a deformed child. Cosmo is a part of you.

Together, your powers are double fold. Remember that." Mother kissed my hand.

She closed her eyes. I brushed Mother's hair away from her face. Doctor Panphilia hurried inside with her medical bag and Juliana walked behind her.

"Mother had a cold, and then suffered smoke inhalation from a fire. Can you give her something for her cough?" I asked.

The doctor listened to Mother's lungs and heart. She lifted Mother's eyelids and shook her head. "I'm sorry, but it's too late. She's gone. You should have called me sooner. I suspect she had fluid around her heart or possibly pneumonia. The smoke inhalation increased her condition. Nothing I can do for her now." Doctor Panphilia collected her things.

"But Mother was talking to me, before you came in. She can't be dead." I shook Mother's shoulders. "Wake up! Tell the doctor you're only sleeping."

Mother didn't budge. I punched the headboard.

"Let me see your hand." Doctor Panphilia applied a bandage over my bleeding knuckles. "I'll type up the death certificate and notify the king." She strode out of the room.

I ran my fingers through my hair. "This isn't happening." Juliana embraced me and I cried on her shoulder. I pulled back moments later. "Make her more respectable, before the others see her." I wiped my eyes.

"I'll take care of things. Go to the king. He'll need you." Tears welled in Juliana's eyes.

"You've been a great friend and the best of Mother's handmaidens. What will you do now?" I asked her.

Juliana shrugged. "Don't worry about me. Go."

I stole a last look at Mother and stifled a sob, biting my fist, before walking out the door.

Santurin raced to the door and grasped my shoulders. "Is it true?"

"Yes," I croaked out. I hugged him tight, and Santurin burst into tears.

After some time, he pushed my hands away and wiped his tears. Santurin entered Mother's chambers. I walked to the elevator and pushed the button. When the doors opened, I trekked inside, and pounded the walls of the elevator. I slumped to the floor and wept. The doors closed and the elevator zoomed down to the first floor. The elevator dinged and the doors opened, but I remained on the floor.

One of Mother's handmaidens stared at me. "Did you lose something?" Rashida asked.

"Yes." I covered my face. My shoulders shook as sobs wracked me. It was too much. *First, Father murdered and now Mother gone, all thanks to Grimshaw's schemes. How many more must suffer because of the sorcerer?*

Chapter Thirty-One

DARK, LOW-BROODING CLOUDS MATCHED MY MOOD. I stared at the remnants of the jailhouse. The wind circulated the ashes and irritated my eyes. I blinked several times. Grimshaw was as much to blame as Tiana for Mother's death. What if there were clones of Grimshaw? None of us searched the underground building of Fallow. Someone tapped my shoulder, and I turned around.

Rashida curtsied. "My Prince, it's time."

For a moment, I was confused. "Time?"

"Remember, the funeral procession?" she said.

I wiped my hand down my face. "Right." I followed the handmaiden to the garden area. Mother lay on a bed of balsam over a wooden casket. Her hair fanned behind her on a satin pillow. A thin, gold crown adorned her head. Her cheeks tinted with pink rouge and her lips stained with berry juice, Mother looked elegant in a royal blue gown, yet peaceful. I placed some wildflowers in her hand and flinched at her coldness. Mother appeared asleep. I leaned in to kiss her and that's when it struck me. The make-up didn't cover the unnatural gray of her skin. I bit my fist. She was truly gone. I'll never hear her voice again. She believed in me when I didn't know myself. I swiped at the tears raining down my face.

Cosmo, Sir Jayel, Clay, and I lifted the handles of Mother's casket. Her handmaidens formed a line behind us. Santurin and Mori rode in motorized thrones. The rest of the kingdom followed behind them, including villagers from the other cities.

We paraded to the end of the property where the mausoleum stood. We set the casket down on the marble path.

The high priest lit a bundle of sage and waved it over Mother. "Willow Zavion Azure, queen mother to us all, we grieve the loss of your passing, yet we wallow in the strength you gave us. We honor you with a ceremony. May those that have gone before us, guide you on your spiritual journey." He plunged the burning bundle in a bucket. The priest nodded to the archers as he moved out of the way.

A young lad beat a drum. Yvonne and Ulric dipped their arrows in oil. Sir Edrei lit a match and touched the tips of the arrows. They burst into flame. The archers shot their arrows at the balsam, and it caught fire. Sylvia broke out in song in the forest-dweller's language. I didn't understand all the words, but Mother sang it when Dad died. It talked about how we'll meet again. I shivered and rubbed my arms up and down. Cosmo gazed at me. *Did he feel it too?* I swore Mother's spirit walked among us.

After the song ended, I informed Sylvia of Grimshaw's involvement during the war and the incidents following with Tiana. "He's in the infirmary in locked restraints. Any suggestions what we should do with him?"

Sylvia tapped her chin. "I sense your twin has powers. It might work if we combine his powers with yours and mine."

"What's your idea?" I asked.

"Trap him in a dark mirror world," she said.

"How?" I arched my brows.

"Find a mirror large enough to push him through. Once Grimshaw is inside, write his name on the outside of the mirror. It seals him in. Stay out of his reach though or he'll pull you in with him."

"What's in there?" I dared to ask.

"A world of grays and darkness. Slithery and unspeakable things roam in it. Not a place I'd like." Sylvia shuddered. "I'll stay in the guest room tonight. On the morrow, we'll do the deed. Agreed?"

"Can you stay?" I asked Cosmo.

"I planned on staying for the coronation. Sleeping over works for me," Cosmo said.

"Good. We're agreed." I nodded.

Astra put her arms around Cosmo and my shoulders. "Keeping secrets?"

"Sylvia gave us some advice. Are you staying here for the coronation?" I asked.

"Negative. Mori doesn't like me, besides the king asked me to escort Lady Darshana to Meadowlark. He's upset with her for not keeping close tabs on Tiana. Mori expects me to take Juliana away too. She doesn't want the girl around her husband." Astra glanced at her nails.

"Petty jealousy."

"Where was Lady Darshana?" I asked.

"Tiana dropped something in Lady Darshana's tea. Sir Edrei found her sleeping on the chess table in the main lounge." Astra snickered. "Can you imagine? Most embarrassing. Anyhow, did you know Mori gave Juliana two choices?"

I shook my head.

"Either marry an eligible male or join her mother in banishment." Astra scrunched her nose. "Stupid girl. She chose the latter. I don't get it. Juliana could pick any man she wanted. Mori also gave me my freedom. I plan to live on Meadowlark."

Cosmo clapped. "Wonderful news! I'll have friends and family around."

"Are you riding with us?" Astra asked.

"Aidan and I are spending some time together. You don't mind?" Cosmo asked.

"Whatever. I'm out of here." Astra stormed away.

"I believe she's jealous. I don't know why." Cosmo scratched his head.

"Astra wants everything her own way or she has a fit. Don't let it bother you," I said.

The people parted and strolled back to the fortress. Mori led the way. A mausoleum drawer with Mother's name stood ajar. Santurin and Sylvia scooped up Mother's ashes and placed them in a box inside the drawer.

I thought, *maybe it eased my brother's conscience? He could have delegated it to a servant.*

Cosmo and I followed the line of people.

"Did Juliana tell you she was leaving Azure?" I asked.

"No, maybe it embarrassed her about her mother's banishment and all," Cosmo said.

"Probably." My thoughts wavered. *With the deaths of Tiana and Monica, and now Astra and Juliana leaving Azure, only two of the original handmaidens remained. The rest of Mother's handmaidens married.*

"Anything you want to share? You're deep in thought," Cosmo said.

"Nothing important. Mori requires new handmaidens," I said.

"Let me guess. You have one in mind?" Cosmo asked.

"What do you think about Yvonne? A handmaid position raises a girl's stature," I said.

"She's rough around the edges," Cosmo said. "Can you picture her in a gown? She seems more geared to a tomboy, but you know her better than I do."

"She'd protect the queen better than some wimpy gal afraid of breaking a nail. Never mind. Tell me about the day Grimshaw hurt Damira," I said.

"Something snapped inside me after he killed her. I can't explain it, but a soft, musical voice told me to think of a peaceful place," Cosmo said. "I lay on the floor and Grimshaw kicked me in the ribs. He called me horrible names. I visualized the soothing rhythm of the river, and a warm light filled me. I changed into liquid." Cosmo glanced away for a moment. "I pooled across the floor and Grimshaw jumped up on a chair to protect his feet. I floated out the door and down the embankment to the river. Once there, I transformed into a sea creature and swam around the river. The voice told me not to fear the inevitable. The goddess gave me special powers because I am one of the chosen ones, a child of light. I own the power of healing, but I also transform at will. Together, you and I are stronger. We're two halves of a whole." Cosmo grinned.

"Great. Together, we'll rid the kingdom of Grimshaw. Come on," I said.

We hastened into the main lounge. People stood around and reminisced stories about Mother. Cosmo stopped and listened, as if he couldn't get enough information about her. It wasn't fair he never got to know her.

I, on the other hand, felt chilled, as though death swaddled me. Unable to shake it,

I grabbed a mug of hot cider and welcomed its warmth. *Was Mother with me?*

I glanced at the platters of roasted beef. Food wasn't appetizing to me, but Cosmo filled his plate. He grabbed a piece of sweet potato pie and a dollop of whipped cream. He shoveled the pie in his mouth before we found our seat.

"Sorry, but it called my name. So-o-o good," Cosmo said.

The simplest things delighted him. I asked, "What do you like to do for fun?"

"Living on Fallow, I had little free time." Cosmo sat down at the table and ate his food.

I wanted to know more about him, but it wasn't the right time. He had a rough life compared to me. I sat next to Cosmo and stared into space. Everything seemed different without Mother around. I looked at the assembly of people. They ate the food, but grief weighed on their shoulders. It was depressing. Mother sang, while the musicians played at father's funeral. I slapped my napkin down and stood up.

"Join in if you know the words. Mother taught me this song when I was little." I burst into song about a bird finding its way through the gloom of the clouds.

The others sang along and clapped when it ended. Tears stained my cheeks. I raced down the hall afterwards.

Cosmo chased me down. "Wait!"

I twirled around. "Sorry, everything hit me at once." I wiped my face with my hanky.

"Come with me."

We ran up the stairs to the ancestral hall. I flipped the switch and the hall lit up.

Cosmo whirled around and gazed at each hologram. "Are these all our ancestors?"

"Yes." I recited each name and the history of the individual like I did with Astra. I paused at the last hologram. "This was our father, King Arin. Mother was a bit superstitious and refused to have her hologram displayed until she passed away."

Cosmo stood on his tiptoes and peered closer. "I see the resemblance, but the clones don't do him justice."

"Mori and Santurin posed for theirs but wanted to wait until after the coronation to add their holograms with the others," I said.

"What about us? We should get ours done together," Cosmo said.

"I'll ask Santurin," I said.

"What about Astra?"

"Santurin won't allow it. Astra is a product of an affair, and he doesn't want it flaunted."

"With that logic, I shouldn't be on the ancestral wall either." Cosmo frowned. "I was only a baby and our mother wanted me dead."

"Mother was under duress. First, her husband had an affair, then you're born with a disfigurement. In all sense of the word, you were Damira's son. She loved you with all her heart. Astra also had a mother. Veda raised her as her own. Don't you see? The goddess took care of us, and we turned out okay," I said.

"When you think of it that way…" Cosmo smiled.

"We have each other," I said.

A horn blew and announced the coronation ceremony. We rushed to the west tower room.

A blue carpet lined the aisle and chairs stood on each side of it. High Priest Reynard waited on a platform behind Mori and Santurin. Mori wore a cream-tiered gown anointed with a royal blue cloak. Her hair bound in pretzel braids; gold lace earrings adorned her earlobes. Her back was rigid, and she pushed her shoulders back, and lifted her chin. Santurin wore a cream shirt with cobalt blue breeches. Wrapped over his shoulders, he wore a blue cloak.

Everyone sought their seats. Cosmo and I took our seats up front. The room hushed as the high priest raised his arms.

The high priest said, "We come today to celebrate Mori, daughter of Sylvia Zavion on her coronation as Queen of Azure and to officially coronate her husband, Santurin Azure as King." He nodded to Olivia, Juliana's sister.

Olivia carried a satin pillow with a gold crown atop it. Gems of tanzanite sparkled from it. She walked up the two steps to the platform and halted in front of the priest.

He picked up the crown and hovered it over Mori's head. "I crown thee, Queen Mori Zavion Azure." The high priest placed the crown on her head.

Everyone stood and called out, "Hail, almighty queen!"

Santurin handed Mori a bouquet of roses and she smiled. Sir Edrei carried another satin pillow, with a gold crown upon it, up the stairs. High priest Reynard picked up the crown and held it over Santurin's head.

"I dub thee, King Santurin Azure." High priest Reynard placed the crown on Santurin's head.

Cosmo and I whistled and clapped.

"Hail, almighty king!" the people shouted.

"It's about time," Sir Jayel said.

Rashida and Imani picked up the tails of Mori's cloak and she held her head erect, strolling down the aisle to the applause of the people. Santurin's valet and mine picked up the tails of Santurin's cloak and followed behind the queen. They walked into the hallway and down to the reception room. Someone had placed their thrones inside it. Mori and Santurin sat down.

My valet, Jarvis, stood on Santurin's left and Olivia stood on Mori's right. A line of welcome wishers approached with gifts. Cosmo stood in the line. When it was his turn, Cosmo handed Olivia a tissue-wrapped box. She placed it in Mori's hands.

Mori opened it, and her eyes lit up at the intricate metal box. She ran her hand over it. She opened the box and gasped. She pulled the delicate chain out. On it, hung a pair of swans carved from wood and polished until smooth.

"Beautiful. A rare talent you possess. Thank you, Prince Cosmo," Mori gushed.

"My pleasure, My Queen." Cosmo bowed.

I whispered, "That's what you do for fun."

Cosmo blushed. He handed a wrapped gift to Jarvis to give to Santurin.

"This was unexpected." Santurin ripped off the paper. Inside was a wooden name plate with Santurin's name carved on it. He ran his hand over the polished wood. "I agree with my wife. You have a great talent, Cosmo. I shall place it on my office desk. Thank you."

Cosmo bowed and walked away. I strode over to Olivia and handed her my gift. She gave it to Mori.

Mori tore the wrapping off. In the bottom of the box, was a book on plants, but on top of it, wrapped in tissue, I placed a brooch in the shape of a palette with colored gems of paint."

"Lovely," Mori said.

"Would you consider Yvonne of Zavion as one of your handmaidens?" I asked.

"Although it's true I need more handmaidens, I prefer to pick my own. I'll consider your suggestion though, Prince Aidan."

"As you wish." I nodded. Not sure if Santurin would approve of it, I handed his gift to Jarvis.

Santurin unwrapped the box. Inside, lied a book on baby names plus a book on how to raise children. Santurin chuckled. "Something I can use. Thank you, Aidan. A well thought out gift."

I bowed and left the west tower room in search of Cosmo.

Chapter Thirty-Two

COSMO STUFFED HIS FACE WITH ANOTHER PIECE OF sweet potato pie. I sat down next to him in the reception room.

"Hey, I'm sorry if I embarrassed you. It's great you have a natural talent," I said.

"When I gathered metals and wood for the scientists, sometimes I wasted time by carving things out of the extra pieces. I had no one my age to talk with and it kept me occupied," Cosmo said. "I'm delighted you liked my work." Cosmo pointed at the pie. "Best item on the menu."

"You're going to get fat if all you eat are sweets." I chuckled. "In Mother's chambers is a large vanity mirror. I figure it'd work for our plans. When you're done eating, we'll take a walk there."

Cosmo shoved the last forkful of pie in his mouth. "Ready."

We strolled out of the room and walked down the stairs to the second floor. We strode down the hall to Mother's chambers. To my surprise, the door stood open. We walked in and I couldn't believe it. Olivia, Rashida, and Imani packed up Mother's things. Anger boiled in the pit of my gut.

"Mother is barely gone, and you're cleaning out her room?" I shouted.

"Queen Mori sent us here to organize it," Olivia said.

"How dare she. It's up to Mother's children to go through her things, not the next queen." Aidan whirled around as he felt someone behind him.

Mori stiffened and her lips pressed into a firm line. "These are my new chambers as the new queen. The girls followed my orders. They boxed what I won't use of your mother's things. They'll store them away. Were you searching for something special, Prince Aidan?"

"I'm keeping the mirror and anything else I want, regardless of your position. I'm sure Santurin will agree with me." I narrowed my eyes, daring her to deny me.

"Come, ladies. We'll do this another time when the prince has calmed down." Mori gestured to them to leave the room.

When Mori and her handmaidens were out of sight, Cosmo spoke. "Her intentions were good. Mori sought to relieve you and Santurin from the burden. Take some mementos, before we move the mirror."

"It felt like an invasion. It surprised me to see them in here." I opened a drawer and found an envelope with my name written on it. I slit it open. A ring fell into my hand, and I held it up to the light. Leaves scrolled around the silver ring. A tanzanite bird with topaz eyes and a small nest centered the ring. It was beautiful and worthy of Yvonne. I pocketed the ring, then smoothed out a note included with it, and read it.

Aidan, this was your grandmother's ring. She asked me to save this for your bride. She saw your future and encouraged me to hire the best scholars for you. You'll need your brain to survive whatever lies ahead. Good luck, Mother.

I shoved the note in my pocket.

"I love craftmanship," Cosmo ran his hand over the mirror's wooden frame.

"Father carved the branches that entwine the frame. You must get your talent from him. What do you think? Is it big enough?" I asked.

"Perfect. Let's move it out of this chamber," Cosmo suggested.

"Good idea. I don't trust Mori. Her power has gone to her head. Let me look around here first." I hit the switch on the side of the closet and the door slid open. Removing some silk garments, I inhaled Mother's perfume that lingered, then covered the mirror with them. I knelt on the carpet and opened Mother's chest. The aroma of cedar filled my nose. I fingered old baby clothes of Santurin's and mine. An old, worn book lay underneath them and a red ribbon marked a page. I flipped it over. Pressed inside was a dandelion I gave Mother when I was five.

"I can't believe she kept it all these years." Tears sprung to my eyes. I shut the book and placed it inside my cloak pocket. "I've seen enough."

We wheeled the mirror to the elevator. I hit the down button. When the doors opened, we pushed the mirror inside the elevator.

"Basement," I spoke into the intercom.

The elevator zoomed down. The doors opened in the basement, and we faced a wall of tuff stone; volcanic ash compacted into solid rock. We wheeled the mirror close to the wall.

"We'll leave the mirror here, until Sylvia joins us, then we'll move it to one of the corridors," I said, covering the mirror with Mother's garments.

"All right," Cosmo agreed.

"What if Grimshaw left some clones inside Fallow? No one searched the building after the war," I said.

"I don't like that creepy place," Cosmo said. "The lab isn't far from the door at the end of this corridor."

"Relax. Together we are stronger, remember?" I said.

We walked down the corridor until we stood in front of the door.

"Someone fixed the door." I wiggled the knob, and the door opened. "Come on."

Cosmo held my cloak tail and followed my lead into the darkness.

I stopped in the middle of the path and listened. "What's that noise?"

"Someone left the tanks on. I recognize the pump," Cosmo said. "It connects to the water tank the clones float in. It's up ahead."

Vapors formed in the air. Mildew and something rotten punctuated the chamber and mixed with the coppery taste of blood. Nearly complete, a clone of Grimshaw floated inside a tank of water. A tube connected to his belly button. Cosmo pressed a lever down on the side of the tank. The water seeped out and down a drain in the floor. The clone gasped for air.

Cosmo pulled on some rubber gloves and reached inside the tank. He disconnected the tube to the clone.

I scanned the lab for a weapon of some kind. A sickle hung from a string on a bulletin board. Above it, a sign said, *for emergencies*. I grabbed it and raised the sickle above the clone.

His eyes snapped open. "Please—help me."

I paused with my indecision. The sickle wavered. My mind feuded with thoughts of whether he felt things like a human.

"Pathetic weakling," the clone sneered. "You don't have the guts."

Grasping the clone's hair, I hacked the head off, then I dropped the sickle. It clanged to the floor. I tossed the head and backed up. Revulsion at what I had done, I turned away, and vomited. I wiped my mouth on my sleeve.

"Disgusting," Cosmo said.

"My anger got the best of me. We don't know if the clone possessed magic like Grimshaw or not. One less thing to worry about." I pointed my hand at the head and set it on fire. Grabbing a mop, I wiped up my vomit.

"You know clones don't contain souls. That's the difference between humans and them," Cosmo said, before he walked over to a table with microscopes. He grabbed a box of test tubes marked with King Arin and Cosmo's names. "What do you want me to do with these tubes?"

"Destroy them," I said.

Cosmo smashed the glass tubes on the floor. When he finished, Cosmo glanced my way. "Can we leave?"

We trekked back the way we came. I opened the door, and we headed down the corridor back to Azure. The rank from the clone and my vomit penetrated my nose. I pulled off my stained shirt and rolled it inside my cloak. We strolled further down the corridor until we reached the elevator. I hit the up button. The doors opened, and we strode inside.

"First floor," I said into the intercom.

We arrived at our destination, and I turned to Cosmo, "Find Sylvia and inform her about the mirror. I'll change clothes and meet you in the main lounge."

Cosmo left my side, and I strolled down the long hallway to my chambers.

Removing my things from my cloak, I handed my valet, Jarvis, a bundle of filthy clothes. "Give these to the laundress. I'm taking a shower." I walked inside the bathroom and wrapped the book, ring, and note from Mother in an extra towel. Hopping in the shower, I scrubbed the nasty smell off me with a lather of sandalwood soap. I rinsed off and climbed out.

Jarvis placed a fresh set of clothes on my bed. "Anything else, My Prince?"

"No. You're free the rest of the day," I said.

"As you wish." Jarvis bowed, then walked out the door.

I strolled back inside the bathroom and retrieved the towel with the book, ring, and note. Removing the box from the floorboard underneath my bed, I placed the ring, Mother's note, and the book inside it, then shoved it back in place. After Grimshaw had invaded my room, I hid important things away. Pulling on my clothes, I hurried out the door, and strode down the long hallway to the main lounge.

Sylvia, seated on the red couch near the artificial gas fireplace, stood as I approached her.

"This room reminds me of your father. He was full of energy and life, and everyone flocked to him. And now your mother gone too." She shook her head.

"Yes, not the best year," I said.

Silence surrounded us.

Eager to switch topics, I asked her, "Did Cosmo show you the mirror?"

"Yes, it's perfect. Here he comes now. I asked him for a drink," Sylvia said.

Cosmo strolled inside and handed the glass of water to Sylvia. She drank half of it, before placing the glass on the coffee table. She pulled a paper from her pocket and gave it to me.

"I've written down a spell. When Grimshaw stands in front of the mirror, all three of us say the words together. Understood?" Sylvia asked.

"Yes," Cosmo and I chorused.

"Good. After we say the spell, motion with your hands like you're pushing him, but we don't physically touch Grimshaw. Once he's inside the dark mirror world, one of you writes his name on the mirror. Got it?"

We nodded.

"Prince Aidan, tell security to bring the sorcerer to the basement," Sylvia said.

"I'll talk to Sir Jayel. He hates Grimshaw as much as I do. Meet us in the basement." I glanced at the spell and memorized the words, before giving the paper to Cosmo.

Sylvia and Cosmo headed to the elevator, while I trekked outside to the security building.

Tano polished an airship and gazed up as my shadow fell over him.

"Hey, Your Prince-ship. How can I help you?"

"I'm searching for Sir Jayel."

"He's guarding the sorcerer at the infirmary. Grimshaw spit his morning meal in Matt's face and the lad decked him. Sir Jayel told him to go cool off," Tano said.

"Do I know Matt?" I asked.

"Nah. He's fresh meat from Volney. Sir Edrei picked him and another fella. Said they had potential for soldier material. Both are tall, slender athletic youths. Are you executing the sorcerer?" Tano wiped sweat from his forehead with a cloth.

"No. Something far worse. Excuse me." I hiked back across the ramp, then down the hillside towards the infirmary. My thoughts plagued me on the way across the lawn. When Sylvia first broached the subject of the dark mirror world, I researched through the books she loaned me. One man survived the ordeal, and his notes filled an entire chapter. He talked of a dark world filled with the lowest of creatures and vile things. Nothing grew in that world. He never admitted how he escaped, but he survived by eating cockroaches. Disgusting.

A woman, dressed in a white headdress and the uniform of the healers, dumped a pan of water outside the infirmary doors. I bypassed her and walked inside the building. The place reeked of bleach and the walls were painted in a bright white color. I strode straight to the sorcerer's room.

Sir Jayel jumped up when he saw me. "My Prince, you require my services?"

"Hmm, the goody-two-shoe prince graces me with a visit. How utterly dull."

Grimshaw rolled his eyes. He remained stretched out in leather restraints.

"Unlock his arms," I ordered.

Grimshaw rubbed his wrists after the restraints left his arms. He slapped a full urinal off his nightstand and saturated me with his piss. The sorcerer boomed with laughter. Sir Jayel knocked him out. I wiped my face and shirt with a towel at the end of Grimshaw's bed.

"How do you expect me to get him to the fortress in that condition?" I asked.

"I'll carry the bastard." Sir Jayel released the restraints from Grimshaw's waist and legs.

He heaved the sorcerer over his shoulder. "For a skinny guy, Grimshaw ain't a lightweight. Good thing I worked out this morning."

I led the way back to the fortress and felt thankful for Sir Jayel's muscles. I'd probably dump the sorcerer in a wagon and haul him inside. I'd make sure he felt every bump too. The fortress doors opened, and we walked inside, and down the long hallway to the elevator. I pressed the down button.

"You're going to the bowels of the fortress, My Prince? Not much there, you know," Sir Jayel said. "You're leaving him for the bugs and rodents to feed on?" He laughed and his round belly jiggled.

The elevator doors opened, and we walked inside. Out of the corner of my vision, I caught movement. I whirled, but it was too late. Grimshaw plucked Sir Jayel's dagger from his belt and stabbed him in the back.

"The wily bastard got me. Sorry, My Prince. Save yourself." Sir Jayel's legs buckled.

I leaned against the intercom button. "You'll regret stabbing Sir Jayel."

Grimshaw stepped close and held the dagger against my throat. Sir Jayel's blood dripped from it. "A thousand things I'd love to do. Killing you is too damn easy though." The sorcerer ran his finger across the blade and licked the blood. "A good source of protein, don't you think?" Grimshaw chuckled at the revulsion on my face.

"You won't get away with this," I said.

"When my father left Twyla and me, I scrounged for food and coin. I promised my sister when I became king, she'd be my queen, and we'd never be poor again. You took her from me."

Grimshaw glared at me.

"I can't do anything about Twyla now, but the kingdom is rightfully mine since I married your mother." Grimshaw sliced off one of my ears. "I've heard human flesh is an acquired taste."

I screeched and held the side of my head, blood seeping through my fingers. *What will Yvonne think of her prince? First, I lost my front teeth on the manhood journey and now an ear.*

The elevator doors opened. Sylvia and Cosmo stood on each side of the elevator. The mirror faced the opening. Alarm etched Grimshaw's face.

Together, the three of us chanted the spell: "We summon the strength to release you from our presence. We cast you out to live your days in darkness. We cast you out that you won't harm us nor others dear to us. We cast you out, Grimshaw of Fallow, for all your greed and evil deeds." We raised our hands. "Begone from us, into the mirror world, for there is nothing further to discuss."

"What sick joke is this?" Grimshaw asked.

Afraid he might slip from our grasp; I butted my head into the sorcerer's stomach. He fell into the mirror and the magic sucked him inside. I cringed as phantoms called out to me and quickly wrote Grimshaw's name with a piece of charcoal across the mirror and trapped him inside.

Chapter Thirty-Three

Six days later

I SHOT UP IN BED AND SCANNED MY CHAMBERS. THIS was the sixth night I woke up terrified, after we trapped Grimshaw inside the dark mirror world. I swore he would call me, but that was impossible, unless we underestimated the sorcerer's powers and intelligence. Either that or I'm insane. I covered the mirrors in my chambers. Granted, I never saw his face in them, yet I feared he lingered between the two worlds. After all, he practiced in the dark arts. I searched through my dresser, under my bed, and inside my closet, but nothing appeared out of the ordinary.

I promised Sylvia's son. Gus a cloud-board of his own. Wiley said he'd help me make one for Gus. Eager to begin, I pulled on my clothes, then brushed my hair, before racing out of my room and down the long hallway. I took the elevator to the third floor.

The doors opened and I strode past the west tower room and to the back of the fortress. I stood in front of the wooden door and pressed the intercom button. Minutes later, Wiley opened the door and waved me inside.

"I cut the decks out of the wood while I waited for you." Wiley led me to the back of the room. He handed me some protective goggles and I pulled them on.

"The nose and the tail of the deck points up and the flat center rests on the surface. Today, we're going to use grip tape. It's faster and less messy than paint." Wiley handed me a roll. "Lay it over the board, before peeling the back side off and exposing the adhesive. You want to cover the entire board."

I followed his instructions. "All right. Now what?"

"Peel off the backing and smooth it out. Press down any air pockets. Start in the middle and move outward towards the end. Cut off any excess tape, then sand the edges." Wiley gave me some sandpaper.

I laid the sandpaper on his desk while I pressed out the air bubbles. When I finished, I sanded it down.

"Okay, punch some holes through the grip tape for the connections of the ankle clasps." Wiley pointed to the areas for them. When I finished, he said, "Attach the bearings and clasps through the holes." Wiley got out an EEG headset and some wraparound lights. He waited for me, then hooked up the lights to the cloud-board. Wiley handed me the headset. "Try it out first, before you give it to your little friend."

I shook Wiley's hand. "I appreciate this. If you need anything, let me know."

Wiley walked me back to the door and I carried the cloud-board under my arm. I rushed down the hallway, then raced down the stairs, instead of waiting for an elevator.

Hastening outside, I stood on the cloud-board and applied the EEG headset. Green lights circulated around the board and the clasps hooked around my ankles. The cloud-board lifted, and I soared over the river towards the security building. I whipped back around and flew over the top of the Harmony Waterfalls, and then zoomed back to the security building's roof and landed. I removed the headset and the clasps on my ankles released me. *Gus will love it.*

I walked inside the airship hangar and snatched my key-bob off the rack. Signing my name next to my airship number and the destination per procedure, I unlocked my airship.

I placed the cloud-board with its EEG headset on the passenger seat before I climbed inside the pilot seat. Engaging the airship across the track, I sailed into the afternoon sky. The first lift always tickled my stomach until it evened out. The hum of the crystals energized the airship, as I headed northeast.

I flew over herds of elk in a clearing between the trees. Two bucks lowered their heads and rammed their antlers into each other. The rest of the herd moved out of their way. I veered left and soared over trees. By horseback, it took two to three days from Azure to Zavion. By airship, the time narrowed to two to three hours instead.

The further I traveled; the trees thickened for miles. Up ahead, the jagged teeth of the Fang Mountains came into view. I searched for an open field on Zavion. Shifting gears, the wheels lowered, and I glided the airship in for a landing.

I grabbed my gift and climbed out. Gus, Sylvia's ten-year-old son, waved as he met me half-way on the path.

"Is that for me?" His eyes widened into huge discs.

"Whatever are you talking about?" I feigned ignorance.

"In your arm, My Prince." Gus blew a dark curl from his forehead.

I raised the cloud-board up to my level. "You mean this?"

Gus nodded his head.

"Then you don't want the EEG headset that goes with it?" I asked.

Gus tried to grab it out of my hands.

"Hold on. Let me explain everything, before you fly off," I said.

Gus pouted.

"Put on your headset first," I said.

"Now what?" Gus smiled so wide; I thought his teeth might break.

"Stand on the board and tell it where to go. You control the cloud-board with your brain waves. Give it a try." I backed up.

Gus followed my instructions and soared around me. "Wahoo! Look at me."

"Watch out for the trees!" I yelled.

Gus zipped in between the trees and above them without fear. He was natural.

"I'm going to Yvonne's. Did you want to come or are you all right on your own?"

"How do I stop, My Prince?" Gus called. Worry lines marked his forehead.

"Remember you control it. Tell the cloud-board when you want to stop, and it will. Remove the headset when you're done." I hummed and strolled along, while Gus flew above me.

When I passed by Sylvia's hut, she nodded to me, until she saw her son in the air. Sylvia dropped her clippers. Dead flower heads lied at her feet.

"Look at me, Ma!" Gus called.

Sylvia said, "Son, get down!"

"I fulfilled my promise to Gus. He's having fun," I said. "He controls the cloud-board by using his brain."

"Does it damage his brain?" Sylvia asked.

"No. I'd never harm Gus," I said.

"I've kept technology away from my people, yet on a whim you brought it here. I don't approve of it, but I'll allow Gus some fun. He is the way of the future. Perhaps things may change in his time." Sylvia glanced up at her son. "May the spirits guide him." She sighed.

I walked further down the path. Gus no longer followed me. In the clearing up ahead, Clay chopped wood and stacked it in a pile. Yvonne spread seed on the ground for the chickens. She waved at my approach. I hastened my steps, and she met me halfway. I twirled her around and she giggled.

I placed her back on her feet. "Tell me about your day."

"The usual chores," Yvonne said. "Did you ask Queen Mori about a position for me?"

"Yes. She'll let me know." I smiled.

"Do you ride, My Prince? The horses haven't had their daily exercise yet."

"I do, but it's been some time," I said.

"Good. You ride Alvina. She's gentle." Yvonne grabbed my hand. "Come with me."

We walked through the field, then stopped at the barn. The odor of hay and manure hit me as we strode inside. I covered my nose. Yvonne halted at a stall where a tawny colored mare bobbed her head at us. The mare sniffed my cloak.

"Ah, you want my snack, eh?" I pulled an apple from my pocket and held it out flat on my palm.

Alvina grasped it with her big choppers and crunched away. I rubbed the white star on her forehead, before pulling Alvina's reins out of the stall. Yvonne belted a saddle on Alvina's back, then saddled a black quarter horse for herself.

"This big guy is Midnight. He doesn't allow most people to ride him, but he likes me."

Yvonne kissed his forehead. "Ready?"

I climbed on Alvina's back and waited for Yvonne. She hopped on Midnight and kicked his sides. They galloped across the grassy field. I kicked Alvina's sides and tore down the field behind Yvonne.

"Race you to that fence," Yvonne called. She leaned forward and Midnight picked up speed. Her horse vaulted over a bush and Yvonne hung on.

Alvina surged ahead. I leaned forward and lifted my rear, removing weight off her backside. Yvonne and I were neck to neck. We drew near the fence. Midnight jumped over it, but Alvina halted, and I flew over the fence post.

Yvonne pulled on her reins. "Whoa." She climbed off her horse and raced to my side. "Are you all right, My Prince?"

I landed in a pond and a bull frog croaked near my ear. I raised my hand for assistance and Yvonne grabbed it. I yanked her in.

She sat in the pond water and splashed me. "Unfair. I rescued you."

"You knew Alvina would shy away from the fence, yet you picked it as the end goal." I splashed her back.

Yvonne snickered. "You got me."

"You owe me," I said.

Yvonne arched a brow. "What do you want?"

"A kiss." I pointed to my cheek. "Right here."

Yvonne crawled on her knees and leaned closer to me. She pursed her lips next to my cheek, but I moved, and our lips met. Her eyes opened wide. I deepened the kiss and dipped her over my arm. Her pulse quickened and her face blushed. Yvonne tasted like blackberries. Her hand played with my hair. I grabbed her arm and kissed the inside of it. Yvonne shivered.

"We should get back before Pa sees us." Yvonne stood and wrung out her buckskin dress.

As I stood, something wiggled in my breeches. Yvonne stared at the bulge and turned away. I removed a large goldfish and held it to her neck. The goldfish sucked, and Yvonne screeched, slipping and landing on her butt in the pond.

"You." She tossed water at me.

Clay rushed over. "What happened? I heard Yvonne scream."

I helped Yvonne up. Embarrassed, Yvonne ran inside the house. Clay glared at me.

"She screamed over the goldfish. Look." I held up the fish. "Nothing happened," I said.

Clay grabbed the reins of the horses and led them to the barn without a word.

Were my chances of courting her over?

My boots squished as I trekked down the path back to my airship.

Chapter Thirty-Four

MY BOOTS SQUEAKED AND I DRIPPED WATER DOWN THE long hallway of the Azure Fortress. I wanted to change out of the wet clothes and hurried to my chambers. To my surprise, Cosmo stood outside my door and punched the intercom button.

"Aidan are you in?" he called.

"No. I'm behind you."

Cosmo twisted around. "What happened to you?" He pinched his nose. "And what is that smell?"

"Hello to you too." I sniffed my shirt. "A horse threw me in a pond. I need a shower. You're welcome to wait in my room." I punched in the code and the door opened.

"What were you doing on a horse?" Cosmo sat on my bed.

"It's a long story. Give me a moment." I stepped out of my boots and clothes, and then strode inside the shower.

When I finished, I pulled on some clean clothes and told Cosmo the details of my day. "All because a damn horse threw me into the pond."

Cosmo laughed. He wiped his eyes, before he spoke. "Yvonne probably didn't expect to find her brother walking in on you two. Give her some time." Cosmo paused. "I came to inform you about Sir Jayel."

"He's not dead, is he?" Worry knotted my gut.

"He survived the stabbing from Grimshaw, but now Doctor Panphilia thinks he may never walk again," Cosmo said.

"Sir Jayel is a fighter. If there's a way, he'll find it. I don't know if I'd handle it as well as him. Too bad my magic couldn't heal him," I said.

"I played cards with him, and he moved his toes. I think the doc is wrong about him," Cosmo said. "Sir Jayel beat me twice and said I owed him. I asked him what he wanted, and you know what he said?

When I didn't answer, Cosmo said, "A visit from Astra. He likes a girl that is not afraid to fight. Astra impressed Sir Jayel with her warrior skills when you two practiced. Wanted to know if she was spoken for."

"And what did you tell him?" I asked.

"I'd arrange a meeting," Cosmo said.

I laughed.

"It's not funny." Cosmo frowned.

"Maybe you should ask how she feels about him, before you force her into a meeting," I suggested.

"I didn't think it through. Gosh, I hope she doesn't sock me. Last time she got mad at me, I had a sore arm for a week." Cosmo picked up a wrapped parcel from the floor. "Wiley dropped this off when you were in the shower. He said he made an extra one for you. Whatever that means."

I unwrapped it while Cosmo watched.

"A cloud-board. Now I have my own again. Grimshaw destroyed my other one with a missile during the war." I admired the bright orange color with black designs. Included with it was an EEG headset.

"How does it work?" Cosmo examined the cloud-board and turned it over.

"The headset works on your brain waves. Did you want to try?" I asked.

"I don't know. Is it safe?" Cosmo scratched his head.

Explaining the procedure to Cosmo on the way down the hall, I stopped at the hall storage unit and took out the cloud-board Juliana used.

We walked outside and onto the bridge. Mori and Santurin strolled along and greeted us.

"Lovely day," Mori said. "What are your plans, gentlemen?"

"You'll see." I winked.

Santurin groaned. "I should take you inside, my love."

"Don't be a silly goose. They're young and harmless." Mori ran her hand down his cheek.

"You don't know Aidan like I do," Santurin said.

"Cosmo, put your headset on and stand on your board," I said.

He did as I instructed, but a look of apprehension showed on his face as Cosmo looked down. "I don't know. Transforming is easy for me. I'd rather change into a bird."

"Look in front of you, instead of down. You want to glide across the sky, not fall. Watch me," I said.

I shoved off the bridge on my cloud-board and the clasps clicked into place around my ankles. I soared across the sky and around the spire on the roof of the fortress, before coming back. "Are you ready?"

Cosmo shook his head. "I can't." He tore off the EEG headset.

Disappointment dashed my joy. *I missed Juliana. At least she knew how to have fun. If not her, then her cousin, Varick. Was there no one to join me?* I pouted.

"Let me see that thing." Santurin stood on the cloud-board Cosmo vacated. He placed the EEG headset over his forehead.

"What are you doing?" Mori asked.

"Something I should have done a long time ago." Santurin shoved off and Mori screamed. Santurin zipped across the sky and over the top of the security building.

"Wahoo! Way to go, Santurin," I flew over to his side and he whirled around me, then flew across the river. I followed behind him.

"You complained I never took risks. I'm proving you wrong." Santurin glided under the Harmony Waterfalls and whipped his wet hair back. "Refreshing."

I zoomed under the arches of the bridge over the Hope River and Santurin copied me. We flew past Cosmo and Mori. Santurin blew a kiss to his wife and Mori smiled.

Happiness filled me. All these years, I wanted Santurin's respect and to do things together as true brothers. Finally, I had it. And Santurin appeared happy and relaxed too, instead of uptight.

"Race you to the spire," Santurin said.

Epilogue

THE VOLUNTEERS AND I CLEARED THE DEBRIS FROM Fallow in preparation for the planting. I held out my arms like wings and buzzed around Mori and her handmaidens. My sister-in-law smirked and shook her finger at me. Pregnancy agreed with her. At least today, she was happy. I stopped my foolishness and passed out the flowers.

I knelt and planted a four o'clock plant in the soil. Tapping down the roots, the flowers spread out in various trumpet colors. They were known for ridding the land of contaminants. We also planted dogbane. They grew tubular with white bell- like flowers. They produced a milky latex sap, and sequestered lead in their biomass. There were other flowers, I didn't know their names, but they stored toxins within their tissues and broke them down, eliminating the toxins all together. It would be a slow yet cost-effective process. And in a few years, Fallow would have better air quality.

I winked at Yvonne. Mori brought her into the circle of her hand-maidens. Yvonne and I spent hours walking and getting to know each other better, when she was off duty. I planned on marrying her in another year or two, but I'm waiting for the right moment to propose. Santurin suggested I not rush into things. We were both young, but in my heart, I knew Yvonne was the one.

Each night, I gazed at my grandmother's ring. Patience was a hard thing for me. I'd been impulsive far too long, almost like second nature.

I ran my tongue over my new front teeth. Doctor Panphilia's brother placed implants in my mouth. I still wasn't used to them. After the tree knocked them out on my manhood journey, I thought I'd never eat an apple or corn on the cob again. My long hair covered my stubby ear. I still couldn't believe Grimshaw sliced it off in the elevator those months ago, but I'm able to walk on my own, not like Sir Jayel. He relied on a wheelchair to get around. Yvonne considered my stubby ear a battle scar, yet it bothered me.

I'm not sure when it happened, but I love Yvonne. Maybe it's the twinkle in her eyes when she teases me or the simple act of tucking her hair behind an ear? Or the highlights of gold and red in her hair when she sits in the light? Maybe it was the day our hands barely touched, and a warmth ignited in my belly? It doesn't matter. I can't imagine a day without her. And that book of poems Mother gave me on my last birthday came in handy. I read one each night to Yvonne.

I miss Juliana to confide in. She resided on Meadowlark with her mother. Mori was jealous over her husband's attraction to Juliana. Santurin held a grudge against Lady Darshana for not keeping tabs on Tiana that fateful day of Mother's passing. Mori was wrong about Santurin's attraction though. He didn't feel that way about Juliana. She was like a sister to him. He loved Mori.

Clay visited Juliana on Meadowlark from time to time. She claimed he wasn't the one for her, but it didn't stop Clay from trying. I also missed Varick, Juliana's cousin. When he moved to Waverly, a part of me went with him. He had been my best friend. His father kept him busy learning estate affairs. I hoped to visit him soon.

I earned respect from Santurin, when Grimshaw made him ill, and I took responsibility to run things for the kingdom. The best thing this year was when Santurin cloud-boarded with me. He took a risk. We were true brothers now. I've also grown up some. I quit lying to him and playing pranks, while Santurin quit mocking and bullying me. We lost both of our parents and relied on each other. Strange what life brings.